WHEN THE SKY FALLS

(OR *A IS FOR ADONIS*)

PHIL EARLE

ANDERSEN PRESS

First published in 2021 by
Andersen Press Limited
20 Vauxhall Bridge Road
London SW1V 2SA
www.andersenpress.co.uk

2 4 6 8 10 9 7 5 3 1

Lyrics for 'Vane Tempest' by The Lake Poets, written by
Martin Longstaff, are reproduced with kind permission
by BMG and Sony/Membran

British Library Cataloguing in Publication Data available.

ISBN 978 1 78344 965 1

Printed and bound in Great Britain by
Clays Ltd, Elcograf S.p.A.

'An EXTRAORDINARY STORY with historical and family truth at its heart, that tells us as much about the present as the past. Deeply felt, movingly written, a remarkable achievement' MICHAEL MORPURGO

'COMPLEX, DARK, INTENSE AND MYSTERIOUS, *When the Sky Falls* is an astounding work of fiction. The characters have the knotty awkwardness of real people, and the whole book has that unfakeable FEELING OF TRUTH. For years now Earle has been one of our FINEST WRITERS for young people and here he is at the height of his considerable powers' ANTHONY McGOWAN

'When *the Sky Falls* is heart-racingly good. POWERFUL, KIND AND THRILLING. An urgent reminder that when we have the courage and compassion to stand up for other animals as well as humans – they often save us right back' LAUREN ST JOHN

'A BOLD and BEAUTIFUL story' ABI ELPHINSTONE

'Packed with ADVENTURE, MYSTERY AND A WHOLE LOT OF HEART, *When the Sky Falls* feels like an instant classic' LISA WILLIAMSON

'A RAW AND BEAUTIFUL story about the power of kindness and hope' ANNA JAMES

'A POWERFUL, REMARKABLE story. It is heart-soaringly wonderful' JENNIFER BELL

'A RAW, TOUCHING TALE of a boy in WWII Britain whose biggest war is with himself. Powerful, convincing, full of heart and love' MICHELLE HARRISON

'Phil Earle writes from the heart: a story about LOVE and FRIENDSHIP and how animals can connect people in the darkest of times and allow them to heal' GILL LEWIS

'Enormously POWERFUL AND VIVID – a real heart-wrenching evocation of the Blitz'
LISSA EVANS

'BEAUTIFULLY WRITTEN, heart-tugging and fierce. I loved it'
JENNY DOWNHAM

'A writer whose words hold a CLARITY OF COMPASSION and can carry any reader to a world that feels as real as one's own' NON PRATT

'A lovingly crafted piece of work with a POWERFUL EMOTIONAL ADVENTURE at its heart – how to survive, how to love others, and how to let them love you. One of those books that makes you forget where you are when you're reading it. Highly recommended'
MELVIN BURGESS

'I was gripped by this POWERFUL STORY OF FRIENDSHIP set against the backdrop of the Blitz. I read it in one breathless sitting and felt like I was walking alongside Joseph every step of the way. It's A RAW, BEAUTIFULLY TOLD STORY. I loved it'
JENNY McLACHLAN

'*Kes* meets *The Machine Gunners* in a story that MADE ME THINK AND FEEL and remember why we need to love and be loved'
TOM PALMER

'Impressive depths and fathoms of emotion and COMPASSION run beneath a highly affecting story of lives and landscapes ravaged and torn apart by war. Based around a true story, it will touch heart and mind alike'
JAKE HOPE, CHAIR OF YLG

'I knew I was going to LOVE it from the opening lines'
MARCUS SEDGWICK

'Absolutely wonderful. I literally couldn't stop reading it. Continuously exciting, increasingly moving, and the whole effect is AMAZINGLY POWERFUL. A truly brilliant performance. It deserves accolades and prizes but, more profoundly, it's a fabulous gift for readers who, I think, are going to LOVE IT FIERCELY'
SIMON MASON

For Pete, who planted the seed . . .
and for Louise, who brought it to life.

I look into your eyes, and I can see
Another life and a mind worth reading
When you look into mine,
I hope you see not a boy,
but the man you made me

When you were down the mine,
under the sea, You held a dream
that you passed onto me
You said, 'You can be the man,
you want to be
Just keep in mind
what my own dad told me'

Because there will come a time
There will come a time
There will come a time
Oh, there will come a time
There will come a time
For people like me and you

'Vane Tempest', The Lake Poets

1

The platform was a battlefield: seventy yards of carnage transplanted straight from the coasts of northern France.

Smoke billowed; people clung to each other. There were cries of pain, howls of despair as loved ones were ripped apart. There were silent tears too, quiet reassurances whispered into ears: that this was temporary, that it changed nothing, *I am still your mother, your parent.*

Against the tide of devastation walked a boy: tutting and huffing at the tears and carrying-on. He looked just like any of the other evacuees in the station: regulation case, tag and gas mask box. But instead of being shoehorned onto a train, he was marching away from one, having just arrived.

He had no idea where he was heading, nor any real sense of who he was to look for, but he knew he wanted no part of the drama going on around him. He scoured the crowd, cursing at the smoke that bit his eyes. It didn't take much to light the end of his fuse, and the long journey down had been more than enough to start him smouldering.

He seethed under his breath, then over it, not caring who heard. He'd give it a minute; see if anyone presented themselves. And if they didn't? Well he'd just sneak onto a train and be pulled back north. He'd hide out in the guard's van, amongst the musty sacks of letters from soldiers begging to come home. He knew how they felt. He wanted to go home too, despite everything. He certainly didn't want to be here.

It had been two months since his father had marched to war. Long months, both of them, and every day had hardened him, tightening the cog in his gut, winding up his anger, his fury.

He peered again at the faces by the barrier, not knowing who he was looking for, nor how he'd react if someone had the audacity to smile or beckon him forward.

He didn't know the woman he was meant to be meeting, nor did he want to, and now that she'd failed to present herself, he was not disappointed.

I'll go home, he said to himself. Didn't have to be to his grandmother. The cow. He'd not go anywhere he wasn't wanted. Not any more. He'd find an empty place. There were plenty of them around. He'd live off scraps, whatever he could find. He'd not let anyone stop him. No one would dare.

But as the boy spun to return north, he felt a hand on the strap of his box. Not a gentle hand. It clutched at him like a barn owl would a mouse.

'Joseph Palmer?' The boy recognised the tone, he'd heard it plenty of times before. A bobby, he was sure of it.

'Joseph? Is that who you are?'

A face craned over his shoulder and into view, too close to focus on. He couldn't see the chin strap of a policeman's helmet, just a shocking frizz of greying red hair that sprung in all directions.

'I'm here to collect you, lad.'

A woman. A hard face – lived-in. And a deep, gravelly voice. The boy looked in her eyes and dared her to look back. She did, and seemed about as happy to be there as he was.

'Don't know what you're talking about, Missus. I'm just leaving. Sending me to the country, they are, with the others.'

The woman gripped harder at the strap. 'With an accent like that? I don't think so, Joseph.'

The boy didn't like the way she was holding him, or how she was challenging him, even if it were true. He shrugged his shoulder, then swung it, all the time eyeing her angrily, but her clasp didn't give a bit.

'Get your hands off me, will you? I don't know you. Get your hands off me or I'll make a right scene.'

The woman didn't doubt it. She could feel the power in the boy, despite his meagre frame.

Much of her would have been only too happy to walk away, she neither needed nor wanted this, but there was a promise, wasn't there? She might have made it a long while back, but it was still a promise, and she didn't have it in her not to keep it. Or at the very least, to try.

'Joseph,' she sighed, 'I know it's you. So you can kick and scream and deny it as much as you want. I've grappled bigger beasts than you, my lad, and I've not lost yet.'

The woman turned on her heel, pulling Joseph with her,

despite his spirited struggles. But within ten yards she felt her progress thwarted. The boy had put the brakes on.

She turned, ready to bite. But as she made to speak, she saw it wasn't Joseph who'd stopped them, but a suited man who'd taken hold of Joseph's other arm, leaving Joseph stretched and angry in the middle.

'Are you this boy's grandmother?' He didn't look like he was about to congratulate her.

Joseph felt her bristle at the suggestion.

'I'm not, no.'

'But you are responsible for him?'

Joseph could tell she didn't particularly like that either, but the man had her there. The second she'd arrived at the station, she'd crossed that uncomfortable line, and she was now responsible for Joseph, whether either of them wanted it or not.

'I am.'

Joseph flinched at this, before bucking between them like an unbroken stallion.

'Well, he's stolen from me.'

The words stopped the boy's thrashing, just for a second, before he stepped up a gear, releasing himself from the man's grip, but not hers. She held on effortlessly.

'Is this true?' she asked Joseph, ending his thrashing with one firm tug, though she saw a wildness shoot into his eyes.

'He's lying,' he spat. 'Idiot's got nowt I'd want. *Nowt.*'

Her eyes moved from the boy to the man.

4

'He says he's taken nothing,' she said, as if the man couldn't translate Joseph's unruly northern twang.

This did nothing to appease the gent. 'Then he'll not mind opening his case.' He ripped Joseph's luggage from his hand and took a step back as the boy aimed a kick at his shins.

'I'd suggest you keep the child under control,' he said, and struggled with the case's clasp, before realising there was only a loop of twine holding it shut.

It surrendered quickly to his demands, and the case fell open.

The woman leaned in, wincing at the god-awful smell rising from inside.

'If there's anything in there belonging to you,' she told the man, while recoiling from the cloying stench, 'why on earth would you want it back?'

But the man was not to be deterred, his hands flinging aside socks and underpants that looked like they had reluctantly survived the trenches some twenty-five years earlier.

'Aha,' he cried, as he came upon two large wedges, wrapped in brown paper. 'Care to explain this?'

Joseph didn't flinch as he gathered his shabby clothes back into the case. 'Sandwiches.' He shrugged. 'Mother made me them for the journey down.'

The woman sagged visibly and at that moment Joseph knew he had given himself away, to her at least. He had no idea why this woman had volunteered to take him in, or of the link that existed between them, but she clearly knew he had no mother: he saw it in her eyes. And her knowledge bothered him.

'Nonsense,' yelled the man. 'You are a thief, and I'll prove it.' With a grandstanding flourish, he ripped the paper from one parcel to reveal a block of cheese so substantial it could wedge open a stable door. As if that wasn't enough, he then revealed enough sliced bacon to feed a sizeable platoon in the other.

Both were responsible for the smell. Both had been out of a cool pantry for too long.

'You see?' he spat as he wrapped them back up. 'The boy is a liar, and a thief. He took these from my bag while I slept. I want an apology from you, Sunshine, and I want it now.'

But he would not get one. He had lit the boy's fuse, and Joseph now lurched forward, fists raised, forcing the woman to pull him back by the scruff of his neck.

'Enough!' the man shouted, pointing over to the ticket booth. 'There's a policeman over there. Two, in fact. One word from me, my boy, and you will find yourself in real bother. As will you, my dear,' he added, pointing disdainfully at the woman. 'You should be ashamed, with everything going on, to let your boy run wild like this, taking whatever he likes.'

It seemed to Joseph that while the woman could accept the man's words about him, something had snapped when his attention turned to her. A snap that propelled her towards the man, then beyond him, ripping the parcels from his grasp as she passed.

'What on earth do you think you're doing?' he said.

'Exactly what you asked,' she replied without looking back, making the man scamper to catch up. 'If it's the law you're after, then let's get it over with. They'll be surprised to see one man in possession of such large rations, though. But I'm sure there must be a legitimate reason for it, what with you being so morally upstanding and all.'

The man's face flushed. 'Madam, wait . . .' he blustered, though the woman, if anything, accelerated.

'I won't!' she insisted. 'This is an awful, squalid business, and if there has been a theft of *any* kind, then we need to have done with it. Immediately.'

'Well, perhaps . . . I was a little . . . rash. I mean, it's clear the boy is troubled. I could see that from his demeanor on the journey from Yorkshire. Perhaps it would be best . . . for him . . . if we were to forget it ever happened.' He made to wrestle the parcels from the woman's grasp, but found no give in her whatsoever.

'Now that would never do, would it?' she said, deadpan. 'I can't, with good conscience, allow for *any* crime to take place, and for the guilty party to go unpunished. As you said, these are difficult times. We need to be standing together, not stealing from each other.'

The policemen were mere strides away now, and the woman began to wave the parcels in their direction. Joseph reckoned the bobbies could probably *smell* them, and half expected them to bolt in the other direction in revulsion.

Instead, they stepped forward, towards the woman, which was enough to see a river of sweat break across the man's brow. With a desperate lunge, he ripped one of the parcels from the woman's hand, and ploughed back into the crowd, out of sight.

With a movement equally deft, the woman grabbed Joseph by the hand and changed direction, making it appear she was waving at someone near the exit and not at the police at all. The officers stood down, and the pair weaved through the scrum towards the street.

Joseph allowed it all to sink in. He had no desire to be in this place, with this woman, and after what he'd just seen, he didn't like his chances of getting a single thing over on her, either. Not that it would stop him trying.

'Cheese for supper then,' he said. 'Call it a gift from me, Missus.'

The woman didn't break pace. Nor did she look in his direction. Instead, she let the parcel fall from her hand into the next passing bin. Joseph's face fell a mile.

'Eat that and you'd be glued to the lav for a month,' she said. 'That might suit *you*, but some of us have better things to be doing. So, let's get two things straight. I'll not tolerate thieving. Steal as much as a glance in the future and I'll turn you in myself. And secondly, I'll thank you not to call me Missus neither. My name is Margaret Farrelly. My friends call me Mags. So to you, I'm Mrs F. You hear me?'

The boy said nothing and showed nothing, either, his emotions securely locked down. For now.

'We must dash, so no dallying. If that siren sounds, we don't want to be anywhere near here, believe me.'

The boy followed her without changing his stride.

He did look skywards, but could see nothing. No sun, no bomber, and most importantly, no hope.

2

Joseph had no idea how far from the station the woman's home was, but he was starting to wonder whether they would reach it before the war ended.

The bus crawled through the streets, feeling every bump and hole with a shudder that travelled through its wheels and up into the bodies of its passengers.

Joseph fizzed and bubbled, his turned head resting on the window, adding to the vibrations.

He'd never seen anything like it: never been in the city before, *any* city, but in his head, it had never looked like this. He'd expected tall buildings, stretching into the sky, all brick and stone and permanent, not rubble and smoke and carnage.

His eyes fell on the first floor of one building, the front wall obliterated, fragments of chairs and tables scattered: a single framed picture somehow clinging stoically to a nail. It was a painting of a tropical beach: paradise, smack-bang in the middle of hell.

The house next to it was equally shambolic, and no less surreal. Again, the front wall had surrendered, but there was no furniture to be seen, only a capsized wooden box, from which poured Christmas decorations. Baubles sat wedged beside fallen timbers: stray pieces of tinsel blinked and shone.

Ten minutes later and only a few yards on, he saw a boy, little older than himself, perched on a crate in front of a bookshop. The door and windows lay scattered at his feet, beside a very tidy pile of books. The boy was flicking his way through a large volume. When he reached the end, he pulled himself up, clambered through the rubble, and returned the book to a shelf.

Joseph found his top lip curling in disgust. Why the boy didn't shove the books under his coat and make off with them, he had no idea, but more fool him.

There had been little in the way of conversation between Joseph and Mrs F since they'd left the station. She had tried, but there had been no conviction in her efforts, and as Joseph merely offered monosyllabic grunts in reply, the pair were left to listen to the voices of other passengers, not a happy sound to be heard amongst them.

'Found him on the corner of Lunham Road, they did. Some of him anyway, his left leg and wallet were seventy yards on. Not that there was anything in it . . . his wallet, that is.'

'We've not seen the end yet, you know . . .'

'There'll be sirens again tonight, you mark my words. The phony war wasn't as bad as we thought, eh?'

The voices became noise to Joseph, static, the kind that used to crackle out of Dad's wireless, no matter how hard he tried to tune it in.

He exhaled, hard, though it did nothing to dispel the frustration buzzing in him. The bus had stopped again and was showing no sign of moving, clouds belching from its back end in protest.

'Enough,' tutted Mrs F, pulling her bag from the floor but leaving Joseph's where they were. 'We'll do the rest on foot. Come on, before they enlist us to clear the rubble.'

Joseph struggled behind her, not caring when his luggage clouted each and every passenger unfortunate enough to have an aisle seat. He clattered down the rear stairs too, and through the open exit at the back of the bus.

It made him wonder if anything in this city had a door any more.

'Keep up. I don't have the time or inclination to be searching for you between now and home. Today's been long enough as it is.' She forged a path past the bus and the toppled building blocking its path, and beyond a group of kids playing a macabre game of Finders Keepers in the rubble.

There was no end of sights and sounds for Joseph to drink in: houses without roofs, roofs without walls, newspaper men and bible-clutchers both shouting about the end of the world. But if any of it did impress or bewitch him, he refused to show it on his face, and followed Mrs F sullenly, leaving enough of a gap so it didn't look like he was obeying her.

'Almost there,' she barked, which was a relief. His hands were turning blue. Early February was no time to be out without gloves, and his hands burned with cold as they clung stiffly to his baggage.

Finally, she turned left onto a street called Calmly View,

which looked identical to every other they'd seen so far, in that only half of it seemed to be left standing.

'Right, this is us,' she said, pushing at a gate that was as reluctant as the boy behind her. The front door opened more easily, revealing a hallway darker than the street.

'Shoes off at the door. Outside stays outside.' Though she made no effort to remove the boots from her own feet.

'Sitting room is on the right. Sundays only. Leave your shoes by the front door and pile your luggage neatly by the stairs. You can move it shortly. Follow me.'

Joseph wondered what was behind the door in front of them. A flick of a switch revealed a starkly lit room that seemed to match the woman's personality: cold and lifeless. Barring a tin bath tacked to the wall and a series of austere family photographs, there was little else. The stove was unlit, much like her heart, Joseph thought to himself. From the tiny amount of wood and coal piled next to it, it didn't look like it would be warming any time soon either.

'Cold in here,' he said.

'Yes, well, best get used to it. That's the last of the coke, and we've not had a delivery in weeks. Not since the last of the lads from the coal yard was conscripted.

'Lavvie is through the back door and on the left. Don't be wasting paper in there. And don't be flushing unnecessarily. Same's to be said of electricity. No reading in bed, unless it's by candlelight. In fact, scratch that. Can't say I like the idea of you and a flame alone together.'

Her words bounced off him. There was little chance of *him* bothering a book at any time.

'Look.' She was staring at him now, her gaze heavy and uncomfortable. 'I know you don't want to be here. And you aren't daft, you can see I'm hardly thrilled myself, but here we are. Your gran, she's a good woman. Loyal. And I owe her a real debt.'

Joseph felt himself bristle. He didn't share her opinion of his gran.

'She helped me, see. Many years ago now, but that's irrelevant.' Joseph saw Mrs F's expression change, like she'd gone momentarily back to that time, but didn't like what she saw.

'Why? What did she do?' His gran had done little for him. It had felt like she couldn't wait to pack him off soon as the march of Dad's shiny boots had stopped echoing in their ears.

'That's between me and her,' Mrs F said uncomfortably. 'And it's certainly not something to be discussed this evening. Your gran wrote to me. Told me she was struggling to handle you, your behaviour. Your . . . moods.'

Joseph's fists clenched at his sides. But Mrs F did not notice.

'She asked me to have you for a spell. Just while your father is away.'

The anger in him grew. He didn't like her mentioning his dad. And besides, she didn't know anything. Doubted very much his gran had shared the important stuff with her.

'Well, I don't need you. I can look after myself.' He had half a mind to collect his case and walk straight back to the station.

'Not according to your gran, you can't. According to her, you're argumentative, aggressive and surly. You've been in more scrapes than she can keep up with, and she's scared. Both for you and for her. That's why she wanted me to help.'

Joseph thought about arguing with her, but realised she'd just see that as proving her point.

'I made a promise to your gran,' she went on, 'that I'd keep you safe, as much as I can here anyway, and when I make a promise, I like to keep it. So my advice to you is, keep off my toes and I'll keep off yours. We don't have to like each other, we don't even have to pretend, but until your dad comes home, I'm the best you're going to get. Now, your room is at the top of the stairs on the right and your bed is made. That's the last time I'll do that for you, so make the most of it. Do you want anything to eat? I'll be needing your ration book and identity card, though Lord knows if they'll accept it down here. You'll be registered to a shop up at home. Well? Do you have it?' Her hand went out, awaiting payment.

He reached into his pocket for his crumpled book as she ranted on, not pausing to breathe, 'If you are hungry, it'll have to be something small, mind. I've not much in.'

The boy shook his head. The fire in his gut would only incinerate any food he swallowed anyway.

'Then take yourself off to bed. We've work to do tomorrow. Me *and* you.

'Oh, and if the siren sounds, get yourself dressed and down here quickly. No dallying, you don't need to be presentable if Hitler knocks, just prompt.'

And without so much as a goodnight, she unlocked the back door and barrelled through it, leaving Joseph to stand there alone.

3

Joseph prowled his room.

In the hours he had spent up there, he hadn't bothered to try and sleep. There was no point. It was too cold, for starters.

The room was nothing but a small box, with an iron bedstead and an upturned orange box for a bedside table. To Joseph it felt like a coffin with the lid nailed down.

He didn't want to be here: in this room, this house, this city, but like everything in life, it seemed he had no choice in how it played out. At the same time, deep in his gut, he knew he was to blame.

He did not like this woman. How dare she suggest Gran was decent or caring? She was neither of those things. If she were decent, he'd not be here. He'd still be at home, left to do as he pleased. It had suited him fine, the way things were, and if it bothered her? Well, it just showed her weakness. He paced harder, and heavier, the room shrinking with every step until he felt he could touch each wall merely by stretching out his arms.

He made for the window and wrenched open the curtains, hopeful that the sight of outside (as alien a landscape as it was), might make him feel less trapped. But there was nothing to see, quite literally, as every inch of the glass had been covered in blackout paint.

His shaking hands reached into his pockets and removed his penknife, but no matter how hard he scratched with the blunt blade, he couldn't remove the daubed paint. It was sticky and thick, most likely a tar mixture rather than paint itself. All Joseph wanted was to carve a bullet hole into it, to prove there was life outside this prison and his own head, but even that wasn't possible, and he felt himself beginning to lose control again.

He grabbed the bedside lamp, turning it, club-like, in his hand, throwing the shade to the floor. He didn't feel the plug rip from the wall, the only thing he felt was the window yield to the club, shattering around it, then an overwhelming feeling of disappointment, when the street outside offered neither light nor any respite to his anxiety. The only things it did prompt were an icy blast of wind, the bark of a dog, and an angry voice telling him to *Keep it down, there's a war on out here!*

Suddenly his bedroom door flew open, revealing the silhouette of Mrs F.

'For the love of God,' she spat in shock and disappointment, wrapping her dressing gown tightly round her to keep out the cold, before turning to walk down the stairs.

Joseph didn't move.

Two minutes later she thundered back in, clutching a dustpan, brush, and piece of jagged plywood that she threw onto his bed.

'You don't honestly think I can get that replaced do you? I

don't have the money, for starters. And I doubt very much that I could find any glass that hasn't already been broken by the Jerries. Anyway, you'll pay for that to be replaced when the time comes,' she said, pulling a hammer and nails from her dressing gown pocket, 'but for now, you can fix it yourself.'

And that was that. No lecture, barely a tone to her voice. Instead, she backed out of the room without bothering to slam the door, leaving Joseph to pick up the hammer from the bed.

He looked at the window, had no desire to fix it just because she had told him to, but at the same time, he didn't fancy dying of hypothermia. Besides, he could see it was an easy job. He knew how to work with tools, and the hammer felt good: heavy in his hand.

Minutes later, the plywood was tacked crudely to the window frame, much to the delight of the already irate neighbour.

And when he was done? Well, Joseph didn't know what to do with himself, so he prowled some more, stewed some more, and cursed his luck repeatedly, until finally, his energy ran out. He sat on the floor, pulling the blanket on top of him, so he could ignore the bed Mrs F had made in one final, wilful protest.

His eyes opened to the most grotesque of sights: Mrs F, standing above him, arms folded, nostrils flared.

'You've made a real pig's ear of repairing that window,' she sighed. 'And as I said last night, you'll be paying for it yourself. That, and any others you decide to break, so think on.'

Joseph didn't move. It couldn't possibly be morning. He'd only just closed his eyes, for Pete's sake.

'And what are you doing down there? Your rent doesn't go up if you sleep in the bed, you know.'

Joseph pulled the scratchy woollen blanket right up to his chin, exposing his toes to the cold. He didn't want her looking at him in his vest and pants.

The woman, annoyingly, seemed to read his mind.

'I'd cover myself up too, if my underwear were the colour of yours. I suggest you bring your clothes down with you. If we get them scrubbed now and hung over the stove, they'll be dry by the time we get home.'

'Where are we going?' Joseph mumbled.

'I told you last night. Work. Paying for that mess.' She pointed at the window. 'Now, be down in five minutes. And don't forget your laundry, otherwise you'll be wearing out my stair carpet unnecessarily.'

Joseph dressed slowly. Not because there was anything better to do, just because he was damned if he was going to do what she told him.

He bundled up the rest of his clothes and carried them downstairs to the backroom, which smelled strongly of porridge. It was the first pleasant smell to invade Joseph's nostrils since he'd arrived, waking his stomach with an impatient growl.

'About time,' Mrs F offered in way of a greeting. 'You were lucky there was no air raid last night, or you really would be tired.'

Joseph had never experienced an air raid, but he'd heard reports about them on the wireless. About the mess and the smell and people sleeping in church halls because there was nothing left of their house. He'd heard about kids his age who thought it was all the most exciting adventure, roaming the streets trying to find shrapnel and bullets and helmets afterwards. Pathetic, he'd scoffed. Though there was one report on the news about a group of kids finding their own machine gun, sawing it clean off a crashed German bomber, and hiding it. That sort of adventure, he wouldn't mind. *Imagine that*, he thought, *having your own machine gun?*

'Come on, your porridge is on the table,' Mrs F barked, without turning from the meagerly-lit stove. 'There's already a pinch of sugar in it so don't be looking for any more. I suggest you fill your boots now, as there'll be precious little else until supper.'

He had no interest in conversation. He was hungry. So he dropped his laundry at his feet and looked at the table. There were two steaming bowls on it, but one serving was much smaller than the other. Guessing this was his, he sat before it, only for Mrs F to switch the bowls round.

'No, this one's yours,' she said, a slight flush to her face.

Joseph didn't care. He pounced on it, almost forgetting to use the spoon at all.

Three mouthfuls in, he felt her eyes on him, frowning, of course. Was her face permanently fixed in that position, or was she saving it just for him?

'What?' he said.

'When was the last time you ate?'

He shrugged. 'Yesterday probably.' Though he knew exactly when and what it was: an apple stolen off a stall before he got on the train. His grandmother had made him a sandwich, but he'd dumped it in the bin without her seeing. He didn't want anything she'd made.

Anyway, he thought, he had porridge now. And although it didn't have enough milk or sweetness to it, he didn't care, and he fell on it again, ramming it into his mouth until his pupils dilated. He was careful not to let her see though – after all, the woman didn't care about him. She was on his gran's side. She'd made that only too clear.

'You might as well have mine too,' she said, spooning her porridge into his bowl.

'What's wrong with it?' he spat through a full mouth.

'Nothing. Not hungry, that's all. When you've finished, you can get your hands in that bucket. There's suds already in there, and a brush. Your clothes will think it's their birthday.'

But Joseph had no idea how to go about getting clothes clean. And even when he tried (just to get her to leave him alone) she found fault in his every move.

'Don't be wringing it out like that, not till you've soaked it properly . . .

'Keep the water in the bowl, not on my rug . . .

'Can you not see that stain ther—'

'*If* I'm doing such a lousy job,' he finally snapped, sluicing water all over the floor, 'wouldn't it just be easier for you to do it yourself?'

But the woman didn't step forward or change her expression. 'No, it wouldn't. It'd be a lot easier if you learned quickly how to listen and take orders. Now, once you've wrung them out properly, lay them flat on the rail by the stove. If they're all bunched up, it'll be Christmas before they're ready to wear. And dry that floor up, too. We leave in fifteen minutes, so be ready. And be prepared to graft. We've a long day ahead.'

Joseph swore under his breath as she blustered from the room and up the stairs. Probably in search of her witch's broomstick, he didn't wonder.

He had no idea where they were going, but he knew one thing. The day had to get better, surely.

4

There was little to celebrate in the sight of buildings reduced to ashes, but it did make Joseph feel a couple of things, other than his usual anger.

Firstly, he was shocked. How could he not be? He'd seen photos and grainy footage of the Blitz before, but nothing had prepared him for the *smell* of it. There was gas in the air and plenty of it, so much, it was a wonder that the cigarettes of the many bystanders hadn't seen the whole street burst into flames. But there was another smell too: a cloying smell of charred decay, and as it invaded his senses for the first time, Joseph wondered if it would ever leave him.

It was an assault on the eyes as well: not just the buildings reduced to dust, but the other things around it. Joseph hadn't expected to see a gaggle of nurses in full white uniform digging amongst the rubble, for starters. Wasn't that what the home guard was for? Shouldn't they be at the hospital, putting people back together again? He asked Mrs F as much.

'War might bring out the worst in some people,' she said, 'but it brings out the best in most.' And she thanked the nurses as she passed.

The other feeling racing round, apart from Joseph's queasiness and shock, was a strange sense of gratitude, because the endless, smouldering houses warmed the air from Baltic to merely freezing.

He didn't ask where they were going. He'd already learned better than that, and instead he allowed his mind to wander, imagining the most fitting place for Mrs F to work.

Hair salon? Unlikely, given the electrified shock of frizz barely tamed by her coarse woollen hat.

Cafeteria, maybe? He shook his head. He'd tasted her porridge and reckoned no one else would pay for the privilege.

Hospital, then? It was a definite possibility, seeing how she'd thanked those nurses. But she didn't exactly have the bedside manner. A grin hit his face as a more likely location lodged in his head.

The funeral home. No one would answer back or challenge her there. Plus she was as cold as the cadavers she'd lay out in readiness.

The image of her applying make-up or fixing neck ties on corpses was enough to occupy Joseph's mind for a good few minutes, the images becoming more elaborate and macabre in his mind, until he lost himself entirely and ploughed into the back of Mrs F, who had stopped abruptly in front.

Righting him with a firm tut and a strong arm, she told him they had arrived, before wrestling a huge padlock and chain that wrapped snakelike round two metal gates.

Joseph took a couple of steps back, focusing on the imposing stone pillars that stood either side of the gates, and the two letters that sat, proudly above them: oo, they read.

The building didn't look in any way as enticing as the letters suggested. In fact it looked desperate, like it would happily beg a German bomber to put it out of its misery.

It didn't take long for Joseph to work out what the building was, of course. He wasn't daft, far from it, and quickly realised where the third letter should be.

'You work in a zoo?' he asked, not wanting to sound impressed, despite a twinge of excitement.

Mrs F turned, the chain coiled effortlessly in her arms like a sleeping python.

'Work in it? No, I don't work in it. I *run* it. Like my brother did before he went off to fight. There's very few people who work *in* it, Joseph, because it's 1941 and there's a war on. So by my reckoning you make up one third of the workforce. Best get used to it.'

And she laid the chain around his neck, the unexpected weight almost taking him off his feet.

'Now, close that gate and follow me. Before one of the residents thinks breakfast has arrived early.'

He knew she was joking – well, he at least hoped she was, but there was something immediately strange about the place: ghostly, still, unsafe. As they passed cage after cage, there was no sign of movement, though his ears picked up disjointed, jarring cries that were always in the distance and impossible to place.

There was one noise that persisted, a growl that rumbled over them, growing louder and louder as they paced on.

It didn't trouble Mrs F, not in the slightest. In fact, she looked so unconcerned that Joseph wondered if only *he* could hear it.

He didn't like it, and found himself reaching for a shard of wood that lay abandoned on the floor. He gripped it tight, his knuckles turning white. *What am I doing?* he thought. This was ridiculous. He didn't get scared.

Mrs F still showed no sign of distress. What did she know, that he didn't? How could she not hear it, or be feeling the same rising panic that was engulfing him?

He wasn't going to ask her though, of course he wasn't.

Mrs F walked on, whistling tunelessly, until suddenly, from the shadows, a scruffy black tornado whipped past her, launching itself at Joseph's chest before he could even raise his weapon.

He tumbled to the floor, gravel pulling through his shirt and at his back, a wail leaving his throat that was more primeval than anything the inhabitants in the cages could muster.

He felt his shoulders tense and arms flail as the creature's muzzle snapped repeatedly at him. The wood fell uselessly to the floor. He wanted to bite back but found himself pinned, powerless, not just by the animal, but by fear itself. He waited for pain to rip through him, but instead he heard a different bark from a different beast.

'Tweedy. No!' snapped Mrs F.

Then: 'Friend. Boy.'

Instantly, the growling stopped, and Joseph felt the

pressure from the animal's limbs relent. It was still on top of him, still pinning him flat, but its jaws were no longer searching for the juiciest part of his neck. Instead, its muzzle was less than an inch from his face, two chocolate brown eyes hiding behind a mess of straggly hair, thick and unkempt like an old man's eyebrows.

Joseph didn't know what was going to happen next, and still half expected teeth, but got instead a tongue: long slobbering licks that started at his chin and didn't stop until his hairline.

'Get off!' he yelled, embarrassed. The dog's breath reeked. Hot and stale, like its tongue had spent far too long up close to another dog's backside. Or its own. Whichever it was, Joseph didn't want it anywhere near his face, and pushed the animal off him, surprised by how easily it moved: completely at odds with its initial power.

He rolled onto his side, head (and nose) clearing, though he felt a wave of shame engulf him as he saw the dog properly for the first time.

He wasn't sure what he was expecting: a German Shepherd perhaps, the sort he imagined Nazi officers strained to contain on a leash as they terrorised a cowering crowd. Something with heft and power coursing through it. But to Joseph's embarrassment, he saw only what looked like a longhaired miniature whippet.

Not a puppy, there was too much grey in its matted coat for that, though it was bounding around now like a youngster, snapping at its own tail with dizzying speed.

It was, quite possibly, the scruffiest-looking thing Joseph had ever laid eyes on. Its beard was a mess of food and Lord knows what else, and its fur carried what looked like a small collection of flowering bushes.

Joseph wondered when it had last been bathed. Though to be honest, it looked like a bath was way too late for it. The most sensible option would be to shave it from ear to tail and start all over again.

'Terrifying beast, isn't he?' Mrs F said, appearing above him, a wry smile on her face. 'Almost the scariest thing in the whole place. He lives with me, usually, but with you arriving I left him here last night. Takes his guarding duties very seriously.'

She pulled a morsel of something from her pocket and tossed it at the dog, who hoovered it up and sat to attention for more.

'Is he yours?'

'Hard to say,' she replied, bending to the dog, wincing as she did so. 'Found him sleeping in the hippo enclosure seven months ago. Don't know how he got in there, but they didn't seem to mind as long as he left their food alone. In fact the hippos were sadder to leave him than anything else when they were shipped out. Lord knows if big beasts like that can actually cry, but they didn't like leaving the daft dog behind. Wouldn't get in the lorry until he led them in.'

It was the most the woman had said to him since he arrived, and he heard a different tone to her voice, saw the

29

tiniest softening in her body, too, as she carefully pulled the foliage from the dog's fur. It rankled with him. She could show a straggly mutt such care, but manage only orders and demands of him.

The dog, now freed of its leafy cargo, turned its attention back to Joseph, sniffing at his hands before circling him in short, fast bounds. Begging him to play, howling excitedly.

Joseph gave him no time, walking on instead towards a large cage, feeling like he was on the inside of the bars, not outside them.

'I wouldn't get too close to that one,' Mrs F said, 'Adonis isn't keen on new people.'

'Sounds like someone else round here,' Joseph muttered, ignoring her and wandering closer still.

It was dark inside the cage, too vast and shadowy to see where it ended, though he could make out a ramshackle hut at the back, with wooden walls and a corrugated tin roof. He thought Mrs F was winding him up: that the cage was as empty as most of the others, so he picked up a stick, about as long as his arm, and began to run it along the bars as he walked.

The echo of the metal was a pleasant noise, almost musical, and Joseph enjoyed how the stick, bouncing off the bars, sent shudders up his arms and across his chest. He reached the end of the cage, spun on his heels and started to rewalk its length, repeating the process, ignoring Mrs F's second warning.

But as he reached the middle of the cage, he felt the world spin on its axis.

There was no warning, no siren, just a tsunami of movement and an ear-splitting noise. Something crashed against the bars, ripping the branch from his fingers and sending him skittering backwards in shock, tripping and falling unceremoniously to the ground.

The noise continued. Noise wasn't even the word. Joseph had never heard anything like it. It tore at his ears, so loud that his hands flew to his lobes, not only to cover them, but to stop the blood that he felt must be flowing. What sort of place was this? he thought. What on earth was he doing here? Was it a punishment? Because he didn't deserve this, did he?

The chaos didn't stop. Whatever was in the cage continued to throw itself against the bars, long hairy arms reaching through, clawing for the boy as he scuttled away on his hands and knees.

It was a monkey, he thought. No, it was bigger than that. Way bigger. Angrier, too. Angry enough to push Mrs F into action, moving towards the bars as Joseph dashed from them. Through gasping breaths Joseph watched her walk slowly closer, arm outstretched, hand open and flat, but head lowered, never once making eye contact with the monster inside.

What was she doing? Had she not seen what was in the cage, the way it was behaving? It'd rip her apart. She was mad.

Mrs F, though, appeared to be completely in control. As she neared the cage, her pace slowed further and she started to talk. Well, make noises really. A succession of grunts, low and

31

guttural, while the arm that wasn't outstretched snaked into her pocket.

She reached the bars, a matter of inches from where the animal still rocked, agitated, and let herself slide down them until she was in a crouching position, a mirror image of the animal inside the cage. Slowly, with her head still down, she took a carrot from her pocket, and pretended to eat it. The animal watched her, its movements slightly blunted.

She pretended to take another bite, and a third: then, almost in slow motion, she allowed her arm to reach through the bars, the beast's hand brushing hers as he took the carrot from her grasp.

And then? Nothing. The animal tucked into it, while scratching at something on his belly. A flea probably, Joseph thought, as he watched Mrs F mimic him, her own hand rubbing at her stomach.

The carrot lasted seconds, and before he'd even finished his final mouthful, the creature turned and stalked into the shadows. Mrs F stood too, shaking the stiffness from her knees.

'Don't worry. Adonis takes some getting to know. You'll be cleaning his cage out in no time.'

'You go in *there*? When he's actually in there too?'

'Of course. I can hardly send him out for ice cream, can I? And he's not likely to shovel up his own muck if I leave him a spade. Sometimes I wait till he's asleep, sometimes not. It's all about trust.'

'You wouldn't catch me in there,' he mumbled.

Mrs F didn't hear him, but she wasn't finished. 'Lesson number one,' she said. 'Always listen to Mrs F.'

There was a pause, a heartbeat.

'Lesson number two – always listen to Mrs F in the zoo. *Especially* in the zoo. I'll tell you lesson number three as soon as I make it up.'

And without offering him a hand, she walked on, the stupid dog circling her.

Joseph's eyes didn't leave the cage. He still couldn't comprehend what he'd seen. All he knew was that Adonis (if that was the name of the creature), clearly didn't like him very much. Just like everyone else in his life.

5

As entertainment went, the zoo fared badly, and not just because of the foul mood that enveloped Joseph after his introduction to Adonis.

He couldn't stop thinking about what had just happened. What was it about him that made others react like that instinctively? Was he *so* vile and repulsive? Should he have acted differently? Retaliated, maybe? He didn't know. Maybe, he thought, it summed everything up. Maybe he was only getting what he deserved. All these thoughts bubbled and stewed within him. He didn't have a clue what to do with any of them, so he settled as usual for feeling angry.

'Stupid monkey,' he murmured, too close to Mrs F.

'Don't let him hear you call him that,' she replied, throwing a pair of stinking overalls his way. 'He's not a monkey. He's a gorilla. Silverback. Pride of the zoo, that one. When it was open.' Her words tailed off and Joseph could see why. There was precious little to feel proud of around here any more.

The boy pulled the overalls on reluctantly. They were covered in a crusty dung, sitting like scabs at regular intervals up and down the legs. He wasn't sure what jobs awaited him to deserve such an outfit, but he was sure they weren't going to be pretty.

First things first, though, Mrs F insisted on a tour to give him his bearings.

'I won't be telling you where things are twice,' she added tersely, 'so stop your sulking and pin your ears back.'

They started in the aquarium, or what would've been the aquarium had it contained any fish. Or water. Joseph was no expert, but he was pretty sure the only thing living inside the tanks now was algae: it clung to the glass like overcooked spinach on a Sunday dinner plate.

'It's not exactly the Ritz in here, is it? Could you not have cleaned the place up a bit?' he sneered.

'Well you know what they say,' she smiled back icily. 'Why keep a dog and bark yourself?'

God, he hated her. Whatever he said, she always had an answer. And his gran must've known that when she sent him here. Still, he'd bide his time. Get his own back on the woman. She could be sure of it.

As he walked round the aquarium, he noticed a vast amount of sticky tape that zigzagged the length and height of the tanks. There seemed no pattern or reason to it: it had the look of a birthday present wrapped by a four-year-old.

Joseph traced the tape with his finger, forehead creased as he tried and failed to understand its mystery.

'In case a bomb drops,' Mrs F said, eyes moving skywards, even though they were standing inside. 'The tape might stop the glass from shattering. It'd cost a small fortune to replace it.'

'Where did the fish go? They dead?'

He felt her stiffen beside him.

'Some of them, yes. Some were moved into the pond outside, the ones that could survive the cold, but the others . . . well, food was so expensive that . . .'

Hesitation. Joseph spotted it and didn't let it go unnoticed.

'What? They died of starvation? Or did you sit there with a fishing rod like a garden gnome?'

He saw her anger ignite, saw it swell and swirl quickly across her body. He liked it, hoped he'd finally got under her skin. But she blindsided him again with a clipped and icy response, calm.

'No,' she said. 'I didn't have a rod, just a set of steel ladders and a net. I had to fish them out one by one, then watch them die. Some of them lasted too long, though, they were writhing about in agony, so I had to put them out of their misery.'

Joseph deflated. What could he say to that? The thought of it was horrible, and for all his spikiness, he didn't know if he could've acted in the way she did. Nor admit it so matter of factly.

So what should he do? He knew what his dad would say. He'd fix him with a steely look, tell him to say he was sorry.

But his dad wasn't here. He'd left him too, whether he wanted to or not. And now he was stuck with this woman, who hated his guts.

'Sounds 'orrible.' They were the only words he could muster.

'Yes, well, it's done now, isn't it?' she replied, marching on. 'So let me show you the rest of it.'

The tour continued, not that there was much to see.

'That was the elephant's enclosure . . .'

'The old lions' den . . .'

'Penguins swam in there . . .'

Most things were referred to in the past tense – all the glories gone, animals transferred to zoos in the countryside or put down before they starved to death.

Mrs F looked more relieved than anything when they passed an aviary of rather dejected-looking birds, but failed to see the funny side when Joseph compared their foliage to Hitler's moustache.

There were camels and ponies, and snakes too, tucked away in a decrepit building (none of them venomous, much to Joseph's disgust) and a pair of scarily thin wolves, prowling their cage at the sight of the boy. At no point did Joseph feel threatened or in danger of them, though, not when he saw inside their mouths: more gums than teeth on display.

'So much to see,' he said sarcastically, but again, she wasn't biting.

'It's far from how I'd like it to be, but there's little I can do about that now. My family's run this place a long time, my father before my brother, so I owe it to both of them to have something left when this madness ends.'

'How do you feed them?'

'Well, they don't have ration books, do they? So I do what I can. I forage, and I beg, and I do deals with people. Just like you'll be doing from now on, too.'

'Me?'

'Yes, you. Which reminds me. Time to get to it. Muck won't move itself.'

'Muck?' Joseph sagged, fearing what lay ahead.

'There's two tons of manure needs shifting from the camel enclosure. We need to get it delivered by the end of the day.'

'Someone *wants* camel dung? Really?'

'Really. There's a war on, in case you didn't wonder. They've turned the local football pitches into allotments, but the earth's all clay and no goodness. Bit of this on it, and they'll be growing pineapples in six weeks.'

'So where's your truck, then? We loading it onto the back?'

'Trucks need petrol. And oil. And we haven't got either. So we'll be using the power we do have. The animals produced it, so they have to do their bit to shift it.'

This was all well and good, but camels weren't known for their dexterity with a spade. That part was left to Joseph. He was told to shovel every last bit of manure onto two huge sheets that sat outside their cage, while managing not to upset the beasts.

'Don't be getting too close to their back ends,' Mrs F instructed from the other side of the bars. 'They're known to kick at a second's notice.'

Joseph didn't reply but made two clear mental notes: to stay away from their rumps, and to wreak some kind of revenge on the woman in return for this fresh hell. But she wasn't finished yet.

'Oh, and be careful about the front too. They're spitters, all of them. End up with a lungful of that on you and you'll be stinking of it for days. Even after I've hosed you down.'

If ever two warnings left a boy paralysed and paranoid, it was those, and what followed was a queasy dance, with Joseph shuffling continually out of range of the camels, who looked to him simultaneously irritated and amused.

The other problem was that as jobs went, it was incredibly boring. Where was the fun in scooping endlessly? The smell didn't get any easier to bear and Joseph couldn't work out how the animals were pooing so much when food was so difficult to come by.

As the boredom increased, he took more breaks, his attention falling outside the bars for anything even vaguely interesting, which was how he spotted Mrs F inside Adonis's cage, spade and pail in hand.

Letting his shovel fall into the hay, he stepped outside the cage, eyes widening.

So she wasn't joking about cleaning Adonis out? And if she was in there, then where was the ape? There must be a way of locking him inside his hut, he thought, but then he caught sight of Adonis, loping slowly in the woman's direction.

Joseph felt himself gasp. Had she seen? Did she know he

was approaching? Should he warn her, or would that just send the ape into a dangerous funk?

All he could do was watch, holding his breath as Mrs F finally felt Adonis's presence, dropping immediately into a crouch, sitting on her haunches, head down towards the dirt. The ape prowled closer, only stopping when he was within touching distance. He could now, quite literally, end her life with one attack, but still Mrs F didn't move. She remained still, other than her back rising and falling with her breath.

What now? Joseph thought. How on earth was she going to get out? If she knew, she showed no signs, though she did start to make small movements that mirrored Adonis's again: a scratch to the chest or leg. Then, a new movement, her hand in her pocket, pulling out a fistful of grass that she slowly offered to the ape as if he were a god. She did it with her head down still, and slowly Adonis took the grass, and looked at it, before pushing it inside his mouth.

When it was gone his hand snaked out once more, and patted Mrs F roughly on the top of her head, twice, before sauntering slowly away.

Joseph felt himself finally breathe out, not daring to look away until Mrs F finished the job in hand and let herself out of the cage.

He shook his head in confusion. He couldn't decide whether the woman was unbelievably brave or stupid. Either way, he couldn't ever imagine feeling confident or comfortable enough to do the same. Not when Adonis had taken such an instant dislike to him. It made him feel irritable, though not as irritable as when Mrs F spotted him and told him to get back to it.

He had no idea how long it took to finally finish his job, but judging by the blisters that lined his palms, it was too long. Still, at least for once he wasn't feeling the cold.

'Right,' Mrs F sighed, 'Part one done. *Finally*. Part two is delivery, but I'll need to help you with that. Can't trust you with our mode of transport.'

She walked into the cage, picking up a harness at the door. With no hesitancy she hooked it over the largest camel's head, leading it placidly outside. Connecting two long ropes either side of the camel, she attached them to one of the sheets, creating a bizarre manure sledge.

'Allotments are two streets away. You might get a few funny looks, but I'd imagine you're used to that.'

'I'm not walking *that* down the road.'

'Why not?'

'Folk'll laugh.'

'And?'

'You might not care, but I do. It's a camel towing dung, for goodness' sake. With me at the front!'

But Mrs F was already shaking her head. 'Do you honestly think Daphne here will move for you? The dung would be fossilised by the time we dropped it off. No, I think we'll start smaller and work up to it, thank you very much.'

What followed next plunged Joseph deeper into despair,

as Mrs F led from a much smaller cage two miniature ponies, who answered to the names of Stan and Ollie.

'You have GOT to be joking.'

'Have you not noticed yet I don't do jokes?'

'Well, whatever game this is, I'm not playing.'

'You'll do as I bloomin' well say,' she barked.

'Or what? You'll send me back home to my gran? Well good luck with that, we both know she don't want me.'

The woman sighed. 'Joseph, for the love of God. Just do as I say, will you? Just this once.'

He shook his head.

'Look,' she went on, 'you don't want to be here, I understand that, but I also know that despite what you may think about your gran, you'd rather be back home. I don't know what she's done to upset you so much. And I know that you'd feel closer to your dad at home, even if he's not there. So the best way of getting you home is by playing the game. By showing your gran that you're not all bad, that you can do as you're bloomin' well told.'

Joseph's head spun. He didn't like the way she spoke, as if she knew exactly what was going on up there. And he certainly didn't like her talking about his dad. She didn't know him, about how much Joseph missed him every day, nor how angry he was that he hadn't been there when he really did need him. Mrs F had no right to bring him up. He shuffled from side to side, steaming, feeling his fingers clench and unclench. He could sense Mrs F's eyes on him and knew she wanted him to say something.

But he couldn't do it. He didn't know what words to use, didn't think for a second that this woman would understand any more than his gran had. He was angry. In fact he was more than that, he was furious, and to his mind, he had every right to be. He just wanted her to shut up. And to make her do so, he snatched the ponies' reins from her to show he was ready.

So, with an encouraging shout and a clout to her rump, Daphne loped into action, a fearless Tweedy keeping up momentum by snapping at her heels.

Wishing only for this day to be over, or for the ground to swallow him up (whichever was quickest), Joseph followed the same prompts as Mrs F, only to very different effect. Stan chose that moment to let go of his bladder: a yellow waterfall that added shamelessly to the crust on Joseph's overalls.

If the boy had had any tears left in him, then he would've stood and wept.

6

It felt like the circus had come to town.

Joseph remembered it well. Not the show itself, Dad hadn't had enough money to buy tickets, but the procession through town beforehand, the announcement that the greatest show on earth had arrived.

With the procession came the acts: muscular strongmen, graceful acrobats, fearless lion-tamers, and, bringing up the rear: the freaks. Bearded women, tattooed men, a child joined to its sibling at the waist, all drawing gasps and laughter from the crowd.

Joseph remembered being mesmerised by them, repulsed, confused and intrigued in equal measure, but never had he wondered how it might feel to be in the show before: to be the one being pointed and laughed at.

Today he had found out. The memory was now seared into his brain, playing on endless repeat like a scratched gramophone record, even when he pulled himself under the lukewarm bathwater to escape.

Mrs F had insisted on them both washing when they got home, and set about boiling the kettle until the tin bath steamed on the hearth rug.

She made no effort to make Joseph get in first, banishing

him to his room while she 'sorted herself out'. He retreated happily, and lay on his bed, listening to the tick of the clock and the faint wail of Mrs F singing through the floorboards. Finally, she called him down.

'The water's still hot, and there's soap on the side there. Don't be using it all, mind. That's got to last us until the end of the month.'

Joseph shrugged. He wouldn't put a dent in the soap. He had no desire to get in the bath at all. Instead, he stood there, motionless, only removing his clothes when he heard her bedroom door close upstairs.

He wouldn't stay in long, he decided. Didn't like the idea of lying in water that had already held her.

He couldn't remember the last time he'd been in a bath. Grandma had long since given up asking him to do anything, and bathing had been way down the list. But once submerged, he had to admit that the water, still warm despite being second-hand, eased his muscles, if not his mind.

Today had been humiliating. The allotments may only have been two streets from the zoo, but it felt like miles. While Daphne made slow but steady progress with her cargo, onlookers cooing at an exotic beast in such a mundane setting, Stan and Ollie were nowhere near as obliging or awe-inspiring. They stopped whenever he drove them on, added to the manure pile more times than anatomically possible, and generally made him look like an ass at every given opportunity.

The kids standing on the street, watching, thought it was

hilarious. They pointed and laughed. Some practically rolled in the gutter, though others weren't laughing after they strayed too close to Joseph and received a well-aimed kick. It was these occasional successes that released the pressure in his head and stopped him from dropping the reins to chase them down the street.

But even now, with his head under the water, Joseph could still hear their laughter, and feel its heat on his face.

As he pushed bubbles up to the surface in disgust, though, he heard a new, muffled sound that definitely wasn't his ears filling with suds. This was a long continual drone, which even from his position, sounded urgent, immediate.

He tried to ignore it, but it got louder and louder, until finally, begrudgingly, he broke through the surface, ears popping as the wail of the air-raid siren ripped through the closed windows.

Planting his hands either side of the tub, he made to push himself out of the bath, just as the door opened to reveal Mrs F, hair wilder than ever, plus Tweedy, seemingly revelling in the chaos.

Mortified, Joseph let his naked body fall back into the bath, not caring about the wave that leaped onto the floor as a result, and for once Mrs F didn't seem angry, even when the boy yelled at her: 'Haven't you ever heard of knocking?!?'

'No, and neither has Adolf.' She threw a rough towel in his direction as she picked up his festering pile of clothes. 'So wrap that round you and get out here pronto.'

Torn by not wanting to do *anything* she said, but terrified by the prospect of the world caving in around him, he pulled himself from the bath, and, shrouding himself in the towel, followed her through the back door.

Cold wasn't the word for what hit him. So icy was the wind that he expected to look down and see the dripping bathwater turning into icicles.

It burned his skin as he staggered in her wake to the bottom of the garden and the air-raid shelter.

He'd seen them at home, of course: ramshackle affairs that looked like they'd collapse under the force of a sneeze, but it had never bothered him. He didn't think for a second that the Luftwaffe would bother coming after them so far north. But here? This was the city, Hitler's prime target, so he had expected something a lot more robust than what he found. There were two untidy piles of sandbags against the back wall and on top of these, a crudely shaped corrugated iron roof. On the front wall, if you could call it that, sat another sheet of metal forming a sort of door, which Mrs F was pulling aside.

'Get in!' she yelled, as her eyes flicked skywards.

Joseph saw little point, for all the protection it offered, but he begrudgingly did as she said. It was strange to see her flustered and nervous. Until this point Joseph had thought she could blow a Nazi bomber from the skies with her temper alone, but this was different. *She* was different.

It wasn't much warmer inside, despite the small, claustrophobic space. Tweedy's whirling tail whipped the two of them in turn, proving a nuisance as Joseph tried to pull on his clothes without losing hold of the towel.

'Get yourself decent. We'll have guests any second.'

Guests? thought Joseph as he wrestled his sweater on. It was hardly the place for high tea.

Just then the door flew open and in piled three shivering bodies.

'Fancy meeting you here,' a woman sighed at Mrs F, followed closely by a tank of a man, clutching a semi-sleeping child and a lantern. They peered curiously at Joseph through the darkness, making him feel self-conscious.

'These are the Twyfords,' Mrs F told him. 'Sylvie, Thomas and Rufus.' The child wriggled in his father's arms: the closest thing to a greeting on offer, as the adults continued to stare.

'And this is Joseph. I was telling you about him, Sylvie,' Mrs F continued. The two women exchanged a look that said nothing and everything at the same time.

'Ah,' replied Sylvie, re-examining him in more detail, before moving as far away as possible, which wasn't easy in such a cramped space.

'Right then, I'll be off,' said Mrs F, a statement so ridiculous given what was happening outside, that even Joseph challenged it.

'Off? Off where?'

'Work,' she answered, incredulous that he even asked.

Joseph frowned in the half light. This hardly seemed the time to be mucking out.

'Sylvie said you can stay here with them till it passes. Tweedy too.'

This pulled quite a reaction from Sylvie. 'Now, Mags, I did say that I would babysit the boy, but we didn't discuss the dog. And you know my opinion on that.'

Joseph frowned. Opinion?

Mrs F was quick to respond. 'Would you rather I took Tweedy with me and risk him getting hurt?'

'I'd rather you did what most people have done, to be honest. I don't wish to be rude, Mags, but most folk have seen it's cruel to keep pets alive during the war. Plus, they're hungry beasts, aren't they?'

'He's not eating into your rations, Sylvie. Only mine. And I will never *ever* put down a healthy animal when there is no need. I don't have time for this, Sylvie, but as you're sat in *my* shelter in my yard, I'll thank you to keep your opinions to yourself. Now, Joseph, you look after Tweedy, do you hear? Don't let him out of your sight. And get yourself to bed as soon as it's over. I'll be home not long after.'

Without a further word, and before he could interrogate her more, she threw the door open and dashed into the siren-filled night, which sent poor Tweedy scuttling to the door to try and follow.

To Joseph, it was another clear example of how terrible his life had become. The world was fighting itself, dragging the only person he cared about away from him to war. And now he'd been sent to a city where a bomb was *more* likely to fall than where he'd come *from*. Here he was, left at Hitler's mercy in a damp, wet trench with what felt like a cardboard roof, alongside a family of complete strangers and a dog crazier than Adolf himself.

Tweedy, it seemed, agreed. Instead of calming down, he continued to spiral out of control, pawing at the mud walls like a deranged prisoner, howling when they refused to give in to his demands. Every minute or so he would stop, not because the Twyfords were shouting at him to do so, but because he kept pulling on Joseph's sock with his teeth to join him, almost imploring him.

Joseph knew only too well what it was like to be left without a choice or a say, and he knew he didn't like it either.

'It's all right,' he said reluctantly, without adopting that babyish voice most people used when speaking to a pet. 'She's coming back soon.'

But no matter how many times he stroked his back, or rubbed at the matted fur that clung beneath his jaw, Tweedy was inconsolable, and after one final frantic burrow, he changed tack completely and threw himself against the door, dislodging it enough to pull himself triumphantly through and out into the night.

'You are joking!' Joseph moaned. How on earth had he managed to lose a dog in an air-raid shelter?

'What have you let him out for?' Sylvie yelled.

'I'll get him back in,' snapped Joseph. He didn't want to

spend any more time with these people than necessary. It was clear they were looking down their noses at him.

The door was jammed, so he pulled himself through the gap, hearing Sylvie tell her husband to follow behind. 'Do you want to face Margaret's temper if anything happens to either of them?'

But from the cursing behind Joseph, it was clear Mr Twyford had no desire to leave the shelter.

Joseph looked for the dog, hoping he was merely chasing his own shadow in the yard, and yes, there he was, doing exactly that.

'Come on, boy,' said Joseph, taking a calm, quiet approach that felt quite alien to him. 'Back inside now, come on.'

But the dog wasn't interested. In fact, he picked that moment to show he could be just as stubborn as the boy. Instead of obediently padding back underground, he tore in the opposite direction, and leaped the fence into next door's yard.

'I don't believe it,' Joseph groaned. What had he done to deserve this? And more importantly, what was he going to do about it?

He weighed up his options, which were equally simple but unappealing: chase the dog and possibly risk a Nazi bomb. Or lose the dog, slink back to the shelter, and risk the wrath of Mrs F.

What sort of a choice was that? It wasn't like he owed Mrs F a damned thing, but he had little desire to sit in a cramped pit with the world's grumpiest man and his miserable wife.

God, he thought, *what the hell do I do?* He looked to the sky. Silent but for the siren. Empty. Not a bomber to be seen.

What harm can it do? he said to himself. He'd corner the dog, drag him back to the shelter, then pretend he was deaf as well as rude.

He ran to the fence and clambered clumsily over it.

7

His plan, however, soon ran aground.

Firstly, because of the damn dog, whose whippet genes had propelled him out of next door's yard, plus the next six, at the most terrific speed.

His jumping was impressive too. Joseph peered, slack-jawed, through the inky darkness as Tweedy cleared fence after fence like a Grand National winner, leaving the boy to trail like a rag-and-bone nag. Jumping had never been his forte, unless it was onto someone's back before wrestling them to the ground. Scratches bit at his legs from abrasive fence panels and one aggressive rose bush, but as Joseph stumbled over the final obstacle, he caught sight of Tweedy skittering around the corner and away from Calmly View.

'Bloomin' mutt!' He grimaced, forcing his legs to go faster as he gave chase. 'Get BACK here!' he yelled, his voice echoing, the only noise to be heard now the siren had finally stopped. The street was so quiet and dark, Joseph could've been forgiven for forgetting he was in the city at all.

He cursed the darkness as a kerb tripped him up. If it weren't for it being the clearest of winter nights, and the moon coating the horizon slightly, he would've found any progress practically impossible.

But as Joseph pulled himself to his feet, he spotted a second flash of light: a slice of blinding orange, streaking across the horizon, followed by a series of pure white spotlights, zigzagging endlessly.

What the hell is that? he thought to himself, before realising it was a bomb exploding in the distance, followed by the home guard searching for the perpetrator. It would have been exciting, if it wasn't so . . . *real*, and it became realer still when the noise of the explosion rumbled through, like thunder following lightning.

He couldn't be sure how far away it was, but it gave his chase renewed purpose. If the bombers were getting closer, then he didn't want to be out here hunting a stupid dog any longer than was necessary.

He wouldn't run away, though. He was no coward. He'd run from nothing in his life, so he'd find the dog. Not to please Mrs F, but himself. No one else.

He caught sight of Tweedy, or thought he did, sniffing casually at a telegraph pole, but his footsteps served as too much of a warning, and the dog bolted again. The only response he got when he shouted to Tweedy was from a warden, yelling at him to 'Get yer backside off the street, before someone blows it up!'

Joseph ignored him, of course, and ran on, following the dog as best he could, though at times he went on luck rather than judgement. Did the damn thing never get tired? *He* was, but just as he felt he couldn't take another lungful of air, he spotted something. A landmark that he recognised.

A set of gates, framed by two stone pillars, and beside them, a persistent, straggly mutt dragging itself through the tiniest of gaps.

The zoo. Of course it was. If Tweedy was reeling from the chaos around him, what else was he going to do but follow his mistress?

Although this place might offer some kind of sanctuary from whatever Adolf was dropping, it also offered up the prospect of a whole new war. Because when Mrs F saw the pair of them staggering into view, she wasn't going to be happy.

Well, sod her, Joseph thought. It was her stupid dog's fault, after all.

But as he took a step inside, there was another flash of light, another rumble of destruction. Not close, but closer, and enough to see the silence in the zoo broken: there was braying and squawking, and howling from the underfed wolves.

All Joseph wanted was to find the dog. Not to try and drag it home without Mrs F seeing, he wasn't daft. If he tried to do that then Tweedy would make an even worse noise than the din invading his ears right now.

Perhaps if she spotted them at the same time, then her anger might be mildly diluted. Joseph thought about this for a moment, then realised she'd be livid either way. But did he care? He did not.

So he wandered round the zoo, only flinching when a further explosion lit up the horizon. He walked past the aviary, the birds zipping quickly around it, almost in Spitfire formation. The camels looked animated instead of lazy for once, searching for something to kick or spit at in agitation, while the wolves were too busy howling to look hungrily in Joseph's direction.

Whichever path he took, there was no sign of Mrs F. Was she even there at all? Maybe she had further secrets. He wouldn't be surprised. His father aside, he'd not met an adult who was as honest as they claimed to be.

But then he approached Adonis's cage. He didn't want to. He'd avoided it on purpose, didn't want to be anywhere near him or his anger, and as he neared the cage he picked up a rock just in case. He wasn't afraid to throw it, either, if there was any repeat of their first meeting.

There was no sign of the ape, though Joseph could hear him groaning from the shadows. What he *could* see though, was Mrs F, standing some twenty yards from the bars of the cage.

He moved closer, but as he did so, he noticed something very strange.

Another bomb burst on the horizon, close enough to jolt her instinctively into a pose that made no sense whatsoever. It wasn't a calm pose. She wasn't reassuring the ape through the bars this time. She was standing, legs apart, and clutching beneath her chin a rifle.

A rifle that trembled in her grasp, but was pointed and ready to fire, directly into Adonis's lair.

8

Not much shocked Joseph these days, but this didn't make any kind of sense.

What on earth was she doing? The first time he'd seen her in front of this cage, she'd calmed the animal in a way that he hadn't known was possible. The time after that, she'd been *inside* the bars, with nothing to protect her. It had been like she'd understood what the animal needed. No, more than that, he thought: as if she *loved* the beast.

So why was she now looking like she was ready to end its life just as easily?

'Mrs F?' he gasped, voice fighting with another explosion off in the distance.

The woman's eyes flitted skywards, gauging if the German bomber above was any closer than the last. Her focus spun back to the cage as Adonis dashed, panicked, from the shadows. Instantly the barrel trained back to the animal, the rifle tight under her chin, the strain visible on her face and arms.

Adonis made his displeasure felt. Louder. Angrier. Joseph wondered if it was because the ape had spotted him, an even less-welcome guest than a Nazi bomb?

But as the tension and confusion built to breaking point,

they were suddenly shattered, as from nowhere bounded Tweedy, rearing up at his mistress, pulling her focus from the cage.

'What the hell are you doing here?' she said, pushing the dog down while swinging the rifle strap over her shoulder. Her eyes swept her surroundings, narrowing when she saw Joseph only yards away.

'I might have known!' she boomed. 'Can you not do anything I ask?'

He wanted to fight back. To tell her this was the last place he wanted to be: that he'd simply chased her stupid dog here. But at the same time he wanted to know why she had a rifle. And why she had it pointed at Adonis.

But he didn't get a chance to ask anything because Mrs F's attention was pulled away by yet another blast. It still wasn't close, but it brought on a din from all corners of the zoo, and galvanised her into action.

'With me. Now!' she yelled, pushing Tweedy in his direction.

Joseph didn't move, so she shoved him on. She was much stronger than she had any right to be.

'Where are we going?' he protested.

'The aquarium. There's a trapdoor to the cellar. You'll get down there and you will not MOVE until the siren tells you to. Understood?'

He didn't want to do what she said, but felt powerless against her speed and strength. It was like being whisked up by a tornado, and by the time he could really resist, he was descending a dark set of stairs, the dog whimpering at his feet.

'Trip me up, I dare you,' he spat at it as the door slammed shut, throwing him into darkness.

It was just the two of them. Mrs F was still above ground with the rifle, doing God knows what. It was no warmer down here than it was in the open air, just damper, plus it smelled appalling, like all the fish from the aquarium had been dumped there to rot.

Joseph did the only thing he could. He sat on the damp bottom step, tensing as the dog pushed into him for warmth, and waited for the siren to sound the all clear.

9

Joseph had known some long, uncomfortable nights: nights wondering why his mum had done what she did, as well as what *he* must have done to cause it, but this night was different. It felt like it would never end. Time ceased to matter. The darkness of the cellar gave nothing away. It could've been morning, for all he knew, but inside his concrete bunker there were no clues to tell him when the bombers would no longer come.

Sleeping was out of the question, too, unless you were Tweedy, and the only reason the dog had snored for the last three hours was because he'd found some comfort on the boy's lap. Joseph had thrown the mutt off the first few times he'd tried, but Tweedy was persistent, and eventually Joseph gave in. Having one part of his freezing torso warmed was preferable to none at all, though it did mean he had to sit bolt upright on his prison's step, left with nothing but his thoughts, of which he had many.

He started in the obvious place, railing against why he was here in the first place, damning his mother, grandmother, even his dad, which was rare. But when even those thoughts grew tired of themselves, he was left with what he had just witnessed: Mrs F, the rifle, the cage.

It made no sense, no matter how many different angles he approached it from. If he wanted to know the truth he'd simply have to ask her.

But how should he approach that? She'd proven herself straightforward, blunt even, but without ever giving anything of herself away. So there in the darkness, he wrote himself a script that he wouldn't deviate from until she cracked under the pressure.

'Come on,' he'd say. 'In the two days I've been here, that ape's the only thing you've been especially kind to. Like when it went for me. Calmed it down, you did, without shouting or being horrible. Then you fed it from inside the bloomin' cage, and don't say you didn't, cos I saw you. It was like you were the best of friends. So why have you got a gun pointing at it now, eh? It doesn't make sense!'

He nodded to himself, that would do nicely. Straight and fair. Even Mrs F couldn't wriggle out of this one.

The all clear finally rang as dawn broke, sending Tweedy skittering up the steps in a frenzy. Joseph stood, trying to shake life and warmth back into his legs and hold the script in his head. It wasn't easy: the lack of sleep had reduced his brain to what felt like trifle.

He emerged from the aquarium, mole-like. The morning was bitingly cold, with a sheen of dew underfoot and clearish skies above: though in the distance there stretched a long band of smoke, evidence of the Nazis' big night on the town. He couldn't help but wonder what he'd find if he followed the smoke to its source.

Mrs F wasn't hard to track down. He found her by Adonis's lair again, though her pose was markedly different from last night's.

She was slumped on her haunches, forehead and hands resting on the rifle's barrel. Any exposed skin carried a strange, blue tinge. As uncomfortable as that pose appeared, it looked to him like she might be asleep.

Not for long though. Joseph's crunching footsteps soon startled her, the gun returning to her chin as she swung it upon him, eyes wild, yet vacant. Like she hadn't a clue where she was.

If he'd been in the mood he might have thrown his arms up in surrender and said something like 'Don't shoot!'

Typically though, she got in first. 'I am *not* happy with you, my lad,' she spat, her daze as short as her temper.

'Eh?'

'What in the name of blazes were you doing out in the air raid? Did I not make it clear you were to stay with the Twyfords until I got back?'

'It's not my fault. Try blaming your little friend here.' He pointed at Tweedy, now coiled between his mistress's legs, looking him straight in the eye. If Joseph hadn't known better, he'd have sworn the mutt just stuck his tongue out in defiance. 'Soon as you left he got spooked and legged it. What was I supposed to do? Leave him to get blown up?'

'Did the Twyfords not try to stop you? You could've been killed!'

'Why would they? I don't belong to them, do I?'

'You should've stayed where you were. Done as you were told.'

'What? And let Tweedy get blown up instead?'

'If necessary, yes!' she replied.

Joseph pondered this and made sure his expression was doing the same. 'Makes sense I suppose, given what you were doing when I found you last night.'

'And what's that supposed to mean?'

'Well, from what I saw, you're not quite the animal lover you say you are.' He allowed his gaze to move, obviously, to Adonis's cage.

He wanted her to know that he hadn't missed a thing. And he sensed a change in her as she bit back.

'I don't know what you mean, Joseph.'

It felt like a weak answer, delivered without her usual strength. And it galvanised Joseph further.

'Yeah, you do. What was happening when I got here?'

Mrs F shrugged, leaning the rifle against her hip, as if to play down its significance. 'None of your business, is what.'

'Oh, right. Just struck me as strange, that's all.'

'What? Keeping everyone safe. That's strange, is it?'

'Safe? Looked to me like you were ready to put a *hole* in Adonis, not keep him safe.'

'Yes well, it's not as simple as that, is it? Nothing is, these days.'

'Looked pretty simple to me. I thought you were here to look after the animals . . . not end them.'

He could see her colour rising: pink, amber, red, crimson. And he loved it.

'Do you think I want to be stood here holding this, pointing it at *anything*?' Her tone was shrill. 'Well? *Do* you? You know nothing, child. No—'

Joseph had her. He'd done it. He allowed himself to enjoy it, holding his hands up in mock surrender. 'No need to defend yourself to me. Though if you needed someone to end the big lump in there, all you needed to do was ask.'

If the home guard had been watching, they'd have been winding up the siren, as Mrs F was ready to blow. Her face was afire, even her hair burned brighter than normal against the early morning light.

Come on then, Joseph said to himself. *Let's see how much fight you've got in you. How hard do I have to push before you pack me off, like all the others?*

But if the woman was going to explode, she wasn't going to do it in front of him.

Instead, she swept past Joseph and out of sight.

The boy felt the force of her mood as it passed and then

sat, looking at Adonis's cage, pleased and surprised that he'd managed to get a rise out of her so quickly. But what was she actually doing with the rifle?

That remained between her and the ape, and he doubted, very much, that Adonis was going to tell him a thing.

10

Joseph sat for a while, but it didn't suit him. It made his ears sting with cold and his brain itch with questions.

Where has she gone? it asked. *What was she doing?*

When he couldn't answer, his mood darkened further.

Why do you even care? he asked himself. *Do you think she's in that office fretting about what you're doing? No, she isn't. She's probably sat with a nice cup of tea.*

He told himself to think or do something else. There had to be another way of occupying his brain, he was in a zoo, for crying out loud. But then again he thought, when the prize assets are two wolves howling for dentures, or an ape in need of a straitjacket, well, it hardly screamed 'funfair'.

Instead, he gave himself a shortlist in an attempt to force the issue.

a. Find Mrs F – hardly tempting.
b. Go back to her house on his own and catch up on the sleep he'd missed – tempting, but without Tweedy to lead him, he'd probably not find his way.
c. Pull on his crusty overalls and find more dung to clear. Or try and find something to feed to the animals.

But as that final thought entered his head, he shook it out angrily. Why the hell would he do that? What possible reason did he have for bending his back to help someone who clearly didn't want him around?

In his mind, she was no different to the others who were meant to have cared for him. In fact, he thought, scrub that, she was worse. At least when his dad was called up, his gran made noises about wanting him, even if that's all they were. It hadn't taken long for her to change her mind.

But this woman? If she hadn't insisted on him washing his clothes then he wouldn't have bothered unpacking his case. Wait till she saw in him the things his mum and gran had. She'd give him a piggyback to the station, just to be rid. Maybe then everyone would leave him be. Maybe then they'd recognise what he already knew, that he was best on his own.

So he dug his heels in, or on this occasion, his backside, and remained sitting on the bench that faced Adonis's lair.

Right on cue the ape chose to lope out of the shadows, stalking on all fours, each step slow and loose, back flat enough to serve a pot of tea from.

'What do *you* want?' Joseph said. The last thing he wanted was to see its face. He wasn't going to move, though. That would feel like defeat, like the gorilla had won on the basis of their first encounter, and Joseph wouldn't have that.

As much as he wanted to look away, he couldn't, for there

was something majestic about the way the gorilla covered the ground. Each placement of his fists seemed planned, navigated, the muscles in his arms and chest rippling as they took the weight of the rest of him. As he strode, his head moved slowly from side to side, eyes piercing, seeking any danger that dared invade his eyeline. He looked in complete control of his surroundings, and the boy envied him for it.

It looked to Joseph as though Adonis's kingdom didn't even end at the bars: they were a mere inconvenience, one that he could overcome whenever he saw fit.

Joseph sat and watched, lips pulled in a snarl. If Mrs F wasn't here to aim his anger at, then he would be more than happy to point it at the animal, and with good reason, he thought. It had scared him witless, for starters, but more than that, like everyone in his life it seemed Adonis had chosen to reject him. Instantly, in this case. And when that happened, the boy had learned to return fire. He could match every bit of anger thrown his way.

Adonis paced the width of his enclosure, left to right and back again, ploughing the same path around six feet from the bars. The grass there had long been trampled, replaced by a parched, cracked earth that trembled regardless of how slowly the ape placed his feet.

It wasn't until he'd covered the entire space half a dozen times that he finally came to a halt, sitting with his weight resting upon his gigantic fists.

Adonis's gaze landed on Joseph. The boy's pulse quickened. He hadn't taken his attention from the ape, not once, in the hope that eventually their eyes would lock, but when they did, it was not what he expected.

The ape didn't blink when he looked at him and his pupils blazed with an orange fury. It was pure animal, *primal*, the boy thought, without realising that his own eyes flared with the same intensity.

Joseph looked hard at the scars dotted on the animal's face. They were old, some half-hidden by hair that had long grown back, but they were worn like trophies, as a warning to anyone who dared get too close.

The boy would not back down or look away, though, and it was Adonis who tired of the stand-off first — a loud, unexpected bark surprising Joseph, knocking him off balance. After a second, quieter noise, Adonis pushed his fists into the ground, and started his languid movements again. In seconds, Joseph was left to look only at his rear.

What had he done this time to deserve that?

It brought something up in Joseph. Too many times he'd been judged too quickly, and he was damned if it was going to happen now with a dirty, stinking ape.

He jumped from his perch and stooped for the nearest piece of rubble. Pulling himself into a side-on position, he trained his arm on Adonis, who had sat once more.

Here it came. His own revenge. A feeling he loved and was well-versed in.

His shoulder tensed, eyes narrowed, as his arm pulled back.

This was it. He would *not* miss.

11

'I wouldn't rush if I were you,' said a voice behind him. 'He probably won't move now for the rest of the day.' It distracted him: the rubble fell pathetically short of its target.

Joseph turned, ready to fire in that direction too, and there, leaning on a wall, wearing a pair of much cleaner overalls, was a girl. His age or similar, hair not much longer than his own.

Embarrassed by his excuse for a throw, and angered by the interruption, he bent for another rock.

'He won't budge, no matter what you throw at him. Believe me.'

Joseph winced in irritation. Who was she? More importantly, why did she think he wanted her advice? He let fly: the rubble scything from his arm and troubling the bars this time, but not Adonis, who didn't flinch. He simply stared off into the distance.

'You're Joseph. Syd.' It wasn't an introduction. More a statement of facts, delivered in a voice that was clipped and posh, like you heard on the wireless.

At the sound of her name, though, Joseph gave her a second glance, wondering if she were actually a boy after all.

'It's Syd with a Y,' she said, filling in the blanks, but Joseph didn't acknowledge her, hoping she'd take the hint and push off.

But that, it seemed, wasn't Syd's way. 'Seems your tongue didn't make it onto the train with you, did it? Or maybe you've nothing worth saying.'

Now that *did* test Joseph. He had plenty to say, just not to her. And what was it with the people down here? First Mrs F, then the idiot Twyfords in the bunker and now this one – did people in the south have their kindness dug out of them with a spoon?

'What do you want?' he barked. It was a mistake, of course, and he realised this as soon as it came out.

'It speaks!' she mocked, taking his words as an excuse to march beside him. 'I was beginning to think you were mute, but it turns out you're just rude. Still, at least I know now. And I don't *want* anything by the way, though thanks for the offer.'

Joseph did all he could to keep his mouth closed, but it mattered little. There was no chance of prising even the shortest of words in.

'What I *wanted* to do, before you interrupted me with your attempts at conversation, is tell you why Adonis is sitting there like that. I mean, it's clear you don't like him; it's plastered all over your face. But to be honest, I don't think that will bother him too much, because what you will learn very quickly is that Adonis is rather selective about who he pays attention to these days.'

'These days?'

'He was never a great chatterer, to be honest, and he was never a performer either, not like the penguins. Most you ever got was that he'd come out of his hut and walk around for a bit till he got bored. But now? Well, he's a quiet, withdrawn old man.'

'Withdrawn?' Joseph snorted with derision. 'He nearly throttled me the other day.'

'Did he? How odd. You must've really provoked him. He's been very quiet since they took the others away.'

He had to ask. 'Others?'

She plumped herself up, knowing she had his interest. 'That's right. Adonis had a mate. And a son. Terrible business.' She paused, her voice catching in her throat, leading to a rare pause, before, 'I hate this war. All of it. All it does is take.'

Joseph frowned. 'So where are they now? His family?'

'Gone. His mate was rehoused in a zoo out of the city after his son Malachi died. Mrs F reckoned Aphrodite would die too if she stayed here. Thought the grief would kill her.'

Aphrodite? he thought. What kind of name was that for a monkey? He didn't say it though, opting instead for, 'Living with Adonis can't have helped. Irritable beggar.'

'Well, that's where you're wrong,' Syd replied. 'Inseparable, they were, the three of them. Rarely seen without standing in each other's shadows. That's why the public loved them. That's why it changed them both so much when Malachi died.'

Joseph listened, but doubted most of it. It was a lot easier to just hate the beast. 'So you're telling me, that that thing in there is *grieving*?'

'You don't have to be sat crying to be grieving, you know,'

she said. 'You don't know him like we do or saw what we did. When the baby got sick, Mrs F tried to tend to him, but it wasn't easy. She couldn't get close; Adonis saw to that. Even if Mrs F could've got near him, there wasn't much she could do. Vets are hard to come by, and even if they weren't, they're not allowed to "waste" medicine on animals.'

'So he wouldn't even let his own son get treated.'

'What? He's an ape, you fool! He couldn't tell us how he was feeling. He was just trying to protect his son. Like any parent would. From the second Malachi got sick, Adonis didn't leave his side. Not for a second. The only way Mrs F could even retrieve the body after he died was to sedate Adonis.'

'So what actually happened to his missus?'

'Same thing that happened to a lot of the other animals here. Shipped out once it became clear the war wasn't passing quickly. A zoo in the countryside had space for her. Bigger enclosure, more food, less chance of having a bomb dropped on her.'

'But they didn't want Adonis? Not that I'd blame 'em.'

Syd's face looked pained. 'No they didn't, but not for the reasons you think. It was because no one has enough money, have they? Or food. Plus Adonis wasn't like Aphrodite. He's older. It was a surprise when he fathered Malachi, but *she* was still young. The new zoo wanted to pair her with a male already there. There was no *point* in taking Adonis too.'

Joseph shrugged. All this talk of mothers leaving was too

close to the bone, so he kept his focus on the ape in the cage. 'So basically, he's sulking. That's what you're telling me?'

'I'd like to see how you'd feel if that happened to you,' Syd barked back, 'because I can tell you now, losing people is the *worst* thing imaginable.'

'No, I'll tell you what the *worst* thing is – it's being told what to do or how to feel by a stuck-up kid! I mean, what did you even come over for?'

Syd gathered herself before carrying on, as calmly as she could. 'I came over because we're going to be working together. Because like yours, my life hasn't been exactly simple lately, but thanks to Mrs F, I've got something to keep my mind off it. I came over here to say hello, because to be honest, you looked sad. And I thought, stupidly, that I might be able to help. But you were too busy throwing stones at Adonis.'

He wanted to tell her to sling her hook, that she knew nothing about him and if he had his way she never would. But for once, he kept control. He realised she might actually be of some use to him. 'Well, if you want to be a friend, you can start by telling me about that rifle Mrs F keeps in the office. And why, when I arrived last night in the middle of the raid, she was pointing it straight at Adonis.'

But it seemed Syd had run out of charity. 'Tell you what, *friend*, why don't you ask her yourself?'

And she moved on without looking back, leaving Joseph both on his own, and in the dark.

12

'Joseph Palmer?' came the yell the following morning. 'Get your backside down here, or my hand'll be itching.'

He did not answer. He was perched, fully dressed, on the end of his bed and wanted to spend as little time with the woman as possible. He gave it another ninety seconds: long enough to not seem like he was doing as he was told, but not too long to have to endure another telling off.

There was little to look forward to. Another freezing day at the zoo: humping waste about, sorting rotten food from the edible, and, of course, the prospect of more anger from Adonis, sat on his throne. Plus now there was Syd to factor in. Little Miss Know-it-all.

No wonder he descended the stairs slowly.

'About time,' Mrs F said, when he finally appeared. 'I've more to do than summon you repeatedly from your pit, so remember this, please. Breakfast is six forty-five. Not six fifty-five or six fifty. And I'll not be serving you either, so you'll do well to remember that. If you want to eat, then you'll be down here, prompt. You hear?'

He gave the shallowest of nods.

'Right, well. It's Monday. So you know what that means.'

'The zoo again?' he huffed.

'Not till this afternoon. You've got school first.'

'School?'

'That's the one. You might have heard of it, though from what your gran told me, you haven't stepped inside one for a while.'

'Yeah, well, I wouldn't believe everything she tells you. Anyway, I didn't think school would be open. All them kids at the station were off to the countryside.'

'Most of them. But evacuation's not compulsory.'

'Still, no point me going to school.' He felt his heart race anxiously at the prospect of lessons.

But Mrs F was having none of it. 'There's every point, my lad. Now, you'll need your gas mask box, and I've cobbled you something resembling a uniform. Some old stuff from one of the neighbours. There's an apple, some bread and a bit of cheese on top of your mask in the hall. And from tomorrow, I'll expect you to get it all sorted yourself.'

She let the last of her words fall away, as if embarrassed that she'd done this much already, and wiped her hands rigorously down the front of her dress.

'I'd rather not go, though,' he said, not wanting to make it sound as big a deal as it actually was. 'I'd be more use at the zoo with you.'

He felt her quizzical gaze upon him, knew it was suspicious, the notion of him wanting to spend more time in her company.

'And you will be. After lessons.'

'Gran wasn't bothered about me going in the end.'

'Well I'm not your gran, and I don't believe that's true anyway. So get yourself sorted and wait by the gate. Someone's going to walk you there. I've to be at work.'

This was his moment. His big one. Too often already, the woman had had her way. So he couldn't let her win on this, surely. His mind raced to the last time he'd been at school. The laughter, the pointing fingers and humiliation. He couldn't do it. Not again. So he sat on the kitchen chair, wrestled a hunk of stale bread from the loaf, and shoved it all into his mouth until his cheeks bulged. He knew this would rile her. Bread, stale or otherwise, was scarce. This way, he didn't have to explain why he wouldn't go.

But Mrs F was onto him. 'Don't you worry, my lad. You don't need to speak. You just need to listen. You ARE going to school. You ARE going to listen. And you ARE going to learn. And you can start with learning how to tie your shoelaces. You've got ten minutes.'

Ten minutes later, he was standing at the gate, box dangling from his neck, shorts and shirt fitting him so badly it looked like he'd shrunk in the wash. He did not like it. It made him appear weak and puny: a target.

He turned the waistband of the shorts over several times, so they finished above the knees instead of below them. But as he did so, the material at the bottom flared outwards, so when he stood with his legs together it gave the impression that he was wearing a skirt, his scrawny legs apologising all the way to his feet, hiding inside a huge pair of strangers' shoes.

'You can do this,' he whispered to himself, more in hope than belief, but when his school escort arrived, he revised this thought dramatically.

'Well, don't *you* look quite the picture,' said Syd, sporting a smile that said something else entirely.

You ARE joking me, he winced to himself, though he didn't say it. He was practising his gruff exterior, ready for the rest of the day. 'Isn't it time you were evacuated?' he asked, brain half wondering why this hadn't already happened.

'It may well happen yet. But till then, lucky me gets to be your babysitter.'

'Bring him to the zoo straight from school, Syd, won't you?' said Mrs F, marching through the front door and gate without pausing, leaving the two of them on their own.

'Why you?' he said, sullenly.

'Because Mrs F asked me.'

'She asks *me* to do loads of things. Doesn't mean I do any of them.'

'Maybe you should try.'

Joseph didn't like the sound of that. 'Why do you even like her?'

'Because she gave me a job. And support. And help. You know, for someone who acts like they don't want me around, you don't half ask a lot of questions.'

'Doesn't mean I like you,' Joseph said. 'And call what you've got "a job"? Scraping up dung eight hours a day?'

'There are worse things out there, and besides, sometimes the rubbish jobs are the best. They stop you thinking.'

'Aw, got stuff on your mind, have you?'

She looked at him with disdain. 'The last time I checked, this war affected more people than just you.'

She started to walk, with Joseph slouching behind her.

'Now,' she said, 'there are a few things you need to know about Carr Lane School.'

'The only thing I need to know is why the bloomin' place is even open. I thought all the kids had been packed off.'

'Most of them were, but then because nothing happened and the bombs didn't come like everyone thought they would, some parents wanted their kids back home.'

'Even though the bombings would still probably start?'

'Some families didn't think they had a choice. One boy, Tim, he's in our class, his dad runs a shop, but when he got enlisted, it was up to his mum and gran to keep it going. But then his gran died so he got brought home to help, even though he's only nine. Or there's Wendy, her dad got sent to fight but her mum can't walk properly, so she had to come back to look after her. It's awful really, she's only eight!'

But Joseph wasn't great at sympathy. 'Right. So it's basically all the misfit kids, shoved together in one room.'

Syd was aghast. 'Speak for yourself, Joseph Palmer,' she

said. 'We all have reasons for being here. *All* of us. Now, do you want me to prepare you for school, or not?'

He grunted something that was barely a word, but that was enough for Syd to continue: 'Firstly, Mr Gryce, the headmaster. Watch him! If he warns you once, he won't do it again. I promise you.'

Joseph shrugged, like it didn't bother him a jot.

'You need to be prepared, Joseph. He was an officer in the last war and acts like he still is. He runs the place like it's an army barracks. Same things happen every day, every week, every month.'

'Like what?'

'Like his Friday tests. Last Friday of every month he comes into class and tests each of us on what we've learned. Sets us sums, makes us read out loud. He even invites parents in to watch, like it's a parade ground. I swear he's nearly made *them* cry in the past, never mind us!'

Joseph felt his anxiety grow rapidly. He didn't like the sound of the man, and needed to try and work out how on earth to play him. Every school had a teacher like Gryce: in fact, some had more than one. And what worried Joseph was that every one of them had harassed or ridiculed him as soon as they saw what he was capable of – or should he say, incapable of. That was why he'd stayed away so long.

'Are you even listening?' Syd said. 'I'm trying to do you a favour. Well, you need to listen to this, in fact, the only thing you need to remember is that every time you walk into school, look above the door of the assembly hall.'

'Why?'

'Because that's where Clarence hangs.' She lowered her voice, like someone was eavesdropping. 'As a warning.'

'What are you talking about? Who's Clarence? A kid? Why would anyone hang a kid off the wall?'

Syd groaned, like it was the stupidest question ever.

'Clarence, you fool, is Mr Gryce's cane. Fifteen inches of birch. Believe me, Joseph Palmer, you do not want to feel Clarence on your backside. Not today. Not any day.'

'Wouldn't bother me,' he sniffed, though his palms itched at the memory of something similar. 'Anyway, you can't cane what you can't catch.'

'Ha. Don't you tell me that you were never caned at your old school.'

She was right. Joseph had known plenty of Clarences in his short school life. And other things too. Some teachers didn't even bother with a cane, they preferred a belt. Belts without names. And they were only too prepared to risk their trousers falling down if it meant they could punish him for his idiocy. Even if it wasn't his fault. Even if he really *was* trying.

The memories left him sweating and falling even further behind Syd.

'Come on!' she said. 'Clarence doesn't approve of latecomers. Anything else you want to know?'

There was, of course there was. But it had nothing to do with school. The only answer he wanted was to the question he'd asked her at the zoo. The one she'd refused to answer.

'Yeah, I've got a question. Why did Mrs F want to shoot Adonis?'

13

Syd looked at him like he was insane.

'You are joking, aren't you?'

'What do you mean?'

'You don't really think she *wanted* to shoot him, do you?'

To be honest, Joseph hadn't a clue. The woman had been endlessly short-tempered with him, but he'd seen a different side to her when it came to Adonis. She cared for that ape. That's why it was such a shock to see her pointing a rifle straight at him.

'I don't know. That's why I'm asking.'

'Well you can take it from me that she doesn't want to. Ever. I mean, think about it. Mrs F runs that place out of duty to her family. She gets no money, little support, unless you count me and you, and she's watched it be run into the ground because of those monsters in Berlin. So, do you really think she *wants* to kill the only real prize left in the place?'

'Yeah but I saw her, didn't I? She was stood there, while the bombs were dropping, pointing a rifle right into his cage. So yeah, if she didn't want to kill him, then she was doing a pretty good impression.'

Syd shook her head. 'And you still can't work out why?'

Joseph shrugged, wishing in part he hadn't brought it up.

He was about to be made to feel stupid the minute he walked into school, he didn't need her doing it as well.

'She was doing what she *has* to do,' Syd continued. 'Her job. It shouldn't be like this, but it is. Her job should be keeping the animals alive, but because of Hitler and his raids, well, the rules have changed. Now, every time the air raid sounds, her job, her ONLY job, is to point that gun at Adonis, because when the sky falls, and it will fall, sooner or later, it'll create carnage in that zoo. Bedlam.'

'So she was going to kill the ape to stop it being scared?'

'No, you fool. If the bomb lands on his cage, and blows the bars out, then there will be a terrified, powerful ape on the loose, one that could rip yours or anyone's arms clean off in a heartbeat. And nobody, not me, you or even Mrs F wants that.'

Joseph couldn't believe what he was hearing. 'What, so if Adolf doesn't snuff out Adonis, then Mrs F has to?'

'Exactly.'

'And do you think she would do it? Do you think she could?'

'Could you?'

Joseph puffed his chest out like it was the easiest answer in the world. 'If I had to, yeah. It's only an animal.'

'Only an animal?'

'An animal that tried to grab me the first time it laid eyes on me. Why should I care about it, when it acts like that? So yeah, if she can't do it, then she can hand the rifle over to me.'

Syd's eyes were wide, like she'd forgotten how to blink.

'It's that simple for you? To end a life, like *that*.' She snapped her fingers.

Joseph shrugged.

'Well, I hope you never lose anyone close to you in your life, Joseph Palmer. Because to say something like that, you clearly never have.'

That lit something in him. 'You don't know nothing about me, so don't think you do. You haven't got a clue what I've lost.'

'What, you mean your dad? But *he's* not dead. He's fighting, like everyone else's round here. So don't think that makes you any different. You know, I haven't a clue why you're so angry all the time, but I do know it's not nice to watch. In fact, it's ugly. Anyone else would feel sorry for Mrs F, having to sit there night after night, waiting for the second when she has to pull the trigger.'

'Yeah, well . . .' He felt like he was being told off. 'I'm not anyone else, am I?'

'No, you're not. But maybe you should think about what she's given you. She's given you a chance, when you needed one. A bed, and food. Food she doesn't have. Plus a job, and now schooling. She's trying to help. Just like she did me.'

Joseph stood, hand on hip, wanting to fight back. 'Why did you even need a chance anyway? What's so special about you?'

'None of your business,' she spat. 'But maybe you should think about this. If you continue to push Mrs F away, then where does that leave you? Because from what I can see, she's your last chance. Without her, you're on your own.'

And she stormed on, through the school gates, not realising that Joseph already knew this. He'd felt on his own for a long, long time, and school was not going to make the situation any better.

14

Stepping inside a school was not a pleasant experience for Joseph, but while this one smelled the same as the last, and the anxiety it dredged up in him was identical, everything else was markedly different.

The size was different. It loomed over the boy the second he walked into the yard, and felt no less intimidating once inside, either. As much as he hated to admit it, Syd had been right, too – there was something unnerving about the sight of Clarence hanging menacingly on the wall. It was ridiculous to think that a thin stick could be watching you, but Joseph felt its presence anxiously, under no illusion that they would become more intimately acquainted sooner rather than later.

He took in the rest of his immediate surroundings: stone walls pocked with holes and flaking grey paint, a wooden floor, dusty and parched, and an honours board, out of date by two years. But there was one thing missing, especially given the scale of the building – and that was pupils.

Aside from Syd, he hadn't seen a soul, and while Joseph welcomed this in some ways (no one had irritated him so far by trying to engage him in conversation), it made every footstep slap an echo eerily around the place.

If he'd thought about it he would've also realised that an

absence of pupils spelled bad news for him. Fewer pupils meant less chance to hide: both his challenging moods, and his educational shortcomings . . .

'You, boy, yes, you!' came a voice, louder than Joseph's footsteps, and bouncing off so many walls that it took him a few seconds to work out where it was coming from. 'Come here.'

The voice came from a man, who on first sight, was clearly the headmaster, Mr Gryce.

Joseph took him in. He looked a little like Clarence: whip-thin and aged. He must've been pushing sixty, and moved quickly across the wooden floor, but without the accompanying footsteps. Joseph found it eerie. Were his feet beneath his gown even touching the floor? Was he some kind of spectre?

'Now,' he said, voice quick and harsh, 'you must be the boy. Margaret Farrelly's charge.'

Joseph had no idea what a charge was, and so hesitated, which wasn't appreciated.

'So . . . You are . . . ?'

'Well, I'm here.' The words came without thinking.

'And you will soon be wishing you weren't, should such insolence continue. Now, name.'

'Joseph.'

'And did your mother deem to give you a surname as well?'

The boy knew the answer to this, obviously, but was

momentarily thrown by the mention of his mum. Right now he hated her more than ever.

'Well?'

'Palmer.'

'Palmer, what?'

'Nothing else.'

'Palmer, *SIR*.'

Joseph saw a pulse throb in Gryce's neck. Then the man pointed, without uttering another word, in the direction of Clarence. He'd done it again and he knew it. Alienated someone from the word 'go'.

'Palmer, SIR.'

'You will do well, round here, to remember one thing, Master Palmer. *Manners maketh the man.* Fail to remember this and you and Clarence will become the firmest of friends. Now, follow me.'

Joseph did exactly that, marvelling again at how only his own footsteps could be heard on the parquet floor.

They swept down a long dark corridor, until they reached a classroom at the end. With a sweeping flourish of Gryce's arm, Joseph was introduced to the rest of the class. All nine of them. Syd, two older boys, and six younger children, some barely of school age. Syd might have denied it, but from first sight, they *were* an odd bunch.

'Miss Doherty, children – this is Joseph Palmer. He will be joining you from this point on. You know where both Clarence and I are, should you require our help. And Master

Palmer, I shall look forward to seeing your progress during my Friday test at the end of the month.' He looked at his watch. 'Do be ready.'

And with that threat burning itself deep inside Joseph, Gryce ghosted from the room.

Miss Doherty, in a break from tradition in this city, approached Joseph with a smile. It made him suspicious.

'Joseph, hello, my name is Miss Doherty. You're very welcome. Why don't you come and join the others?'

He eyed the rows of empty chairs. He was going to stand out here very quickly, and it scared him.

'Is this it, then?' he asked.

She looked confused. 'I'm sorry?'

He pointed at the empty bank of desks.

'Yes, the others were all evacuated – mostly to Yorkshire.'

'Lucky them,' Joseph said quietly.

'So it's just we few, we happy few,' she said.

There was a singsong quality to her voice that suggested she normally taught much younger children.

'So, Joseph. Tell me about your old school.'

'Nothing to tell,' he said quietly, fearing anything he said would give away the fact that he could remember little. He'd blanked a lot of it out.

'Well, was it a large school?'

'Not really.'

'Small, then. How lovely. And the teachers there. Good, were they?'

'Mostly like him,' he motioned in the direction Gryce had left. 'Only good when they had a piece of wood in their hands.'

She blushed, and wrung her hands together, as if trying to squash such an unpleasant image.

'Well, Joseph, perhaps you could come and read to me. Just for a minute, so I can see where you've got to.' Her words seemed to lack any kind of certainty, like she already knew she had hit on a sensitive spot.

And she was right, it sent Joseph into a spin. 'My glasses are broken,' he blurted. It was pathetic, but it was all he had in the moment.

'Oh dear. Well, let's try anyway shall w—'

'I *can* read.'

'Of course,' she said, surprised by his irritation. 'Of course you can. I mean, you are clearly, what, eleven years old.'

'I'm twelve.'

Cue more blushing. 'Lovely. So, why don't you pop yourself on that chair over there and read me a page of the book on the desk. That way, we won't strain your eyes and I can find you something you *really* want to get stuck into.' She waved her fist encouragingly, like so many did in the war effort posters.

This was hell. A hell that he had visited on too many occasions already. The classroom was quiet, and he knew it would stay that way if she forced him to read. His eyes scanned the room and the other kids. The smaller ones wouldn't say a thing, but the older boys? He knew, he just *knew*.

Slowly, he walked across the classroom floor, hoping for

some kind of miraculous intervention, ignoring the eyes fixed on him.

He breathed deeply, brain still empty of excuses, but filling quickly with anger at what was about to happen. But as he reached the desk, and made to sit, he heard from behind him: 'Bloomin' Northerners. Why don't he clear off back where he came from?'

Followed by: 'No, this should be good. Cos if he reads as well as he speaks, then I don't reckon he'll be troubling the top of the class.'

And that was it. The fuse sparked and spat, and so did Joseph. They'd given him everything he expected and feared: and with a simple whip of his arms, the book, the desk and the chair, all went tumbling.

15

The second desk went over quickly, but not as dramatically as the third, fourth or fifth. By then, Joseph had found a devastating rhythm, one that saw the other children skittering to the furthest corners of the classroom.

He didn't notice, how could he, when the rage consumed him?

A chair toppled, then two more, the echoes shrieking around the walls.

Can't do this, he thought to himself. *Not again, not here.*

He'd smash everything, burn every book in sight, before they tried to make him read a word.

He looked to the windows. They were huge, reachable, and to his panicked brain offered the best chance of escape, as the door would lead him only into the clutches of the headmaster.

He searched for a chair within reach, unaware that Miss Doherty was moving closer, each footstep slow and cautious, not unlike the movements Mrs F had made when approaching Adonis's cage.

The difference was, though, the teacher didn't know Joseph in the same way, and after a growled response, she abandoned her approach, palms held high, apologetically.

'What is it, Joseph? What is it?' she asked, panicked. 'Was it what Bert said? Bert?' she implored, 'I think you owe Joseph an apology.'

But it didn't come. Bert Conaghan, known for the power in his fists rather than the decency in his character, was cowering behind an upturned desk with Jimmy Rodwell. They'd laugh and mock the situation come breaktime, but in the moment were too shocked to say a word. Unlike Mr Gryce, who had ghosted unseen into the room, Clarence in hand.

'Miss Doherty!' he boomed. The teacher was the initial, unfortunate focus of his displeasure. 'I could hear this melee from my office. What on earth is going on in here?'

'I'm sorry, Headmaster. Joseph is a little upset. I can only apolo—'

But Gryce wasn't interested in apologies, or in the boy's welfare, and he sped effortlessly across the classroom, collaring Joseph by the scruff of the neck, as you would a disobedient dog.

Although wiry, Joseph was not a light child, and when you factored in the intensity of his anger, there was no way an ageing man should've been able to restrain him, but that is exactly what Gryce did, and with one hand, he lifted the boy from his feet and positioned him head-first across the nearest desk.

This was not the first time the headmaster had caned a child in front of an entire class. It had been a common occurrence

94

throughout his tenure: a deterrent to others. It was, however, the first time he had ever caned a child on their first day.

And as for Joseph, he'd lost count of the number of canings he'd received, in private or otherwise, but it didn't stop him bucking and kicking under the headmaster's grasp. Didn't stop his arms and legs going rigid with shock and pain, when Clarence first made contact with his backside.

He'd known this would happen, one way or another, when Mrs F told him where he was going that morning, but that did little to dilute the humiliation or pain of it.

'I WILL NOT TOLERATE SUCH INSOLENCE IN MY SCHOOL,' came the roar from above him, and with every strike, Clarence tattooed the sentence onto his skin, not stopping until Joseph's limbs finally fell limp, defeated.

Then, and only then, did Gryce stand upright, slicking a strand of lank hair back across his forehead as he caught his breath.

'Miss Doherty, I will leave the child with you. See to it that there are no repeat performances. I do not wish to be disturbed again.'

Joseph did not move until he heard the door slam shut, and even then he only stood when he felt the gentler touch of his teacher's hand on his shoulder: bolting from her to the safety of a space beneath the window, where he crouched on his haunches, arms pulled around his knees, head buried in the same place.

'All right, children,' Miss Doherty said, voice thick with

emotion, 'if you can pick up any furniture close to you, and return your books to where you were, we will read silently until the bell for playtime.'

The class followed her instruction out of shock, but also out of a very real fear that Clarence was still twitching in the corridor. Desks were scraped and chairs righted, until silence reigned, and the only noise to be heard was the occasional page turning, though how much was being absorbed was debatable.

Joseph stayed where he was, resisting and recoiling from every approach Miss Doherty attempted, not even moving when the bell rang, and the children were dismissed.

It took a glass of water being placed at his feet to break even the tiniest hint of his trance.

'You should drink this.'

He didn't move.

'I'm sorry you had to endure that.'

He didn't believe her.

'Joseph, I don't understand why you reacted like that, but I *did* hear what Bert said. It clearly hurt you.'

Joseph sniffed and pressed his head into his arms. No one could hurt him. Certainly not a kid.

'And is it true, Joseph? What Bert said? Is reading difficult for you?'

He pushed his chin further into his knees, eyes so focused on the ground that he was in danger of burning a hole in the floorboards.

'Please, Joseph. Talk to me. Because . . . well, I don't see what else could've upset you so badly? You'd barely walked in the door. So I'd like you to come sit with me, just for a minute, so I can see where you are with your reading. Then I can help you.'

He shook his head. How could he allow himself to do that after what had already happened? It was like she *wanted* him to lose his temper again. Well, he wasn't going to do that. He'd sit as long as he had to. Till Christmas, if needs be.

His stubbornness showed.

'Joseph, I want you to listen to me now. Mr Gryce is going to question me about where you are with your studies. And on top of that, there are his monthly tests, where he will expect you to read aloud. Now, you might be prepared to lie to him, but I'm afraid I'm not. So the choice is simple. You can either come and read with me now, or you can leave it to chance the next time he pays a visit. I know which I'd prefer, and I think you do, too.'

She left him at that point, returning to her desk and pulling the chair out next to her, as if posting a very public invitation.

This was a standoff, but he refused to back down. Even though he wasn't watching her, Joseph could sense her restlessness, caught her looking at the clock on the wall, forcing her to approach him, just before the bell sounded to mark the end of playtime.

'Take this home with you then, please,' she sighed, placing

a book in his lap. 'Read it with Mrs Farrelly and ask her to send a note back, letting me know if it was too easy or hard.'

Joseph said nothing, but allowed the book to rest on his lap. It was a small, yet painful victory, and he'd had precious few of any kind since arriving here. Heaven knows how he'd hold on to that feeling once Mrs F sat down with him to read.

16

The walk to the zoo was a slow one.

He didn't want to go there, granted. Didn't want to start a conversation with Mrs F about his reading, and wasn't overly happy to be escorted by Syd, who thankfully stayed a pace ahead and was unusually quiet (presumably due to what had happened in class).

But this wasn't the reason for his laboured pace.

He walked slowly because of the shooting pains he felt with every step, courtesy of Clarence. He'd been mostly numb at first, in his body and brain, but as the day progressed, and his isolation deepened and adrenaline dropped, he'd struggled to work out which hurt more: his backside, or his pride.

'Sweets,' said Syd, turning suddenly.

'What?' Joseph answered, confused.

'Sweets. That's what you need now. I mean, before the war, that's what you'd have, to cheer you up. Bloomin' Hitler. Couldn't even leave us those, could he? I'm guessing you're a lemon sherbet fan.'

She was wrong. It was Jelly Babies for Joseph. Though he could barely remember how they tasted any more.

'Do you want to stop for a while?' Syd asked, her voice soft – kind, even.

'Why?'

'Well, I can see you're not comfortable. And I know how much being caned hurts.'

Joseph doubted very much that Syd had ever done anything to warrant a visit from Clarence, but if she was lying then she was covering it well.

'No point,' he sighed. 'Not like I can sit down, is it?'

'Hardly,' and she grinned at him, exposing a row of tombstone teeth too big for her mouth. 'There's not a cushion fat enough to numb the pain, from what I remember.'

'I can't believe you've been caned. What did you do? Refuse to shut up?'

'There's lots you don't know about me,' she replied. 'And vice versa.'

'What do you mean?'

She stopped and thought for a second. 'How can I put this? You seemed . . . very quick to lose your temper. And all right, I've seen you do it before, but, well . . . not like that. It was scary. Not for me. It just looked scary for *you*.'

Joseph shrugged but kept his guard up. 'Didn't bother me. She should've left me alone, that's all.'

'But she's a teacher. What else should she have asked? I mean, you're a new boy in a new school. A question about how good you are at reading was always going to be at the top of the list, wasn't it?'

He said nothing.

'Because,' she went on, despite Joseph's scowling, 'if you

haven't learned to read yet, it's not the end of the world, you know.'

'I *have* learned.' He tried to work out how much he wanted to say. 'Tried, anyway. Tried bloomin' hard.'

'But . . .'

'But what?'

'But you still can't read?'

'No, but it's not my fault.' His voice went up a tone defensively. 'It's the words.'

'What, the words are to blame?'

'Well, yeah.' He blushed. 'Sounds daft, but it's true. They won't stay still on the page, will they? Every time I try, right from the first day of school, they won't have any of it. They move about. Dance, almost. I can hear what noise the teachers say they *should* make, but how am I supposed to make sense of it if the ruddy things won't stay still?'

Syd didn't have an answer, which made the insecurity of being honest even worse for Joseph.

'You think I'm mad, don't you?'

'Not mad, n—'

''Cos that's what they all think, all the teachers I've ever had. I've thought it myself, too. Every time I've tried to explain it, they think I'm mad, or lazy, or both. That's why I didn't want to go in this morning, not cos I'm idle, but cos I knew I'd end up on the end of one cane or another. It *always* happens.'

Syd opened her mouth but couldn't find the words.

'Forget it,' he said, 'what do you care anyway? It's not your problem, is it? It's mine.'

'Doesn't mean I can't help.'

'Why would you do that?'

'Are you serious? People help because it's what they do. People help because they care.'

'Not 'bout me, they don't.'

'Maybe,' Syd replied, sadly. 'Or maybe they've just given up because you won't let them.'

That brought a scoff from Joseph. What did *she* know?

'Well, the offer's there,' Syd went on. 'Might not be anything I can actually *do*, but I'll try. You know, if you want me to.'

She trotted on. The zoo gates were in sight. And she clearly had work to do.

'Oh, Syd?' He'd remembered something. Something important. 'You'll not tell her about what happened today will you? Mrs F, I mean?'

'What do you think?' she replied. 'You'll have to trust me, won't you?' And with a smile that he didn't see, and certainly wouldn't have appreciated, she bustled on.

Trust, thought Joseph to himself. It was hardly a currency he dealt in, but as it was all he had, it would simply have to do.

17

He found Mrs F sitting in her office. She stood as soon as he entered, sheepishly, like she'd been caught with her fingers in the biscuit barrel. Joseph may have only known her for days, but he knew she wouldn't have been sitting for long: the flush to her cheeks and stained overalls told him she'd been busy.

'How was it, then?' she barked, by way of a greeting.

'What?' he replied.

'Parachuting into occupied France,' she said. 'School. What else?'

'Fine,' he said, eyes not meeting hers.

'And . . . ?'

'And what?'

'Well, is that it?'

That wasn't it. Clearly it wasn't. The ache across his backside screamed otherwise, but to admit he'd been caned on day one would merely confirm what she already thought of him. And he was damned if he was going to give her that satisfaction.

'So, what did you do?'

'You know. Stuff.'

'What, maths? Spellings? Reading?'

'All those, yeah.' The thought of the final one sent a red-hot streak of pain spiralling through him.

'Were the other children welcoming?'

'Not many others there,' he replied, which was a better, more convenient truth than anything else he could offer.

She eyed him suspiciously, probably filling in the blanks herself, thought Joseph.

'Right, well,' she said. 'Have you any homework to do? Before you get started here?'

The reading book in his bag was barely thirty pages long, but in that moment, it felt like he was carrying a dozen bibles. It was a burden that he simply couldn't share with the woman, so he shook his head. Shovelling more camel dung was preferable to reading with her. Or explaining why he couldn't.

'Right. Well, your overalls are where you left them, and the wolves and camels are due a meal.'

He said nothing, just accepted the orders and shuffled back towards the door.

'Oh, and when you've done that. You can sort out Adonis, too. His feed is already by his bars.'

Perfect, thought Joseph, feeling more imprisoned than the ape he was about to serve.

He shuffled slowly round the zoo, turning his nose up at any greeting that came his way. Not that the residents were great conversationalists: only the birds seemed to chirp at his presence, and even then, they seemed to be laughing at him.

He started with the camels, or rather, they started with him. Joseph had it in his head that camels were lazy beasts, prone to loping rather than sprinting, but at the first sight of him clutching a bale of straw, they came alive, pinning him in the corner of the cage, putting his fingers at risk as they fed greedily. He considered retrieving the book from his bag: he'd see if they were hungry for knowledge as well, but as they pushed him harder into the bars, he settled for leaving without being devoured himself.

The wolves were equally welcoming, but as with the camels, Joseph was under no illusions about why. When they saw him, they saw dinner: a veritable steak in comparison to the offal that slopped inside the bucket. Mrs F really wasn't joking when she said that she took whatever food she could find. He was no lover of liver or tripe in the first place, but the serving he was carrying looked and smelled like it should've been eaten weeks ago, staining Joseph's hands with a stench that he feared he would never shift.

All he could do was hurl the meat from a safe distance, flinching when the wolves fell ravenously on it, turning on each other when the rations were all too quickly gone.

He was relieved when the bucket held nothing but blood and the smell of death. The only problem was, now the wolves had been seen to, his 'to feed' list included only one word: *Adonis*. It took gritted teeth to make him shuffle in the direction of the ape's kingdom, finding him imperious on his muddy throne, eyes fixed on the zoo's entrance.

'Oi! Food,' Joseph called at him, without enthusiasm. Adonis didn't spare him a glance, or even a blink, which didn't surprise the boy, but served as a sad reminder of how he was regarded. He wasn't sure how he was going to feed the ape, and get the woman off his back, if he was so invisible? He didn't fancy approaching the bars like she had. He doubted he'd walk away with his arms still in their sockets if he tried.

Instead, he pulled a handful of grass from the pail and waved it in the air. 'Come on,' he shouted. 'Grub's up.'

There was no movement from inside. Not even a glance.

'Come on,' he huffed. 'Give me a chance! I mean, you'll take food off Mrs F, won't you? And don't think I didn't see her in there with you either, being all chummy. So what's wrong with my food, then? I'll get a right rollocking if you don't eat nothing.'

He couldn't imagine how it would feel to be inside the cage with Adonis. The trust they must have in each other, to know that nothing was going to go wrong. Although he didn't really know it, it was a trust Joseph had barely felt in his whole life.

Begrudgingly, he swapped the grass for a cabbage that had seen better days, and waved it in Adonis's eyeline. 'Any better?'

Not a flicker. His eyes didn't move from the zoo's entrance.

'It's no good staring over there,' he said, 'looking for your sweetheart. I know what happened. Syd told me. She's gone, and she's not coming back, so come and take this off me, then you can do something else. Hang off a tree, beat your chest, I don't know, cos what you're doing right now is a waste of time. I'm telling you this for nowt – once they go, they never come back.'

It may have been a coincidence, but Adonis chose that moment to notice the boy, head turning slowly, eyes singeing the space between the two of them. Joseph felt himself stiffen. Was Adonis going to charge at him again? He was scared, but didn't want to be, so he pushed his chest out in defiance and vowed not to blink unless the beast did first.

'Do you want this?' he asked again, though he felt less confident when the ape slowly heaved himself to his feet and stepped towards him. It took every bit of bravery he had to hold his ground. It didn't matter that the bars divided them; there was a force to the animal's movements, a power that seemed magnified by the slowness of its stride.

'Oh, you *are* hungry are you?' What should he do with the food? Hurl it through the bars? Or dare he approach like Mrs F had done?

He daren't do that. Adonis already felt too close for him to safely stand his ground, so he took a step back, while throwing the food through the bars.

If the 'feast' excited Adonis, he didn't show it. His pace didn't change, his gaze didn't leave the boy until there were mere feet between them. Then, and only then did it shift, as he lowered himself into a sitting position, and surveyed what was on offer, as if perusing a menu.

Joseph watched as the leaves were sniffed and poked before being grumpily discarded.

'Picky, aren't you? Not keen on cabbage, eh? Better than sprouts, I can tell you. But only just. And there's nothing better in here for you, pal.'

He tried a manky head of broccoli instead, but when it was propelled back at him at speed he took another step away, dumped the bucket on its side and retreated to the bench, keen to rest, but finding no way of sitting without his backside reminding him of his shocking day.

What was he going to do about school tomorrow? He had no intention of talking to Mrs F about his reading but knew Miss Doherty wouldn't forget either. The instructions were clear: go home, read with Mrs F, and return with her view . . . or face Gryce and Clarence.

It left him with the most terrible of choices. Humiliate himself in front of the woman or face another freshly flayed backend. Well, forgive me, he thought, if both choices seemed as enticing as the contents of the wolves' bucket.

Just then his thoughts were interrupted by the sight of Mrs F and Syd in the distance, lugging a bale of hay while deep in conversation.

It may have been due to his already fragile state of mind, but Joseph instantly knew that the subject could only be one thing: him, or more specifically, his shortcomings in class.

Syd wouldn't dob him in, would she? he thought. *Trust me,* she'd said.

He watched her closely; the emotion on her face as she talked, nineteen to the dozen, and Mrs F shaking her head as she listened, every second compounding Joseph's paranoia. She was giving him away. Despite everything she'd said.

He was on his feet in a flash, ripping open his school bag, pulling out the dog-eared book he was supposed to be studying.

Syd might want to humiliate him, to force him into reading for Mrs F, but he wasn't going to have that. Instead, he clutched the book in his left hand and marched towards Adonis's cage, not caring any longer about the consequences, only letting go when he was sure that it would land inside the bars. Then, turning to Mrs F, and in particular to Syd, he let fly: 'Can't read it now, can I? So you can tell who you like: Miss Doherty, the headmaster, Clarence himself, for all I care – in fact you can stick it. Stick it in your pipe and smoke it!'

His voice shook, but that wasn't all, his hands and arms too. In fact as he tried to gather his possessions it felt like his entire body was quivering, betraying him, preventing him from getting away before Mrs F was at his shoulder.

'Joseph, what in God's name was all that about?'

'You know what,' he replied, pointing at Syd. 'And you do too. You couldn't wait, could you?'

'I don't know what you're talking about,' said Syd, 'What do you th—' But she never finished, as her attention was broken by confetti falling around her. Confetti made from Joseph's book by Adonis's fingers.

The three of them stared at the ape, who sniffed at the

remaining pages before dabbing them against his tongue. From the way he discarded them, they were clearly even less appetising than the cabbage.

'Joseph,' snapped Mrs F, 'you need to explain yourself. And you need to do it now.'

But the boy wasn't in the mood for helpful answers.

'What's the problem?' he said. 'You can clean it up next time you're in there having a cuddle. And anyway, Adonis just told you everything you need to know. He likes reading as much as I do.'

And with one last deathly stare in Syd's direction, he stomped away.

18

Joseph fell from his bed.

The siren seemed louder tonight, more urgent.

Did it know something he didn't? He thought, as he dressed. Scuttling down the stairs, seeing his breath in front of him, he found both Mrs F and Tweedy waiting in the kitchen.

'C'mon dog,' Joseph said, heading for the back door and the shelter beyond, only to be stopped by Mrs F.

'You're both coming with me tonight.'

Joseph frowned.

'Don't be thinking for a second it's any kind of reward. I know something went on at school today, no matter how silent you've been.'

'What's wrong with me hiding out back there?'

'Rufus Twyford has a bug. His mother thinks he's contagious, so we'll be giving them a wide berth for a while.'

Joseph didn't believe her. She hadn't looked at him while she said it, which wasn't like her. Besides, he wasn't daft. He guessed there might have been words between Mrs F and Sylvie Twyford after the last raid. And he'd seen the way Mrs Twyford had looked down her nose at him when they'd met. If anyone was contagious in her eyes, it wasn't Rufus, it was him.

It was a look he'd become attuned to. He'd seen it plenty of times over the years, judgement or despair at the way he behaved, and he'd learned to shut it out to make sure he fell foul of it no longer.

As they dashed from the house, the temperature dropped even further, and Joseph felt a momentary pang of longing for the relative warmth of the shelter.

'Now,' Mrs F said, without breaking stride or focus, 'if you're coming with me, you'll do as you're told, do you hear? You'll not leave my side unless I tell you to do so. You can't hide under the aquarium tonight, the timbers in the floor have started splintering under all the shaking, and besides, I want you where I can see you.'

Joseph shrugged. It suited him, meant he could watch her, rifle in hand. So for once he trotted alongside her and Tweedy through the pitch-black streets, only making out their exact whereabouts when the horizon lit up in pain.

It was so cold, though. The nipping in his fingertips and ears got worse with every minute, the wind's teeth biting wherever his skin was exposed.

It didn't go unnoticed.

'You'll be needing this,' Mrs F said, pulling a knitted lump from her pocket and thrusting it into his grip.

It was a balaclava, by the looks of it, though Joseph didn't want it. Was she trying to butter him up or something?

'You're all right. You keep it,' he said coldly.

'Don't be daft. It's yours.' A sheepish look hit her face. 'I knitted it for you.' She seemed to go from sheepish to embarrassed to angry in nothing but a second. 'Oh, stop being so ungrateful and put it on.' She turned her head back to the front, straining into the inky night, allowing Joseph to thrust the balaclava as deep into his pocket as it would go.

Though by the time they unlocked the zoo gates, with the bombs still landing in the distance, his resolve was severely tested, teeth juddering in his head.

'Meet me by Adonis's cage. Feed him if he looks distressed,' she said, before dashing in the direction of the office. 'Check the others on the way, too. And take the dog.'

Needless to say, Tweedy was less than obedient, choosing her without hesitation. Still, Joseph did as instructed, casting a cursory glance at the camels, ponies, wolves and birds before arriving at the cage, straining into the darkness until his eyes finally focused, seeing Adonis sitting regally in his usual pose.

'Aren't you cold?' he asked the beast, blowing on his ravaged fingertips, before shoving them inside his coat sleeves. 'No way you'd find me out here if I didn't have to be.'

The ape looked to him slowly, peering through his eyebrows, responding with the grumpiest of snorts.

'Same to you. And you're not having my coat, so don't even ask.'

Another snort, louder, longer. Joseph thought he could smell the ape's breath.

Mrs F had said to feed him if he was distressed. Joseph

had no idea if this meant distress or just plain grumpiness, so he threw a clump of grass through the bars regardless.

It landed, pitifully, some yards away, but close enough to pique the ape's attention. He pushed onto his front arms and leaned in its direction, before deciding that it wasn't near enough to make him bother moving.

'What's the matter? You want waiter service or something?'

He threw a second clump and it landed closer, but still not close enough to tempt Adonis. It drew merely the same disdain. So he tried a manky carrot this time, closer again, but positioned so the beast would still have to make some kind of effort to retrieve it.

The ape's head turned with a sneer, but then came the lifting of one arm, then another, the body pivoting slowly, showing again the strength that surged through every inch of his body. It may have been hidden by the fur, but there was no mistaking its power as it dipped to retrieve the food.

What surprised Joseph was that Adonis didn't then return to his spot. Instead, he faced the boy, rooted his fists to the floor, his rump following. It was quite a sight to be so close, and a mightily impressive one, too, not that Joseph would admit it.

Everything was now magnified: his bulk, his scars, the intensity held in his eyes. Joseph could see the icy wind blowing at his fur, making it ripple and flow as Adonis lifted his food slowly to his mouth. Joseph couldn't be truly sure if the animal was looking at him, but there was no mistaking what happened next. Adonis devoured the carrot, barring the stalk, in one mouthful, then put his hand through the bars, just a foot or so from him.

But he did not drop the waste at Joseph's feet as he expected. Adonis made to do so, but with a late flick of his wrist he sent the stalk sidewards some yards away, far enough for the boy to have to move to tidy it away.

This drew a surprised laugh from Joseph. One that he couldn't keep in or swallow down. He might be going mad, but he thought that small gesture might be Adonis's idea of a joke. One that said, *All right, pal. If you're going to make me move for my food, then you're going to move to tidy it up.*

'Cheeky beggar! Did you mean to do that?' he asked. Adonis threw his head back jerkily. 'Hilarious. Just hit the bucket next time, will you. Or I'll serve you the wolves' food instead.'

Adonis grunted one last time, before loping back to his regular spot, sitting at the exact moment the latest bomb landed in the distance, louder and closer than before. It drew Mrs F and Tweedy quickly into view.

'Have you fed him?' she asked.

'Oh aye,' Joseph said without taking his eyes off Adonis. 'His majesty has definitely eaten.'

'Right, well step back here with me. Jerry's obviously in a bad mood tonight.'

'Must be contagious,' he whispered, transfixed by the rifle in her hands, which lured him back into the shadows.

'Look, neither of us wants to be here,' she said, 'but neither of us gets a say. This place is my responsibility, these animals – all of them – are my responsibility. Now, I may not like it, but if a bomb were to set Adonis here free? Well, it'd be like Hitler himself walking around town. The damage he would do would be huge. Only difference is, Adonis would do it out of fear. You can't say that about Adolf.'

'So you'd do it then? You'd kill Adonis if you had to?'

'I've no idea. Won't have, either, till that bomb drops, till I can see where it's falling. Maybe it'll get me before I can pull the trigger, maybe it'll take Adonis with it first. All I know is that sometimes, doing the right thing feels completely wrong.'

And with that, she sat on the bench and wrapped her scarf tightly around her mouth: a clear sign that she was done talking.

19

The night was still cold: so cold it forced a single tear from Mrs F's eye.

She wiped it away quickly with a rough woollen glove, but Joseph spotted it regardless.

Was she just cold or had the prospect of pulling the trigger become too much for her? He looked for more signs, but frustratingly she gave none, pulling her hat lower and her scarf higher, the perfect camouflage.

Joseph shivered next to her, but not close. The cold had starved him of energy. There was little of him visible either, bandaged in blankets and scarves retrieved from the office.

He kept his eyes forward, fixed on the bars of the cage, but every now and then he risked a glance to see if she was still awake, if her grasp on the rifle remained tight. It was exciting and boring all at the same time.

An hour passed.

The night darkened, so dark even the stars seemed blunted and useless, and it lulled the woman, pulling her down inside her coat, her breathing deepening until it echoed the grunts from the cage.

Joseph waited till he was sure sleep was just about to grab her.

'I don't think you'd do it.'

Her eyes flashed open, body tensing in surprise, finger tightening instinctively on the trigger.

'Hhhhm? What?'

'Pull the trigger. If you had to. I don't think you would.'

She stretched and yawned, irritated at herself for nearly falling asleep. 'You know everything, you,' she said, eyes slit-like.

'If you're tired, you can let me hold the gun.'

'It's a rifle, not a gun. And besides, do you honestly think I'd let you hold this? You took such an instant dislike to Adonis, you'd be pulling the trigger even if Hitler waved a white flag from Berlin.'

Joseph fell silent, thinking about it. *Would* he pull the trigger if he had to?

Ask him a few days ago and he'd have pulled the rifle clean out of her hands. Damned ape had scared the life out of him. But, as much as he hated to admit it, he had no idea if he could squeeze the trigger either. He'd seen Adonis behave differently at times: not just his playfulness tonight, but the way he was with Mrs F. The way he allowed himself to be fed with her so close by. They didn't even need bars between them, such was their trust. He tried to imagine being able to feed the ape like that, before coming to his senses. It was pointless thinking of such a thing. That wasn't how life worked for him. Friendship and trust counted for nothing. He knew that.

Silence fell, and darkness grew. There were no signs from

above but the sirens hadn't called it off yet either. The night was cold. So cold he resorted to the balaclava she had made him, daring to pull it over his head without feeling guilty for doing so.

The noises from Mrs F told him she'd succumbed to sleep, but he had not. He was awake and prepared to pinch himself whenever sleep dared to sneak up.

Her breathing deepened further and he felt her slump gently against him. His instinct was to push her off and as he did so, her grip on the rifle fell altogether and it slid, gently, onto his lap.

He cradled it, out of fear of it falling to the floor and setting itself off. But the second his hands grasped its bulk, it confused him, making him feel too many things at once. He felt the danger in it, the power in its weight. But with that power came an overwhelming and immediate sense of fear, too. He expected to feel brave, but he didn't. He felt scared.

Was this how soldiers felt, he thought, the first time they picked up a gun? And did it change over time? Did it feel lighter, more normal the more you pointed it? Or did it only feel better when someone was pointing one straight back at you?

He thought of his dad, hundreds of miles away, and wondered if he was doing the exact same thing. Was he scared, too? He hoped not. He hated him for leaving him to struggle here on his own, but at the same time, felt a burning love for him, a desire to know that he was alive and breathing, and coming home.

Rustling broke from the cage, pulling Joseph from his thoughts. Adonis dashed along its length: not loud enough to wake Mrs F, but enough to see Joseph swing the rifle in his direction, pulse quickening.

Could he do it if he had to?

He looked to the sky: nothing. Empty. If they were coming again, they weren't here yet, or even close.

So he waited, just like Mrs F did, hands tingling, and not just from the biting cold. But nothing happened. No one came, and just like her, eventually, he found his own clothes and blankets growing, pulling him under, until finally, and despite his protests, his eyes closed for the first time, the rifle slipping to the ground between them both. He didn't pick it up.

Inside the cage two eyes remained open and alert.

Open, alert and fixed on the boy: keeping guard from a distance.

And they stayed that way, until the all-clear siren finally sounded.

20

A long night meant a long day for Joseph.

He'd pleaded through pinprick eyes to be allowed to sleep on: his head had only hit the pillow an hour or so earlier, but Mrs F was having none of it: 'Do you think anyone else in the city slept last night, either?'

Joseph didn't know or care. All he knew was that his eyes stung and his muscles ached. A bench had been no place to sleep, and it had been especially embarrassing to wake up nestled against Mrs F, stealing whatever warmth she had left. The only thing that eased the humiliation was seeing that she felt the same, scrabbling to collect the rifle from the floor and move herself to the opposite end of the bench.

'I'll not listen to a single excuse, Joseph Palmer.'

He tried to protest, made a lame claim to a sore belly, which failed to raise an eyebrow, never mind a sick note, and ten weary minutes later, he found himself at the kitchen table.

'So what did your teacher say yesterday? Are you up to date with lessons, or do we need to catch up at home? It's a long time since I did any maths or English, but I can muck in if needs be.'

'She's still working it out,' he spat, through an underwhelming bowl of unsweetened porridge. Again, though, he'd noted then ignored the fact that the helping she'd given him was bigger than her own.

'So, no sums to do? Nothing?'

He shrugged. What didn't speak, couldn't lie.

'Perhaps I should come with you today.'

As his mind raced for an excuse, salvation came in the unlikely figure of Syd at the door, who was just as surprised as Mrs F to see Joseph dash to greet her, school bag and gas mask box in hand.

'What's got into you?' she asked, after he'd practically dragged her through the front gate and up the road. He didn't reply, nor did he offer anything for a while, as once the relief of escaping Mrs F had passed, he felt tiredness cloud his every step, slowing him to a crawl.

'Come on. Keep up,' insisted Syd.

'Give over, will you. I've barely slept,' he said.

She shook her head unsympathetically. 'Have you not realised yet, tiredness is something you're going to have to get used to here?'

'What, like your rudeness?'

'I'm not rude, Joseph, just honest. The Germans aren't going to have a night off just because you need to catch up on your beauty sleep, you know.'

He looked around him. He could see that from the landscape. Every corner they turned, it seemed there was another building crumpled in despair, another crater dug into the road.

'Thought they were dropping further away than this last night,' he said. He couldn't lie to himself; he was scared they were so close.

'See that hole up there?' Syd pointed to an especially large crater fifty yards ahead. 'Until last week there was a double decker bus in there, blown practically in two. Next night they took down that entire row of shops.' She pointed at more rubble, with naked mannequins scattered in different positions, all of them missing limbs of some description. She flinched, her eyes moving away as Joseph's remained fixed.

'Anyway,' she said, changing the subject. 'I was surprised to see you dash out of the house like that. Can't believe you're so keen to get to school, what with your tiredness and after . . . well, you know, *yesterday*.'

'I'm not *keen*. I just didn't want Mrs F coming with us.'

'Was she threatening to?'

He nodded.

'Oh.' She let a beat pass between them. 'So. Did you tell her?'

'Tell her what?'

'About what happened yesterday.'

'What do you reckon?'

'Well, I can't imagine for a second that you did.'

'Proper genius, you,' he said.

'Well it doesn't take a genius to see that you didn't ask her to read with you either.'

'Oh aye? Why's that?'

123

'Well, because the last time I saw it, Adonis was ripping up your book. I'm not a bad reader, but I'd be terrible if I had to read it in a million pieces, with a silverback breathing down my neck.'

'That's no way to talk about Mrs F,' Joseph said, finding himself way funnier than Syd did.

'She might just surprise you, you know, if you told her the truth. She might want to help.'

'Yeah, course she would.' The sarcasm dripped from him. 'Anyway, there's nothing she could do that'd surprise me. Just like you.'

'What's that supposed to mean?' Syd asked with a frown.

'You know exactly what it means. What was the last thing you said to me when we reached the zoo yesterday?'

'I don't know, "goodbye", probably. Or "see you later." I know it couldn't have been "thank you for the wonderful, witty conversation."'

'You said I could trust you.'

'And?'

'Well, I saw you, didn't I? Talking to Mrs F. Telling her everything that happened at school, I bet.'

Syd stopped.

'Go on,' Joseph continued. 'Deny it!'

'Joseph, I know you think the world revolves around you, but I can honestly say, hand on heart, that it doesn't.'

'So what were you talking about, then?'

'Something else.'

'I don't believe you.'

'Well, it's true. Anyway, why am I even listening to this rubbish?'

'Because you said I could trust you.'

'And you can.'

'Then tell me what you were talking about!' he cried, paranoia running through him.

'I was talking . . . about my parents,' she replied, her voice as sad as his was irate.

'Yeah? What about them?'

She looked at him questioningly. It was rare to see her pause.

'About . . .' she started. 'About the fact that next week it will be four months since they died.'

'They *died*?'

'That's right.'

Blood pumped suddenly in Joseph's ears, making him wonder if he'd heard correctly. 'You're not making this up, are you?'

He had said some silly things to Syd in the very short time he'd known her, but from the thunderous look on her face, he knew that this represented for her a new low.

'Why would I do that?'

His face flushed and he wanted to take it back, but he couldn't, and instead managed only to make things worse. 'I don't know. To cover your tracks.'

'You think I'd make up the death of both my parents, just

so you didn't think I was a liar. Have you listened to what you're saying?'

'No. I mean yes, I mean – oh, I don't know, it's just a shock, what you're saying. I mean, really? That happened?'

She nodded, each movement small and so terribly sad.

'On the second night of bombing. Dad had his conscription papers already and was shipping out three days later. We were all terrified. Terrified *Hitler* would take him. Didn't think for a second that he wouldn't let us say goodbye first, or that he'd take Mum, too.'

Joseph's tired head whirred to keep up. 'But you . . . well, they didn't get you, did they? What happened? Weren't you there?'

'The siren came late. They didn't spot the planes till they were practically overhead. By the time we reached the top of our stairs the bombs were already falling, by the time we reached the bottom . . . well, it was too late. They'd hit.

'I'm just lucky, apparently, but it doesn't often feel like that. Only reason I'm here is because Mum threw herself on me, and Dad on top of her. I didn't know they were doing it. I didn't ask them to. All I know is I woke up in hospital and they'd gone. Both of them.'

'You don't remember anything else?'

'Only what they told me in hospital. They thought they'd found three dead bodies, until they realised I was still breathing. Just. My ribs were broken and my lung was punctured, but it was nothing compared to . . .'

'You don't have to . . .' Joseph interrupted. He wasn't sure he wanted to hear any more. '. . . you know, tell me about it. Not if you don't want. I didn't mean to upset yo—'

'That's just it, though. It's never easy talking about it. But it's better than bottling it up. It's better than imagining that they never existed in the first place. If I did that –' her gaze on Joseph seemed to intensify, making him squirm – 'well, I don't know how I would act.'

'So, who are you living with now?'

'My auntie. She's nice, but she's never had kids. And from what I can see she never wanted them. She doesn't seem to know what to say to me. Maybe that's her grieving, but it's why I'm at the zoo half the time.'

'Cos it keeps you busy?'

'Yes, that, but Mrs F – well, she lets me speak, and more importantly, she understands. And she cares.'

'*Her*? Are you joking me? Only one she has a kind word for is Adonis, and half the time she has a rifle pointed at him.'

'Are you still going on about that? Mrs F . . . well, I know she can be grumpy, and a bit, well, abrupt. But honestly, I don't know what I would have done without her. Her or the zoo. And maybe, if you give her a chance, she can help you too.'

'I doubt it.'

'Rubbish. You just won't let her. But I'll say it again, I'll help. With the school stuff. If you want me to. I won't offer again, mind. It's over to you now.'

Silence fell. A rare one between them. Both of them were

quiet with their own thoughts, Joseph trying to process what he'd just learned.

He had no reason to doubt Syd's news: she was as straight-talking as he was angry, but he couldn't imagine how she carried that around every minute of every day and still managed to smile. Wasn't she angry? Didn't she want to rage at the sky every time it got dark? How did she stay inside when the bombs fell and not want to run outside to throw a grenade of her own? He thought about what had happened to him, about what he had lost, and how furious it had made him.

He watched her for a moment, without her noticing, obviously.

Maybe Syd *could* help him? If he could only drop his guard long enough to let her.

21

The sight of Clarence on the wall soon cured Joseph of his tiredness, replacing it with a sense of dread, which kickstarted his flagging limbs.

Wherever he looked, he sensed trouble – danger, even, in its many guises.

There was Mr Gryce (and Clarence, of course) threatening to test both his manners and his reading, and there was Bert and Jimmy, with whom further clashes seemed inevitable.

Even the prospect of time with Miss Doherty made his heart pump and his stomach churn. Not out of fear; she was a rare gentle soul in this place, though she held the key to relative peace in the classroom. Yet one misguided question or an attempt at getting him reading and the touchpaper would be lit. Of all the dangers that lined his path, though, she was the one he was happiest to run into first.

'Good morning, Joseph,' she said softly, face hopeful rather than confident.

He grunted something in turn, not wanting to encourage a conversation.

'I'm very pleased you're here bright and early,' she continued, but again Joseph decided not to answer. From what the clock told him, he was actually bang on time, and as for bright? Well, the bags under his eyes told him she was wrong on both scores.

'I thought we could start our day with some mathematics,' she said. There was a look on her face, a kind of pleading, like she was trying to gauge if mathematics would rouse his aggression the same way that reading had. He saw her shoulders drop in relief when all he offered was a noncommittal shrug, before sinking heavily into his chair.

It didn't take the rest of the class long to file in – there weren't many of them, after all. Syd appeared first (having *finally* left Joseph's side for a few minutes), with short keen strides that saw her scamper to a seat as close to the teacher's as possible, followed by a gaggle of the younger kids, and then, of course, Bert and Jimmy.

It may have been the time he'd been spending at the zoo, but the second he saw them, Joseph couldn't help but see them in animal form, as the predators they were. There was a slyness to their movements, and a pack mentality that made Joseph think instantly of the wolves, though these two were marginally better fed, and undoubtedly more dangerous.

''Ey up!' boomed Bert in a mock-northern accent that sounded nothing like Joseph's. 'The rag-and-bone lad is back, I see.' Of course Jimmy found this hilarious, unlike Joseph, who stared into the distance, aware of the sudden tension in his jaw.

'Don't be like that,' sneered Jimmy. 'Can't you see this is

hard enough for him as it is? I mean his family must really hate him to send him away to play with all the bombs.'

Their laughter was covered by the scraping of Joseph's chair as he flew to his feet – not to mention the gasps of the other children and Miss Doherty's frantic footsteps as she forced herself between the boys.

'Now that is ENOUGH!' she yelled, eyes flitting between the warring parties. 'Bert, Jimmy, take yourselves to the far table. Joseph, you stay where you are.'

No one moved.

'*Now.* Unless you want me to call for Mr Gryce.'

Unsurprisingly, this saw all three of them do as they were told, albeit reluctantly, Bert kicking sneakily at Joseph's chair leg as he passed.

'Now, children,' Miss Doherty went on, 'on your desks you will find your maths textbooks. I expect twenty minutes of silent work as you pick up from where you left off last time.' She turned to Joseph, without moving any closer. 'Joseph, I have left a short test for you so I can assess what you already know. Please don't feel intimidated if there are sums there that are beyond you. Just, you know, do your best and let me know when you have finished.' And she scurried off behind her desk, fearful of being caught in a similar crossfire to last time.

Minutes later she noticed Joseph's hand in the air – an improvement on him turning over desks.

'Yes, Joseph?' she asked.

'Finished, Miss,' he said, sheepishly.

'Really?'

He saw her forehead wrinkle in surprise and heard Bert laugh sarcastically. But he pushed his anger down after being told to bring his work up to her desk.

'Let me see now,' Miss Doherty said, her pencil tracing his answers, eyebrows raising higher and higher as she scribbled tick after tick after tick. 'Too easy for you, these, clearly!' she said, and Joseph sensed excitement in her, not that he understood why. Sums like this were easy.

'Try this page,' she said, handing him a different book which housed a lot more numbers than the first. He did as he was told without fuss, or enthusiasm, but still found himself in front of her again ten minutes later, looking at the same long line of ticks and an even bigger grin on his teacher's face.

'Joseph!' she beamed. 'Where did you learn to do this?'

He shrugged, not out of churlishness, but out of honesty. He didn't know. He'd always found sums as easy as he found reading hard. 'They're just puzzles, aren't they,' he said, quietly enough so only Miss Doherty could hear.

'Well that's true,' she replied, much louder, 'but some are also puzzles that I'd not expect you to be able to solve for another two years. So I'm surprised. Delighted, obviously.' She paused, her eyes not leaving his. 'In fact, would you excuse me, just for a minute or two.' And after picking up his books, she bustled from the room, leaving Bert and Jimmy with the opportunity they'd been looking for.

'Oy, Einstein,' leered Bert. 'Where've you got the answers hidden, then? Cos you definitely didn't work 'em out yourself.'

Joseph didn't look away, though nor did he focus on Jimmy's face. His blood, still simmering from the earlier barbs, caught fire, the heat in his chest spreading quickly.

'Can't see old Gryce believing you, either. Wasn't just your arse he marked first time round. Was your card, too. He'll work out you're a cheat – even if Miss can't.'

Joseph was over the desk before he knew it. He'd heard enough, his fist full of Bert's jumper, pulling the boy towards him.

'Say that again. I dare you.'

The only thing was, Bert *did* dare. This was the sort of confrontation he loved, though opportunities these days were precious few. War robbed people of different things, and ironically, given the battles raging across Europe, it had cost Bert the fights that had fed his ego so satisfactorily since he'd started school.

'What's your problem, Palmer? Truth hurt? You're a cheat.'

Joseph gripped harder. 'You don't know anything 'bout me.'

'That right? See, I reckon I know plenty. Doesn't take much to work out that you don't belong here. And that no one wants you here, neither.'

Joseph didn't think he needed help. He was rarely in fights when he didn't come out on top one way or another, but on this occasion, he was beaten to the punch.

Not by Bert. Or Jimmy either. But by Syd, pushing Bert so

hard that she almost sent him *and* Joseph crashing over the desk to the floor.

'That's rubbish. There's plenty of people want Joseph around, so don't you dare speak for me, Bert Conaghan.'

Bert looked at her, incredulous. 'This has got nothing to do with you. I mean, who are you, his sweetheart, or something? Get lost.'

This of course merely spurred Syd on.

'Make me,' she replied. But Bert didn't have to, as Jimmy stepped in instead.

Syd may have been able to beat them with her intellect, but physically it was a mismatch, and Jimmy made her back-pedal by lifting her by the arms and sitting her on a desk.

All eyes were back on Bert and Joseph now, and Miss Doherty was still nowhere to be seen.

'Come on then, Palmer,' Bert spat, fist cocked.

Joseph knew what the boy was doing. He was goading him because he didn't want to throw the first punch. That way, he could say he was only acting in self-defence. But what Bert didn't know, was that at that moment, Joseph didn't care about blame, or punishment, or even another short dance with Clarence. All he wanted to do was inflict the anger he was feeling on the runt in front of him.

So he did exactly that: a single straight jab that parked Bert on his backside, demolishing a chair on the way down.

That was the point when pandemonium should've kicked in. Joseph expected it.

There *was* a groan from Bert as he looked around him, disorientated, looking at the floor in confusion. His hands wrestled with the ground, trying to build a base from which to spring, and Joseph felt the storm coming, and braced himself, only for it to be blown off course at the last second by the return of Miss Doherty.

Her eyes widened.

'Oh dear,' she gasped. 'Oh dear, what has happened here?'

Everyone in the room knew that this wasn't really a question she needed to ask.

Joseph waited for Bert to do his worst. He'd not stand down or unclench his fists, not even if Clarence wanted to kiss his palms. Bert had got what was coming to him and he'd have done it yesterday if he'd had the chance.

Syd, though, was as clever as Joseph was defiant, positioning herself between the teacher and Bert.

'Clumsiness!' she declared. 'That's what happened, Miss. That and showing off. Bert was trying to balance on the chair.'

Miss Doherty blinked several times, as if this answer was having trouble reaching her brain. It wasn't the answer she'd been expecting, nor did it feel particularly plausible to Joseph.

'Bert? Is that true?'

Bert returned his gaze to Joseph, mouth twitching somewhere between a grimace and what might have been a smirk. He'd wipe it off with pleasure, the second Bert piped up with the truth.

But it seemed the truth had been blown off course as well.

'Chair wasn't strong enough, Miss,' Bert said simply.

'I can see that,' the teacher replied, though she was clearly still bemused. 'Well, put everything back and stop being so silly.'

'Yes, Miss,' said Bert, climbing to his feet but with steely eyes still on Joseph.

Joseph watched him go. He was shocked. Bert had had everything he needed to see Joseph packed off to the head's office.

But he'd chosen not to use it. He'd chosen to play along with the lie, and Joseph knew that could only mean bad news. Because whatever Bert was plotting, it had to be worse than Clarence. And that, no matter how brave or pig-headed Joseph could be, was not something he wanted to be on the end of.

22

The ball rebounded off the wall and landed at Joseph's feet.

It didn't bounce. That would demand some air being left inside it.

'Was this thing *ever* pumped up?' he said.

'Course it was,' Syd replied, pointing at an enclosure off in the distance. 'That's where the seals lived, over there. That was their favourite juggling ball.'

Joseph looked over to where Syd was pointing but couldn't imagine what she was describing, couldn't picture the crowds or hear the laughter. Couldn't imagine the zoo feeling anything but dead.

He kicked the ball again. Harder, though it returned in the exact same, unsatisfactory manner. The thud drew Adonis from his hut, eyes on Joseph, as if trying to understand what on earth the boy was doing. Joseph tried to pretend that he wasn't there, watching.

'I can see who you're picturing as you kick that,' said Syd. 'The ball's in better condition than Bert is though. The fool.'

Joseph laughed. He couldn't help himself and it felt good. He knew he owed her for today.

'Thanks,' he said, trying to hide the word beneath another thud of the ball.

'Pardon?'

'You heard . . .'

'No, I presumed you were thanking the ball. I was just confused as to why you weren't thanking me instead.'

'You just want me to say it again, don't you?'

'No, it'd just be nice if I thought you actually meant it.'

He kicked the ball once more, as if the exertion would somehow hide his blushes. 'What do you want? Me on my knees or something?'

Syd pictured it and nodded. 'It's an idea. After all, I did an awful lot to stop you getting caned.'

Finally, he stopped his kicking and looked at her.

'I *do* know that. I'm not *dumb*.'

'Why does everything come down to being dumb or thick or stupid with you? Did I say you were any of those things?'

'No, but . . .'

'Then stop it. You seem to have conveniently forgotten that you're also a maths genius! Anyway, I don't care if you're smart *or* the class dunce.'

'Yeah well, that makes you the only one round here.'

Syd knew what he was referring to. Later in the day, she'd watched in class as Joseph had sat, squirming in his seat, Miss Doherty beside him, a reading book quivering between them. To her credit, the teacher had done things differently this time, taking Joseph to the farthest part of the classroom, speaking to him in hushed tones that no one else could hear.

She'd not flinched when Joseph told her he'd lost his

reading book. She'd simply fetched a new one, then prompted, and prodded, and made all the right encouraging noises as he winced in the direction of the page: 'Take your time now, there's no rush . . . Reading is like building blocks. Once you know how to stack them you can build anything – a skyscraper!' Her wide eyes almost pleaded with him to be impressed.

But it didn't matter how gentle the prod, to Joseph it felt like a fist in the chest, and no matter how quickly he'd dashed through the school gates at the end of the day, with Syd in tow, he couldn't shake the feeling that this was another thing wrong with him.

He tried to shake the thought of it from his head, but it had taken firm root, and no amount of ball kicking seemed to shake it, not that he'd really expected it to.

'What did you say when Miss asked where your reading book was?' Syd said.

'Told her an ape ate it.'

Syd looked at Adonis and remembered the confetti the ape had made of it. She laughed. 'Well, it's more original than blaming it on the dog.'

Joseph nodded and looked at Adonis, who seemed to plump himself up proudly.

'Don't get over-excited,' Joseph told him. 'I don't think for a minute that you did it to help me out.'

'Aw, look, you've offended him!' said Syd as the ape looked away. 'And I wouldn't rule it out, either. They're clever, apes.'

Silence. Joseph had nothing to add. Another kick. Another thud.

'So, I'm guessing you never told Miss Doherty – about the words moving around on the page?'

'Did you *hear* her laughing in there?'

'Joseph, she wouldn't laugh, she's a teacher!'

'Didn't stop the others.'

'So, you didn't tell her?'

He shook his head and tried to flick the ball onto his knee, sulking when he failed.

'You can't keep going on like this, you know. In a couple of weeks' time, Gryce will arrive for his monthly tests. And you know full well he'll be extra interested in you. I don't want to scare you, but it's not a nice afternoon when he comes in. I've seen a girl wet herself before in panic.'

Joseph pulled a face that said he wouldn't fold like that, but Syd spoke on. 'And one boy, well he didn't give Gryce the answer to seven times two quick enough, so he got caned fourteen times, so he'd never forget.'

Joseph may have considered himself tough, but even that made his palms sting in anticipation. 'Miss Doherty warned me about the test again today. Said my maths would help, but that we had a lot of work to do if Gryce wasn't going to be upset.'

'And you want that? Really?'

'Course not.'

'Then what do you need to do . . . ?'

Joseph knew what she was getting at. He knew he only had to ask, and she'd do exactly as he wished. But the words, the 'word' – *HELP* – refused to form on his lips. He tried,

140

he really did, but every time he felt it on his tongue he remembered the other times he'd uttered it, and the crashing disappointments that followed. His gaze dropped to the floor and he kicked the ball even harder.

'Oh, for goodness' sake, Joseph. Let me help you, will you?'

The thought of accepting made his chest hurt.

'I know you're embarrassed about it. I understand why. But you can't let yourself walk straight into Clarence like this, you can't! So I'm going to help you read. And don't even try and say no.'

'Or what?'

'Or you'll find me a more dangerous enemy than Bert or Jimmy.'

Joseph bit the inside of his lip.

'Come on, no one's watching. Only him –' she pointed at Adonis – 'and he's already shown you what he thinks about books.'

He weighed it up and realised he had no choice if he wanted to avoid Gryce's and Clarence's wrath.

So he sat next to her on the bench self-consciously, not helped when he spotted Adonis staring at them again. In fact, it looked like he might have shuffled closer.

'Right,' said Syd, 'I brought this with me.' And from the rear waistband of her skirt, she pulled out Joseph's reading book.

'Where did you get that from?' he said, bemused.

'From your desk, of course. I couldn't give you a lesson without it, could I?'

'But I hadn't *asked* you for a lesson.'

Syd looked at him wearily. 'No, but I knew you would in the end. So let's get on with it, shall we?'

Joseph huffed loudly. How on earth had she persuaded him to do this?

She set the book on his knee, and he felt himself tense as Syd leaned into his shoulder.

'Shall we start with the alphabet?'

He turned his head quickly.

'I'm not a baby.'

'I know you're not.'

'And I have been to school, just . . . not lately.'

'So you know about vowels?'

'Course I do.'

'Go on then,' she prompted. To Joseph she looked like she was relishing the power a little too much.

'Well, it's A and E and I, and that.'

'And the others are?'

'Leave off, Syd, will you?' He made to stand, which made Syd change tack.

'I'm sorry. Tell me, then. What does A stand for?'

'Are you pulling my leg?'

'Just tell me. Then we can move on.'

He didn't so much sigh as huff. She was on the shakiest of ground.

'A? Well it stands for . . .' his mind went blank for a second. 'Well, you know . . .' He thought. 'Air raid and Adolf and anger and . . . Adonis.'

The other words he could understand, but that last one? Why on earth did he think of that? There were hundreds, thousands of As out there, so why choose the ape?

'Can we get on with it?' he grumbled, before Syd had a chance to hang any meaning off his choices.

'Fine. So. Put your finger next to the first word.'

He did as he was told, but as he focused on it, it started again. The word, and all the others around it started to move, *dance*, like they were being tossed around on a high sea. It took every bit of concentration he had to make his finger remain below it, let alone read it.

Syd watched, shocked as Joseph's index finger slid around the page.

'Is it happening again? Won't they stay still?'

He thrust the book away from him and onto the gravel. 'What do you think? Just cos you're here doesn't mean it stops happening.'

'Does it help if you close your eyes a bit? Squint, I mean?'

'Are you taking the mick?'

She clearly wasn't, and after more cajoling he snatched up the book and tried again, through narrowed eyes.

'Now it's a *darker,* dancing mess.'

'Hmmmm,' said Syd, a detective poring over clues. 'Will you try one more thing? Please?'

'If you ask me to read standing on my head, I promise, I'll swing for you, Syd.'

She shook her head. 'Don't be ridiculous. Just humour me and try something on, will you?'

She pulled from her cardigan pocket a pair of old spectacles: severe and angular.

'Whose are those?' he said, pained.

'My auntie's spares.'

'Then what are they doing in your pocket?'

'Well, I wanted to see if they helped you.'

Joseph couldn't believe how premeditated all this was.

'You've really thought about this, haven't you?'

She shrugged. 'I'm just organised. And I want to help. Well, come on.'

Joseph peered at Adonis. Did apes have a sense of humour? Because if this one laughed, he swore he would lose his mind.

'Well? What are you waiting for?' said Syd.

Joseph stared at the specatacles, aghast.

'Come on,' said Syd, 'quicker you try, quicker it's over!'

Against his better judgement, and swearing under his breath, he slid the arms over his ears, without letting the bridge rest on his nose. He kept his hands cupped around the frames too, to hide his appearance, though to Syd it looked like he was searching for U-boats through a pair of binoculars.

'Well?' she said, though she needn't have bothered, as by the time the question was asked, the spectacles were spinning on the floor, hurled in a rage. 'Oh,' she said, though she might have said a whole lot more when Joseph's foot crunched them into the gravel.

'Are you happy now?' he spat, face scarlet with frustration, which barely disguised his shame. 'Well? Are you?'

'I thought it might help,' she said, a trace of pleading in her voice. 'That's all.'

'Yeah, well, you can leave it alone now, can't you? There's summat wrong with me. And not you, or anyone else, can fix it.'

'That's not true, Joseph. And you can't give up like that. You mustn't.'

But Joseph had made up his mind. 'Leave me alone, will you? I don't want your help. Go and save someone else.'

'I won't give up,' she replied calmly.

'I said GO!'

So, reluctantly, she did, leaving Joseph where he wanted to be. Where he felt he deserved to be.

Alone.

The only problem was, he wasn't on his own at all. Adonis remained. And although he did not move, he did tilt his head slightly to the side, eyes on Joseph, a low, slow, repetitive noise leaving his mouth.

It wasn't a growl, far from it – more a groan, though even that wasn't completely accurate. It reached Joseph's ears gently, at odds with his own chaotic thoughts, and although he didn't want to admit it, it stayed with him, helping his mind settle, just a touch.

23

The zoo may have been close to empty, but it still demanded a great deal of upkeep. Mrs F stood at the centre of it of course, barking out orders, coming down hard when her standards weren't met. She may not have Clarence hanging on her wall, but her bark could inflict a pain in Joseph's ears that felt comparable.

There was the daily mucking out, with which Joseph became intimately acquainted. He had also been put in charge of sourcing food for the animals, which was barely more palatable. He'd become acquainted with every butcher and greengrocer within a three-mile radius, loitering at their doors as they closed, taking whatever offcuts they could spare or had seen fit to dispose of.

The smell from his buckets was often putrid, the handle cutting into his frozen hands as he lugged them through the streets, ignoring the kids who ran from him screaming at the smell. The only positive to the stench was that it temporarily quelled the constant, nagging hunger he felt in his belly. Food was scarce, and rationing did little for his constant, irritated mood.

He often felt like he was becoming some kind of awful local figure, a scarecrow, the boy with the raggedy clothes and alien accent, the boy who brought the smell wherever he went. It didn't help that he was also regularly tramping through the streets with Stan and Ollie and their dung trolley on the way to the allotments.

Once there, Joseph had become more adept at driving a bargain, determined to return to the zoo with food for the animals that Mrs F hadn't tasked him with.

'If you want all this manure, then I'll need something extra in return today,' he told the ruddy-faced man there.

'That a fact?'

'It is. There's a lot more demand for the dung this week. So it'll cost you an extra six pieces of veg.'

'Will it now?'

'It will.'

The man glared at him. Joseph stood as tall as he could without resorting to tiptoes.

'You'll take three and think yourself lucky you're not getting a clip round the ear.'

Joseph pondered the offer, then nodded and held out his hand. He'd have settled for two. Plus, he couldn't wait for Mrs F to see what he'd negotiated. Adonis would be pleased too. Veg was definitely preferable to grass.

It was debatable whether the ponies were warming to Joseph and his unique style of encouragement, though the boy was certainly tuning in to their eccentricities. In fact, he'd become rather astute as to what made them tick.

Ollie was governed by his stomach; Stan, meanwhile, was

147

more subtle. Rotting vegetables held little incentive for him, and neither did a Gryce style of discipline. What Joseph discovered, through trial and error, was that Stan was very partial to a tickle below his chin. It couldn't be gentle, his hair was too thick and wiry for that, but if Joseph turned his fist into a claw and rubbed vigorously in a strictly clockwise motion, then Stan's eyes would close blissfully, his head tilting to the side, before ploughing on.

It was a discovery that didn't go unnoticed on one allotment run. Stan was playing up at the zoo gates, in full view of both Mrs F and Syd, who had the much more pleasant job of sweeping the paths. Mrs F watched the boy struggle with the beast.

'Shouldn't we help?' asked Syd.

'Give him a minute. He's not helpless. And I don't mean Stan.'

Joseph could feel their eyes on him, and tried, unsuccessfully, to use his body as a shield as he set to work tickling.

Mrs F could see what he was doing though and when he got Stan moving, finally, it was impossible not to be impressed. She turned back to her sweeping, happy that she hadn't had to intervene.

What she didn't know was that she wasn't the only one capable of watching subtly, from afar. Joseph had become rather adept at it himself. He might have become more intuitive when it came to the ponies, but Adonis remained in another league. The ape was still aloof and enigmatic, which did little to help Joseph's confidence. He had no idea what he was doing wrong. Seeing how Adonis reacted so differently to Mrs F didn't help either, whether she was inside the cage, or out.

He'd watch her approach the bars in the same way she had that first day: the slow, hunched walk, the mimicking of his noises and movements, head down, avoiding eye contact. Her methods never changed, and neither did the results. Adonis would walk calmly and quietly in her direction, then perch across from her, as if sitting before a mirror instead of bars, and pluck whatever offerings she had in her hands. It was a little like watching two friends share a picnic.

'It's not difficult,' she'd tell Joseph, when it was his turn to try. 'Just do what I do.'

But it always seemed to Joseph that his efforts could never match hers. He felt foolish trying to mimic an ape. And as for going inside the cage to clean him out? He couldn't see that *ever* happening.

'No, no, no,' she'd tut as he stomped towards the bars. 'It's no good getting that close then throwing it *away* from him. He's not interested in hunting it down, and besides the poor beggar's in there all day long on his own, bit of interaction is what he needs. He'll take it from you if he thinks you're not a threat.'

'*Me* a threat?' said Joseph. 'I'm not the one who charged first time we met.'

'Joseph, that was a one off, and he was scared. You've got to make him feel safe. Treat him like he were a friend.'

'A friend? He's an animal.'

'And? He has a heart, doesn't he? And eyes, and all those things you have.'

'Yeah but—'

'And he has feelings too. You should've seen him when they took Aphrodite. Tore him in half, it did.'

Joseph couldn't picture it, but he saw the emotion on Mrs F's face.

'So what do I need to do then?' he asked.

'Look at him,' she replied. 'For the first time, actually *look* at him. Realise he's a living, breathing creature that feels the same things you do, wants the same things we all do. He wants to feel safe, Joseph. And you can help him with that.'

Joseph pursed his lips and said nothing. It would be folly to do anything else.

'Try it. Here, take this.' She handed him half a carrot. 'Now walk, *slowly* towards the bars.'

He did half of what he was told.

'I said *slowly*,' she half hissed, half whispered.

He tempered his pace but not enough, Adonis sending a bark of disapproval.

'Look,' she said. 'Watch me again.' She plucked a large leaf from the bucket and began her own slow, respectful approach.

Joseph watched reluctantly. It wasn't just about the pace she moved at: it was the way she held herself: her shoulders rounded and thrown forward, meaning her head fell the same way too. There was little in the way of eye contact, either,

Mrs F looking up through her eyebrows to ensure she wasn't distressing the ape. As she neared the bars the noises started: first from Adonis, a softer, lower noise, not a purr – never a purr – but a more sympathetic rumble. Mrs F followed, mimicking him, both noises and movements, but at no point did she relax or take anything for granted, certainly not when she found herself a mere foot away from him.

Joseph took in the difference in their frames. Adonis could break her in a second, could probably find a way of dragging her through the bars if he pleased, but if Mrs F was worried by this, she didn't show it. Instead, she slowly lifted her arm, until the cabbage leaf moved within Adonis's range.

The ape's head moved first, leaning forward to sniff. There was something snooty about it to Joseph's mind, like a dandy taking in the aroma of a pocket flower, but the image didn't last long, Adonis whipping the cabbage from her grip and falling back on his haunches.

Satisfied, Mrs F moved away from the bars, her movements as slow as before, never turning her back on the beast, not even for a second.

'There,' she said. 'Now your turn.'

'You're all right.'

'No, come on,' she cajoled. 'You can do it. But only if you try.'

So he jammed his hand into the bucket and took a bit of carrot.

'Right,' she said. 'Now, start to walk slowly. Head down, small steps, nothing sudden.'

He did as instructed.

'That's it,' she said. 'That's the way.' Joseph hoped she was telling the truth.

'Now, keep your arm at your side until you get closer. That's it, that's it . . .'

He was ten feet from the bars now, and Adonis didn't seem to have moved. Was it working? He daren't look up to find out, though he did hear a shuffling and a short, sharp grunt.

'Hear that?' Mrs F whispered excitedly. 'He's seen the carrot now. He's telling you he wants it. Whatever noise you hear, make the same noise back. Make him think you're just like him, that you're no threat.'

Joseph turned his ear to the cage, tuning in.

Another grunt followed, then a second and a third. Could he do it? Would he allow himself to grunt without fear of laughter from behind him?

'Come on, Joseph,' she whispered. 'You can do it.'

So he did. Hesitantly at first, barely audible, before allowing his chest to rumble and mimic the same tone.

'That's it! That's it!' came the whisper behind him, and Joseph gave the most furtive of glances at Adonis, head cocked, wide fat finger scratching at his chest. Instinctively, he remembered the other order. It wasn't just noises he had to impersonate, but movements too. So bravely, patiently, he stopped and sat back on his haunches, pawing at his chest in the same way, wondering how long he should do it before moving again.

Mrs F, of course, filled in the gaps. 'Don't wait too long now. You've got it. He trusts you, but he wants that food.' Joseph made to stand, only to be told to slow down.

He started again, slower tentative steps, occasionally scratching and grunting in case it helped. His heart thumped wildly in his chest, only increasing as he edged closer, until he could reach the bars.

Again, he fell into a squat, and fighting the urge to look Adonis in the eye, he slowly raised his arm until it, and the carrot, sat at a perfect right angle from his body.

He waited, blood pumping in his ears. Would it work or was Adonis playing with him?

But just as he felt his arm begin to cramp, he caught a movement from the other side of the bars, and saw, from the corner of his eye, Adonis's arm mirroring his own, snaking upwards and out through the bars. It was working. It was *working*.

Through squinted eyes, Joseph marvelled at the size of the ape's hand, one finger the width of three of his own. He was scared, of course he was. No matter what Mrs F said, the ape was unpredictable, but fear wasn't the overriding emotion and he allowed excitement to fizz through him.

'Hold steady, hold steady!' whispered Mrs F, her own giddiness tangible in her voice.

It was happening, it really was, their fingers mere inches away from each other. Joseph relaxed his grip on the carrot in anticipation. But as he felt it being levered away from him, there came a commotion from behind, a clattering of something against corrugated iron, which broke the moment and drew reactions from all three of them.

Mrs F spun on her heels, eyes searching for the source. Joseph felt his balance tip forwards, towards the bars, but it was Adonis's reaction that was the most pronounced.

Whether it was anger at having his meal interrupted, or fear of another air raid, it sent him spiralling, throwing himself against the cage, head back as he blasted out warning after warning.

Joseph was terrified and scuttled spider-like away from the bars, gravel biting at his palms.

'What was that?' he yelled, but Mrs F had something else on her mind.

'You must never EVER turn your back on Adonis as you walk away. His arms are long, longer than you realise. He could've grabbed you at any moment, especially with such a racket going on. Then what would you have done?!'

Gone was her warmth, and Joseph felt it cut him. Why was she so cross with him? He hadn't caused the racket or asked for it. All he'd done was react instinctively to make himself safe. It felt unfair, especially when he'd come so close to something so great.

'Well, I wouldn't have expected *you* to help, that's for sure,' he spat.

'What do you mean by that?' she said in reply, before another clang distracted her. 'Look, we'll talk about this later.

I need to see what's going on over there. Don't be trying to approach the bars again unless I'm around, do you hear me?'

He said nothing, just stared at her. And as she moved away, he couldn't help but wonder how a moment so close to perfect had crumbled so quickly.

24

It didn't take long for Joseph to disobey Mrs F. A few minutes at most. The reality was, Adonis had still not eaten properly, and to Joseph's mind if the situation remained the same, he would be blamed for it.

Besides, he said to himself, he knew what he was doing now, didn't he? And it wasn't like he was stepping inside the cage. He'd watched Mrs F feed the ape through the bars loads of times, and he'd practically done it himself, barring the interruption. Adonis would've taken food from his hand: and if it had happened once, then it could happen again.

So he pushed himself from his seat and stooped over the bucket, deciding to carry several pieces of food in each hand. That way he wouldn't have to retreat every time he needed more.

With full hands and a quickening heart, he started his approach: head down, shoulders slouched, steps fairylike. He didn't bother to look for the ape's response yet, it was too soon.

Ten paces on and it was a textbook situation. Adonis had sloped closer, and could see that dinner was nearly served, though Joseph didn't rush or move impulsively. He wanted to show the ape that he had been wrong to charge at him before, that he was to be trusted, worthy.

Adonis became more excited, grunting and scratching and Joseph followed suit. There was nothing to fear here, everything was as it should be.

Or it was until Joseph's arm extended outwards. He was careful to ensure that it didn't snake through the bars into Adonis's territory. He knew that any overconfidence would leave him vulnerable. He wanted Adonis to come to him, so he could pull away more easily if necessary. Yet as he spotted the ape's arm move forward, he felt a sudden dramatic shove from behind, delivered with such force that it sent him sprawling against the bars, both arms pushing through them all the way up to the shoulders. His nose made impact with the metal and it dazed him, but not enough to stop him realising he was now incredibly vulnerable. But Adonis didn't attack. He sprinted quickly into the depths of the shadows, invisible in a second, presumably as he tried to work out what and where the danger was coming from.

Joseph pushed himself away from the bars on all fours, before turning on his knees to find two figures looming grimly over him.

Bert Conaghan and Jimmy Rodwell.

At first Joseph was confused. He associated them so firmly with school that their presence here seemed incongruous.

'Hello, dunce,' Bert said, gruffly.

'Aren't you on the wrong side of these bars?' added Jimmy.

A second later Bert had Joseph in a headlock: one that he couldn't fight his way out of.

'Think his head would fit through the gap?' laughed Jimmy.

'Only one way to find out.' And the bully started to run towards the bars, with Joseph tripping along beside him.

As they reached the bars, Bert let go, hurling Joseph flush into them, a shooting pain whipping through his shoulder and upper back. But it was only the start, as Bert followed up with a slap to the face and a kick to the ribs. Jimmy took this as his cue to join in, using his fists as readily as his partner employed his feet.

Joseph curled up into the tightest of balls. But no matter how hard he tried there were too many parts of his body left exposed, and the boys went to town on them. The blows weren't always the hardest, but they came with such frequency that it felt to Joseph like he was being prodded with a hot poker.

Bert and Jimmy, however, weren't done.

'What's happened to the thing in this cage?' asked Bert, pausing.

'Dunno. In its hut? Who cares? Can't have been anything interesting anyway. I mean, looks like the whole place is empty, apart from *this* animal right here.' Jimmy nudged Joseph with the toe of his boot like he was a cockroach.

'Maybe we should give the place a new resident then.' Bert marched to the gate of Adonis's enclosure and began wrestling with the padlock.

Jimmy thought this was the funniest thing he had ever

seen, and bent double, laughing. 'People will queue round the block. We'll make a fortune!'

On the insults went, until Bert realised he would get no joy from the padlock and decided to take his frustration out on Joseph again instead.

'Get him on his feet,' he barked at Jimmy, who duly obliged.

'That's it. Keep his chin up, too. Let me get clear sight of him.'

Bert prowled forwards and shook out his fist. Joseph could already feel the sting of the blow he was about to deliver.

'Now you listen to me, Palmer,' he hissed, his back only inches from Adonis's bars. 'We don't like you, as you might've already guessed. So every time you get in our faces, in fact, every time we even *see* your face, know that this is what's waiting for you.'

He pulled back his arm, fist clenched, packed tight with every bit of hate he could summon. Joseph's eyes were already swelling, but he didn't need to be able to see to know what was coming next.

However, the punch never came. Instead there was a thundering from behind Bert that was swifter and more powerful than anything the Nazis could throw.

Before his fist could even draw level with his own nose, Bert had been pulled backwards and slammed against the bars, at the mercy of the beast called Adonis.

25

Joseph was in pain. In pain and shocked, but it was nothing compared to what must have been going on in the mind of Bert Conaghan.

Seconds ago, Bert had been on the cusp of delivering the most delicious revenge, but now it looked to Joseph like his world had collapsed. The bully found himself clamped from behind against the cold steel bars, where no amount of panicked movement could wrestle him free.

What made it worse was that Bert had no idea what was holding him prisoner. Joseph could see Adonis's fist – the size of the boy's head – between Bert's shoulder blades, pulling his coat so tight that it looked like a straitjacket across Bert's chest.

Words fell out of Bert's mouth, so panicked they were a mere stream of babble that mirrored what was going on in the mind of his fellow bully.

'Wh-what is . . . THAT?' Jimmy pointed, before making the sign of the cross, a gesture that only served to send Bert into a full blown panic.

'What is it?!' he screamed. 'Get it off me. Get it off ME!'

But Adonis was having none of it: instead he squeezed harder and pulled the boy again and again against the bars, trying to find a way of dragging him through. But when the boy's bones refused to give, he roared his disapproval, mouth pushed tight against his prisoner's ear, foul breath making the boy's hair ripple and dance.

It proved too much for Bert, who lost control of his bladder, its contents flowing down his legs and over his shoes. Jimmy had seen enough too, tearing for the gate instead of towards his friend.

'Come back!' Bert yelled, leaving Joseph to realise it was up to him now. He was all Bert had.

But what could he do? Adonis continued to pull the boy against the bars like a toy. Joseph shouted for Mrs F, but his calls were no match for Bert's terrified yells and were easily drowned out.

What could he do? It wasn't like he was armed. The rifle was in the office, locked in the cupboard, and he didn't have anything like the power to make the ape think twice. But he couldn't just stand there and watch, regardless of what Bert had done to him.

So he ran to the bars, not realising until he reached them how he was going to help.

Bert was wearing a thick winter coat, made of the coarsest wool and buttoned from waist to neck. It was a wonder Adonis hadn't ripped it clean from the boy's back, but there was no sign of the seams popping or ripping. Joseph knew he had to free Bert from the coat. Do that, and he would be able to wriggle clear.

So, making himself as small as he could, and using Bert as

a shield (he had no desire to be a plaything for Adonis's other hand), he set about the buttons.

'Please help,' cried Bert. Or that's what Joseph thought he heard.

'Shut up and keep still,' he whispered.

The first button gave easily, pinging open at a push, but the further Joseph moved up, the tighter the coat and more obstinate the buttons became. By the time he reached the fourth (adapting to Bert's jerky movements as Adonis waved the boy around), he was having to use both hands to prise it through the hole.

'He's going to kill me . . .' cried Bert, and while Joseph didn't have time to stop and think about it, he wasn't convinced it was true. The kid was scared, of course, who wouldn't be, and Adonis *was* a beast, a mountain of an ape who could've ripped the boy's head off twenty times already if he'd chosen to. But the truth was, Bert was still alive.

All Joseph could do was hope that Adonis didn't suffer a change of heart.

'Almost . . . there,' said Joseph, and with one, final push of his now-sore fingers, the coat fell open.

The result was instantaneous. Bert fell forward to his knees and crawled mercifully away, while Adonis yanked the coat clean through the bars and set about ripping it into shreds, roaring wildly as he did so.

Joseph turned his attention to Bert, face wet with tears, his legs wetter still. He saw the embarrassment on Bert's face, but the second he touched his shoulder, the bully returned, anger flashing in Bert's eyes as he sprang to his feet.

'Don't touch me!' he wailed, face red and snotty. 'You're as bad as that bloody monster in there, so don't be thinking you've done me no favours.' He grabbed Joseph and pulled him close. 'And don't be telling anyone about this. Nobody would believe you anyway.'

With a final push, he sent Joseph back to the ground. Joseph thought about retaliation, but resisted. Nothing he could do would be a patch on what Adonis had just dished out, so he wanted to leave Bert with the thought of that, fresh in his mind.

Instead, Joseph lay on the ground, catching his breath, feeling his injuries for the first time as the adrenaline dropped, and watching as Adonis tossed the remnants of Bert's coat skywards. It was the most joyful he had ever seen the ape, a far cry from the aggression that had almost cost Bert so much.

Joseph felt confused. He'd witnessed something close to a tragedy, yet at the same time, Adonis had saved him.

But had the ape *meant* to help?

And what did it mean? Were Adonis's actions just a coincidence, driven by fear? It didn't feel like that to Joseph, but at the same time, the idea of a silverback gorilla coming to his aid felt far-fetched. Did animals even have a sense of right and wrong? They were hardly questions he felt qualified to answer, and they felt too ridiculous to ask Mrs F.

Instead, he pulled himself to his feet and bit on the inside of his lip, trying to distract from the pain in his ribs.

For so long now he'd been adept at hiding his pain. But here, in this new city, it was getting harder and harder to keep it from view.

Two words formed in his head. They were not words that he gave thought to often, and rarer still did he say them out loud. But tonight, in front of the cage, they needed to be said.

'Thank you. I owe you one.'

26

Joseph moved stiffly onto the bench and let the icy wind numb him more effectively than any medicine could.

He watched as Adonis calmed. It didn't take long: within a minute he'd grown tired of playing with what remained of Bert's coat, and had taken to scouring the floor of his cage for food.

'You *should* be hungry after all that,' Joseph said. The ape didn't give Joseph a second glance. Instead, he ferreted out what he could find on the floor, before adopting his normal position, gaze fixed as ever on the entrance. It was like nothing had happened.

'What are you up to?'

It was Syd. Joseph tried to sit normally so as not to give his injuries away, but in doing so realised he was shaking, badly.

'Have you not thought about putting more layers on if you're cold?' Mrs F, this time. 'We can't have you up wheezing and coughing all night.'

He tried to get up. It hurt, the pain in his ribs so sharp that he felt faint, his arms buckling as he slumped in front of the bench.

'Joseph?' The voices now were different, concerned, four feet dashing to him, four arms lifting him.

'Careful now. Gentle, gentle . . .'

They lifted him back on to the bench. He wanted to lie on it, but they wedged themselves either side of him, holding him upright, the interrogation starting immediately.

'What happened?'

'Did you fall?'

'Was it Adonis?'

'What hurts?'

'Do you need a doctor?'

The questions came so fast and the pain was so thick that Joseph wasn't sure who had asked what.

'Who did this to you?' Mrs F asked.

He thought about how to answer but could find no reason not to tell the truth.

'Bert and Jimmy,' he said, through cracked lips.

'Who?'

'Two boys from school,' interrupted Syd, not that Joseph minded. He hadn't the energy to explain. 'They've taken a dislike to Joseph, right from the word go.'

Joseph didn't look up at Mrs F, but imagined her face was hardening as she tried to work out what he had done to start off another war.

'It wasn't his fault though,' Syd went on. 'They've been *really* horrid to Joseph. All he's ever done is stick up for himself.'

'And they were here, these lads?' asked Mrs F. 'How did they get in?'

166

'Over the wall I think.' Joseph shrugged. 'Must've been them making all that noise at the gate.'

'And they did this to you?'

He nodded. 'You should see the state of Bert, though.' He tried to smile, but it hurt too much, so he settled for calling Bert exactly what he was.

'I'll be adding to your bruises if I hear that word again,' Mrs F snapped, 'and I hope you *didn't* respond with more fisticuffs.'

'I didn't touch him. Couldn't, could I? Jimmy was holding me most of the time, or Bert. I couldn't tell, in the end.'

There was a brief silence before Syd chipped in again. 'But if you didn't fight back, why is Bert in a mess too?'

He didn't answer at first. It demanded energy that he didn't have. Couldn't they just let him sleep?

'Joseph!' One word snapped him back and had him point his finger at the bars.

'Adonis . . .' he said.

Mrs F was on her feet in an instant: on her feet and marching to the bars.

'Adonis did what? Joseph, listen to me. What did Adonis do?'

Her eyes flicked between the boy and the cage, checking that the ape was all right, that he hadn't been attacked too, but Joseph could see that she was scared. She knew about the beast's temper and what he was capable of.

'Joseph, I know you're in pain, but this is important, you need to tell me, now. What did Adonis do?'

'Bert got too close to the cage. Had his back to it, ready to punch me. And Adonis grabbed him.'

Hands flew to mouths and eyes opened wide.

'Sweet Lord. The boy. What happened to him? Where is he now?' Her eyes roamed everywhere. She knew he couldn't be pulled through the bars, but she looked anyway, and that's when she spotted the rags of his coat.

'Is that his?'

Joseph nodded. 'He was lucky. Adonis grabbed him, but only his coat. His mate, Jimmy, did a runner, so I . . . er . . . I . . .'

'What? What did you do, Joseph?' He heard the panic rising in her.

'I helped him, all right? I didn't hurt him. I helped him get his coat off so he could wriggle free. That's how he escaped. I helped him.'

He felt himself sag, both inside and out. But he didn't fall sideways off the bench as he felt his shoulders being held, gently but firmly, by Mrs F.

'That . . . that was brave. Incredibly, incredibly brave . . . But unbelievably stupid. What were you thinking? You could've been killed. Both of you. Don't you understand that?'

Joseph knew this. How could he not? But he didn't have a chance to tell this to Mrs F because her attention was yanked away by more commotion at the main gates. Shouting. Lots of it. Shouting and rattling gates. Someone was demanding attention. Now.

'Stay here. Don't move. Do you hear me?' And she walked, briskly, towards the main gate, Syd following.

Joseph sat. Just for a second. Before realising he couldn't stay here. He knew that the racket at the gate must be linked to all this. And if that was the case, then his place was there too. Holding his ribs, and catching his breath, he pushed on after them.

27

It was a strange sight that greeted Joseph at the zoo gates.

Its bars acted as a cage in themselves, dividing two parties, both bristling and shouting. There was so much anger bouncing around, it was difficult to say which of the animals involved was the wildest.

It didn't take Joseph long though, to work out who was trying to get inside.

The large man shaking the gates had to be Bert's father. There was the same cruelness in the eyes, the same power in the forearms. He was a bear of a man, much bigger than Joseph's own father, and he couldn't help but wonder why such a huge, fearless-looking person wasn't doing the same as his dad. Risking it all, somewhere in France.

If there was a physical reason why Mr Conaghan couldn't fight, then he was doing an excellent job of concealing it: he shook the gates with such ferocity that the hinges were under threat, and this wasn't lost on Mrs F.

'I've already been told I may lose these gates to the war effort, but until they melt them down into bullets, I'll thank you to leave them alone.'

'Well, if you'd let me in to have this out properly, I wouldn't have to lay a finger on them.'

Mrs F sighed. 'The zoo has been closed for months now. Not my choice, but it has. That's why the gates are locked. To keep people out – for their own safety.'

'Well from what I hear, there's animals inside *and* outside the cages.' He pointed at Joseph.

His words didn't hurt Joseph. He'd heard worse than that. He was surprised to see that Bert had come along for the ride, though, hiding behind his father's heft. He might have changed his wet trousers, but he still wore the same expression, a mixture of hatred for Joseph, and overwhelming fear of what he'd experienced. His eyes kept moving over Joseph's shoulder, in the direction of Adonis's cage.

'If it's animals you're wanting to talk about,' said Mrs F, 'then let's have that conversation, shall we? It's clear there's strife between your son and Joseph, and boys will be boys after all, but I do know this: from the second Joseph walked into that school, your boy made a beeline for him. He looked to belittle and humiliate him in front of every kid there.'

'Well, he would tell you that, wouldn't he?'

'No, he wouldn't. And he didn't. Stupidly, he didn't say a word about it, which is a shame. First I heard of it was minutes ago.'

'And were you told your boy punched my Bert?'

'I wasn't, but it doesn't surprise me either. And to be clear, Joseph here, he's not strictly my boy, but I am happily responsible for him. So if he ever, *ever* came to me and told me about bullies like your Bert, then I'd tell him to do exactly what he did do. Stand your ground. Stand your ground and if you have to, fight.'

Mr Conaghan didn't like that, not a bit. He seemed to grow several more inches, hate filling every cell as his chest expanded and his fists squeezed the bars.

'And if he's too cowardly to do that, then get your pets here to do it for you – eh?'

'Mr Conaghan, please—'

'Don't you "Mr Conaghan" me.'

'Then don't spout such ridiculous comments in my direction. Do you honestly think Joseph could train a silverback gorilla to attack your son? Adonis isn't a dog. He's a wild animal, which is why the gates here are locked. Unfortunately, your son chose to ignore this, and in doing so put his own life at risk.'

Mr Conaghan didn't like what he was hearing, but he was learning that there was little you could do once Mrs F was in full flow.

'If these boys want to fight, then there's precious little that you or I can do about it. But I'll tell you this, he won't do it in my zoo. Not again. Not without me contacting the law.'

But as she drew breath, Mr Conaghan swooped in with a rant of his own that seemed to knock the air from them all.

'If anyone's contacting the law, it'll be me. And I won't be waiting, neither. I'll be doing it now, today. But it won't be about that ruffian of yours. It'll be about your ape. Wild or otherwise, closed or otherwise, a woman, especially one like

172

you, shouldn't be left in charge of such dangerous beasts. And if I get my way, and I will, then it won't be for much longer. I'll see that ape of yours ended, so he can't do any more harm. I'll even pull the trigger myself, if I have to. Happily.'

'Have you finished?' Mrs F blurted back, but there was a change in her tone. She sounded weakened: there was suddenly tension in her shoulders.

'Mrs, I haven't even started. But I will soon enough. I'll be seeing you. All of you.'

And with a final glare, he left, Bert skittering afterwards.

No one said a word. Mrs F stood motionless until they disappeared, before gathering herself and turning back towards Adonis.

28

Sweat clung to Joseph's face as he rocketed upwards, pulling his bed sheet with him. It was swampy and cloying. He gasped, not once or twice, but several times, as if emerging from the coldest of rivers.

Joseph was not usually a dreamer, whether awake or asleep. He'd never had any patience for it: why daydream when the next bad thing waiting was only round the corner?

This probably explained the grip that this particular dream held over him.

It had been night, and they were at the zoo, bombs falling, thick and fast, too many to count, way too many to stop. There was no sign of Mrs F, but the rifle was somehow in Joseph's hands. Not that it was any use: there were no bullets no matter how many times he pulled the trigger.

The thing that made the dream strange was that it wasn't Nazi planes releasing the bombs: they were being hurled by people, huge godlike figures peering round the darkest of clouds, laughing and leering as they propelled the explosives towards the ground. There was Bert and Jimmy, old man Gryce, and Mr Conaghan too, screaming for revenge as he rained his weapons down.

Joseph saw them in the greatest of detail: their faces all

completely recognisable to him, but there was one face which was not. Its features were hazy, vague, at times obscured by cloud, and no matter how hard he tried to focus, Joseph could not make out who it was.

It was a woman. He knew that much. Her arms were long and slender, yet they weren't gentle, far from it. They hurled destruction with abandon, double the number that the others could. And when the others' arsenal ran out, she went on, throwing bombs faster and faster, leaving Joseph to scrabble on hands and knees, feverishly catching each and every one.

But in the end, it was just too much, even for him. With sweat blinding and hands cut to ribbons, Joseph made one last, desperate lunge, but the bomb was too big, too fast, ripping the sky in two.

As it hit the ground, it did not make a sound. Only Joseph did, letting rip with a deafening cry. But it was not loud enough to pull him from the dream; only the response from the woman could do that: 'Shush now, my darling. Don't cry for Mummy . . .'

He tried not to cry. Desperately holding his breath, trapping the wail deep in his lungs. He wanted to please her, to keep her, to stop her from walking away again. He'd be good this time, he promised. Do whatever it took just as long as she stayed.

But as he reached his arms in her direction, she turned quickly and disappeared.

No, he cried, *don't go. I'm sorry.*

And that's when he sat up, awake now, searching for someone who patently wasn't there.

As reality and sleep merged and twisted, leaving Joseph disorientated and whimpering, he heard another voice, another woman, her tone clipped, but reassuring.

'Joseph. Joseph now, come on. It's a dream. A dream. That's all it is.'

He leaned into the voice, feeling the pain in his ribs for the first time since waking.

'Open your eyes now. It's all right. That's enough.'

He peered through sticky eyelids to see Mrs F perched in front of him, shocks of greying-red hair flailing in all directions.

'Well,' she said, levering his hands from her. 'I don't know *what* that was about. Maybe it was what happened earlier, with those boys. And you shouldn't feel bad about that, you know, if it's upset you.'

Joseph allowed himself to fall back to the mattress, embarrassed by what had happened. He really didn't want to talk about it.

'I'll not be sleeping for a while,' she went on. 'So if you want some company, you'll find me in the kitchen.'

Slowly, knees creaking, she stood, yet her eyes remained fixed on the boy, head tilted to one side, even as she moved to the door. 'It's up to you.'

The offer surprised Joseph, as did her act of leaving his

door ajar. She usually closed it with a bang, like she wanted to seal him within the four walls. Not tonight, though.

After a few minutes, feeling his chest rise and fall with a degree of normality, Joseph climbed gingerly to his feet, feeling every jolt of pain, and descended the stairs on jelly legs.

It was vaguely warm in the backroom. The stove was lit, just: a single flame trying to welcome him as he quietly shut the door behind him. Mrs F was sitting at the table, her back to him, shoulders rounded, poring over something laid out in front of her.

'We don't have any milk, do we?' he asked, his voice not loud, but startling enough to see Mrs F jump to her feet and clumsily bundle a pile of documents towards a battered tin that sat open on the table. 'No, no we don't,' she said. 'Sorry.'

'Right.' He pointed at the papers. 'What are they?' He could see old photographs, and letters, some handwritten, others formal and faded, yet he couldn't make out any detail. She'd moved too hurriedly for that, which interested him. The only time he saw her flustered like that was when the siren sounded.

'None of your business, that's what they are!' she said, once the pile was back in the tin. 'And I'll thank you not to sneak up on me like that again, Joseph.'

'You told me to come down. Do you want me to go out and knock?'

'What I *want,* is you not to put me in an early grave by

177

sneaking up on me. I've enough grey on this head without you adding to it.' And she moved past him briskly, putting the tin on the lintel above the fireplace, well out of his reach. She even partially hid it behind an empty vase, as if obscuring it would wipe any memory of it from his mind.

'I thought you'd gone back to sleep,' she added, filling a glass from the tap.

'Don't think that'll be happening for a while.'

'It was clearly quite a dream you were having. What was it about?'

'Can't remember now,' he muttered. He didn't want to give it a second's thought, nor risk her judgement when she heard how strange it was.

'Maybe that's just as well,' she said. 'Still, there's plenty we *can* talk about, isn't there? Water?'

She slid a glass in front of him, and waited for Joseph to speak.

29

They were out of coal, so had resorted to damp wood found amongst the street's rubble. It hissed and crackled angrily in the stove.

Joseph said nothing. He was still pondering the contents of the tin, vainly applying his best X-ray vision to the mantelpiece. He only stopped when Mrs F followed his eyeline and clocked what he was looking at.

'So,' she said, not really aimed at anyone or anything.

'Aye,' he replied. His glass was empty now, but his palms still gripped it. 'Do you think he'll be back?' he asked.

'Who?'

'Bert's dad.'

'Who knows?' she said. 'People like that can be difficult to understand. All mouth and no trousers, some would say.'

'Is that what you think?'

Mrs F shook her head. 'I don't know much, but I do know this. Men like Conaghan don't enjoy seeing women like me anywhere but in the kitchen. Seeing me at the zoo, regardless of what happened to his boy, well, it offends him, threatens him, I reckon. Though whether it's enough for him to do anything about it, we'll see in time, won't we?'

Joseph nodded. He was in little doubt that the man would follow through on his threats. After all, his son had.

'Do you think there will be more funny business at school? With either of the boys?'

Joseph made a gesture that was hard to read, something between a shrug and a shake of the head. There'd be hard stares and puffed-out chests from both sides, he was sure, and it was difficult to give each other a wide berth with so few in the classroom.

Both sides held weapons. Bert knew how much Joseph struggled with his reading, but Joseph, well, he'd seen Bert wet himself for goodness' sake, so Joseph was unsure as to who would *really* have the upper hand.

'You've still not told me about what really happened, you know. About what went on to make them even come to the zoo.'

Joseph shrugged, just as he had every time she'd asked. He knew she was getting more exasperated every time he deflected, but he wasn't ready to talk about it. 'What's the point?' he said, deadpan.

'The point, Joseph, is that if things don't ever get talked about, then they never get out, and things have a way of burrowing down inside you. And as they do that, they spread, they spread and they fester without daylight or air. Sometimes, without you ever realising, it's reached every part of your body, so every step, every breath, every decision you make, it's made up of that thing, that thing that was too horrible to talk about in the first place. It takes you over. Believe me, it rules you. Is that what you want?'

'No.'

'Then look at me as you say it.'

He lifted his head. 'Course not.'

'Then for goodness' sake, talk to me about it!'

He looked at her as his head raced to think of how to explain it. *Tell her like you told Syd*, he said to himself. *You managed it then, didn't you?*

But this was different. She'd judge him, make him feel even thicker than he already did.

Mrs F looked at him expectantly and he grimaced.

Say he *did* talk. Say he told her everything that had happened and how it had made him feel. What good would it do? Could she turn back time and make it *not* happen? Stop the boys from calling him out, or pin back their arms to stop the blows? No, she couldn't. She was powerless. It had already happened, so what was the point in dragging it out?

The only problem was, Mrs F was as stubborn as he was, so if he wasn't going to talk, she was going to ask questions.

'Syd says they went for you as soon as you walked in. That right?'

He nodded.

'Says it was only one comment that upset you.'

A shrug this time.

'Something about you being thick.'

181

'Why don't you just keep asking Syd, instead of giving me the third degree?'

'Believe me, Joseph, I've tried.'

'Maybe you're not trying hard enough?'

'Or maybe she's just protecting you.'

'Why would she do that?'

'Beats me. I can never usually shut her up.'

'Maybe it's not worth knowing.'

Mrs F was on her feet. 'Not worth knowing? I've had *you* top to toe in bruises, a complete stranger of a boy almost ripped limb from limb in *my* zoo, *and* the threat of our most precious animal, our *only* precious animal, being put to sleep. All this because of something happening which isn't *worth me knowing*?'

She paused, her face as angry as her wild hair. Joseph knew this was the point he was meant to come clean, but still, *still,* he could not find the words.

'Then, if you're not going to tell me, all I can do is make a guess. So, here it is, here's my guess. That boy in the classroom, he offended you. He saw something in you, the second you walked in, and thought he could have some fun at your expense. Get under your skin. So he did. He called you thick, a dunce. Told the teacher you couldn't read or write or even spell your name. And you, because you are the most pig-headed child . . . no, *person* I have ever met in my life, you refused to prove them wrong. Because it's easier for you to be angry and use your fists, than choose to engage your brain and *try* for once.'

182

'I did try, all right? I've tried all my life. I know what you're thinking. You're thinking the same as everyone else. That I'm just thick or lazy, but I'm telling you, I'm not. I know about the alphabet, I can tell you about the vowels as well, all of them. But soon as I try to read them off the page, they start dancing.'

'What do you mean, dancing?'

'They won't stay still, the words. They move about. Every time I think I recognise one, it moves to a different place, like it's floating or something. Drives me mad, it does.'

She'd never heard anything like it. She wanted to believe him but had no idea if it was actually true. The boy was no liar and his eyes were blazing as he spoke, but it sounded so . . . ridiculous. Like the ramblings of a madman.

'And it happens every time you read? No matter how big the writing is?'

'Yes.'

She exhaled, thinking for a second. 'Then we should get you to the doctor. Maybe it's your eyes, maybe you just need glasses.'

He remembered the indignity of Syd's aunt's pair. 'Or maybe they can slap the straitjacket on me there and then. Cos I know, I *know* what you're thinking. And I know there's hospitals down here for people like me!' He was on his feet now, blood pulsing, fingertips gripping the table edge, nails digging into wood.

'Only things you need to know, Joseph Palmer, are these: one, I believe you. Two, there might well be doctors, but there'll be no straitjackets and no bloomin' hospitals, neither. Not while you're with me. And three? I don't care if you can't read. No matter what the reason. There's plenty that can't, and I don't judge them either. What I do care about is this temper of yours. It'll land you in way more trouble than not knowing your A-B-Cs ever will. There's so much anger in you, too much for my liking. But I'll tell you something else, it doesn't outweigh the good in you, not by a long chalk. Look at what you did to help that bully at the zoo? Despite what he'd done to you?'

Joseph furrowed his brow and shuffled uncomfortably from foot to foot.

'Oh, I know you keep it well hidden, but I see it, Joseph. You can't hide anything from me. So, from this point on, I'll be asking a lot more of you, and if you do something good? I'll tell you about it, just as I will if you do something that makes my hand itch.'

Joseph took her words in. Well, he took in what he could, and it had been quite a speech. What he hadn't noticed was that he was no longer gripping the table. And his fists weren't fists either.

'Can I ask *you* a question?' he said, the devil still very much in him.

'You can.'

He pointed at the mantelpiece. 'What's in your tin?'

But she didn't answer. As like a boxer, she was saved, though not by a bell, but by a siren. It was announcing the end of this round, and the beginning of a new one.

Their eyes leaped skywards even though they were indoors.

'Right, get yourself down the shelter, pronto.'

'Not with the Twyfords,' he groaned. 'They hate me.'

'Don't take it personally. They hate everyone.'

'Don't leave me with them, then.' He knew they were short on time, so he had a better chance of getting his own way for once. 'I can come with you again. To the zoo. After all, you don't want to leave Tweedy with them next door, either now, do you? They hate him even more than me.'

Mrs F sighed, sagging as she reached for their jackets.

'All right, then. But you do as I say, *when* I say. Right?'

'Right.'

'And you wear the balaclava I knitted you.'

'Deal.'

'And these.' She threw him a pair of knitted gloves. 'I finished them earlier.'

They were pink. Joseph's face told her what he thought.

'No gloves, no zoo. It was the only wool I had. Now. Hurry up, before Adolf comes knocking.'

For once, Joseph did as he was told.

30

The post-school walk to the zoo wasn't a long one, but the day after an air raid, everything felt more tiring, and as with most things these days, Hitler was to blame.

The bombings were at his insistence, and when they came, they came thick and fast. They left their mark on the landscape and on the people too. Joseph was definitely feeling it, despite his bruises slowly healing, a week on. Constant, disrupted sleep in a bed that wasn't his, plus night after night at the zoo, had left him exhausted, and as Syd was about to find out, even grumpier than usual.

It made everything he saw and heard an irritant: the way gravel crunched beneath everyone's feet (even though his boots made the same noise), the way Syd managed to talk on a constant loop without ever filling her lungs, even the way people took their solace in the aftermath of the bombings got under his skin.

'Look at that,' he snapped.

'At what?' Syd wasn't sure if he was talking to her, or himself.

'That!' He pointed a stabbing finger towards a boy, clambering on top of a large pile of rubble.

'He's only climbing,' she said, confused. 'You did it the other day.'

'I didn't have a stupid ruddy flag in my hand though, did I?'

Syd looked again and saw in the boy's hand a clenched Union Jack flag, attached to a jagged wooden pole. As the boy reached the top of the rubble, he stood, wobbled, and held his makeshift flag aloft, before ramming it into the debris. The material fluttered (pathetically, in Joseph's opinion), drawing a round of applause from those below, Syd included.

'What are you clapping for?' Joseph demanded.

'What do you mean?'

''S ridiculous. I mean, what's impressive about ramming a flag in a load of bricks. Does he think they can see it all the way from ruddy Berlin?'

'What is wrong with you?' Syd said, stopping dead. 'Can you not see what he's trying to say?'

'What, apart from "I'm an idiot"?'

'He's trying to say they won't beat us. That they can drop as many bombs as they want, flatten as many houses as they can, but they won't win. That we won't let them.'

Joseph harrumphed something under his breath, irritating Syd still further.

'Joseph, *what* is wrong with you today?'

Walking on, Joseph clenched and unclenched his fists, fighting the conflict he felt pulling at him. He needed help, Syd's help specifically, but to ask for it? Where did he even start?

Fortunately, Syd found a way to make him say the words.

'Right,' she said, striding ahead. 'Well, if you're not going to talk, then neither am I. Goodbye, Joseph.'

'Wait!' he shouted after her, the word scratching at his throat on its way out. 'I need your help, don't I?'

He may have let his voice drop at the end of the sentence, but it was loud enough for Syd to hear. She stopped, and turned. 'No problem. What with?'

Joseph stared at her. He'd expected her to laugh or make him beg, and maybe she would yet, but so far, all he could see was a girl with her hands on her hips, waiting for him to continue.

'You mean you'll help?'

'As long as it's not checking your hair for nits, yes.'

'No chance,' he huffed, knowing he had to just say it now. 'It's Gryce, isn't it?' He felt the fear bubble as he heard his own words. 'And his stupid monthly test. It's not far away now. And I know what you're going to say about my maths being good, but I still can't read, can I? Still can't tie the words down onto the page. I've been trying, but it's no better.'

'I know. And I tried to help, didn't I? But I don't know what else I can do.' She looked worried for him. 'Has Gryce invited Mrs F, like all the other parents?'

Joseph nodded. 'Says she's coming, too.'

'But she knows about the problems you have with the words, doesn't she?'

Joseph looked embarrassed. 'Yeah, I told her. But she can't do anything about it either, can she? And I know what will happen. She'll side with Gryce. Think exactly the same as him. That I'm doing it cos I'm lazy. Either that or they'll say there's something wrong with me.'

'She'd never do that to you!' Syd looked genuinely shocked. 'Look at what she's doing for you. What she's done for me, too. She gave me a job, didn't she, after my parents died. She didn't have to, but she did, because my auntie told her how sad I was. And it's not just the job, either. She listens to me when I need to talk, she cares about me. Just like she cares about you.'

Joseph tried to stop his face from giving anything away but failed miserably.

'Joseph, it's true. Why can't you see that?'

'Do you want to help me or not?'

'I've said I will, haven't I?'

'Good. Because I don't . . . well I can't trust Mrs F but, well . . . I've got an idea. It might sound ridiculous though, and it probably won't work.'

'You're really selling it to me here, Joseph . . .'

'Look, my reading's rubbish, I just can't do it, but what I have got is a pretty good memory. And the book Miss has given me to read to Gryce, well, it's not exactly Shakespeare, is it? I mean, there's not many words in it.'

'So . . . ?'

'So I want you to read it to me, over and over again. As many times as you can bear. Cos if you do that, I reckon I can start to remember it. Learn it, word for word.'

'You think you can really do that?' Her eyebrows were as high as her voice.

'I do,' he replied forcefully, hoping it would help him

believe it. 'It's got to be worth a try. Beats being humiliated. And caned.'

'Then I'll help. I still think you should talk to Mrs F agai—'

Joseph shook his head determinedly and Syd sighed, while smiling sadly.

'Then we'd better get to the zoo as quick as we can, so you can show me just how good this memory of yours is.'

What followed could have been excruciating. For both of them. But while it wasn't without tension and flashpoints, it became clear that both Joseph and his plan were better than first expected.

His memory wasn't bad at all, which fed both his confidence and Syd's patience. In fact, what she saw over the next hour, as they sat on the bench by Adonis's cage, with the ape keeping guard, was how Joseph's stubbornness was also his greatest strength.

'Tell me that line again,' he said.

'*The sky was full of clouds. It looked like rain,*' Syd said, slowly, but not so slowly that he'd feel patronised.

'Isn't that what I said?'

But Syd didn't have time to answer, as there was a loud grunt from inside the cage. The two of them turned to see Adonis, shaking his head vehemently.

'He doesn't think so,' Syd laughed. She couldn't help it. His timing was too perfect.

Joseph felt himself blush. Even a silverback was telling him he was getting it wrong.

'You don't really think he was shaking his head about my reading, do you?'

Syd shrugged. 'Who knows? Maybe? I don't know. Do you?'

'Nah, he's an ape, for God's sake. But then I don't know, do I? I mean, he got hold of Bert when he attacked me.' He felt silly for saying it, but at the same time he had wanted to see what someone else thought. 'So maybe he *was* protecting me.' He instantly felt embarrassed. 'Forget it. It's ridiculous.'

Syd didn't hesitate. 'No it's not. Maybe he just likes you. Ever think about that?'

'I think you should tell me the line again, so I get it right,' said Joseph, as ever the expert at evading subjects. So she did. For as long as he had the will. Over and over again, every time he fluffed one or lost his way. He took his mistakes well enough, not once threatening to quit, swallowing his temper every time he felt it bubble up. They tackled the words in the book a line at a time, half a line, if the sentence was a long one: Joseph repeating it several times before allowing himself to move on. Once he'd memorised the next line, he went back to the start and tried to piece it all together.

'Do you think this can really work?' he sighed. 'Or am I just fooling myself?'

'Do you think you have a choice?'

Joseph shrugged. 'Not really. If I try to con Gryce and he

sees through it, I get caned. But if I don't try and tell him why I can't read, he'll cane me anyway.'

'And it might work. If you read it with enough passion, he might only ask you to do a page.'

'He might.'

'So stick at it, then. I mean, you're doing better than I thought you would.' Syd realised this didn't sound much like a compliment, adding, 'Way better!' before Joseph's face crunched in disapproval.

On they ploughed, though it took an increasing amount of concentration on Joseph's part in particular. He wanted to trace the words on the page with his finger as Syd read them, as he'd need to do the same when in front of Gryce, but of course this invited the dancing words, the usual nausea and inevitable frustration as they slipped and slid around the page.

As hard as he fought, the irritation that grew inside him eventually became too much to hold in, and he slapped the book shut on the bench.

'It's all right,' offered Syd, considering patting his back before deciding otherwise. 'Rest your brain now. We can come back to it later. See how much of it has stuck.'

Joseph was hardly going to disagree with her, though he did instantly fret that the words would fall out of his head the second he stopped.

'We should probably find Mrs F,' she added, pulling them both to their feet. 'I'm sure she's got things that need doing.'

'Oh joy,' said Joseph, deadpan.

'Don't *be* like that,' she tutted. 'And besides, I think we need to keep an eye on her at the moment.'

Joseph was confused. 'I think you'll find it's the other way around.'

'What do you mean?'

'She's *always* watching me.'

'Is there any wonder given what's gone on? Bert almost got his arms ripped off by a gorilla.'

'Who are you calling a gorilla?'

But Joseph's attempts at humour slid by unnoticed. Syd was still thinking of Mrs F.

'She's definitely not been herself though these last couple of days, has she? You live with her. You must have noticed.'

He didn't answer, though he was, unusually, considering what Syd was saying. The truth was, he'd been so wrapped up in his fear of Gryce that he hadn't noticed much of a change in Mrs F. Her temper was still largely poor, though she had taken to wearing an odd expression whenever he returned from school. You couldn't quite call it a smile, but her mouth *was* turning up at each side, like it was being held up by taut, invisible twine.

Joseph thought of yesterday, and how she'd been with him.

'So, how was your day, then?' she'd asked, her voice tepid but her face sunny, which was most off-putting.

'Er, fine,' he'd answered.

'Oh, that's – that's good . . . great. What did you do?'

'You know, the usual.'

'And lessons? Interesting? Tell me something you learned.'

'Stuff,' he'd replied. 'Adding. Taking away.'

She made encouraging noises, then paused, waiting for the question she really wanted to ask.

'And there were no problems still ... No arguments, fights?'

'No, it was fine. Easy ...' She looked briefly relieved, before he added, 'Only three ambulances today.'

So, was she acting differently to normal? He supposed she was. But in all honesty, to his mind it was an improvement on her usual brusqueness. There'd been no dressing down or telling off. If anything, she seemed interested in him, and this was something that he'd not experienced in such a long time, that he wasn't sure he wanted to agree with Syd that there was something *wrong* with her.

'She seems all right,' he said. 'Different, maybe, but not bad.'

'Well, I've seen a change in her,' Syd said, standing her ground, 'even if you haven't. She looks tired. Exhausted, in fact.'

'We're all tired. There's been a raid every night.'

'It's more than that. She's not bustling round the zoo like normal. I mean, when was the last time you saw her clean out Adonis's cage?'

He didn't know the answer to that, but she'd definitely been doing it less this week. He'd spotted way more dung in there this afternoon, but hadn't made a link to Mrs F's mood.

'She can't be sleeping,' Syd went on. '*Is* she sleeping?'

'I don't bloomin' know. I'm not in the same room, am I?'

'Well, you still must know. Is she, I don't know, grumpy every morning? Or short-tempered?'

'If that's how you measure sleep, then it's probably thirty years since she closed her eyes.'

'This is no time for joking, Joseph. You might not be bothered, but I am. You watch her now, when we find her. Watch carefully.'

'But what am I looking for?'

'Just trust me.'

They walked towards the camels' enclosure. But she wasn't there. Nor was she with the ponies or wolves. The aviary was empty too, barring the birds, of course.

'Maybe the wolves ate her,' Joseph said, trying to lighten the look of confusion that had fallen over Syd's face. As usual, he'd judged his comment badly. The expression on her face told him so.

Finally, they spotted her through the office window, slumped back in her chair, hands wrapped around a mug of tea.

'Don't let her see you,' said Syd, stopping Joseph from moving any closer. 'Just watch.'

So he did, though he didn't know what for. Mrs F didn't move. Not even bringing her mug to her mouth.

'What's the point in this?' he said. 'She's not doing anything.'

'Exactly. And when did you last see that? She's *always* busy. You know what she's like. She wants this place to be spotless, to have the same standards as when it was open. But this?' She pointed. 'This isn't like her. And it's not the first time I've seen her hiding in there. There's been other days, too. Last time, she didn't move for over an hour. I timed her!'

'We should ask her, then,' Joseph said, straight to the point.

'What sort of a plan is that?'

'An obvious one?'

'Obvious, and rubbish. Do you honestly think she's going to tell you what's going on just by asking her?'

He shrugged.

'*You* wouldn't, Joseph. Some mornings it takes me half an hour just to get you to reply to "Good morning."'

'All right then, Mrs Detective, you come up with the plan.'

But at that moment, there was movement inside. Mrs F reached forward slowly and picked up a sheet of paper from the desk. It looked like a letter, but from the response it pulled from her, it was no love note. Her eyes narrowed, lips turning into a snarl that quickly took over her face.

She didn't read it for long before screwing it into a ball and throwing it across the room. Then she marched out of the office, sending Joseph and Syd darting into the shadows.

'Where's she going now?' Syd said.

Joseph didn't care, bolting inside as soon as Mrs F was out of sight.

'What are you doing?' Syd hissed.

'I thought you wanted to know what was up with her?'

'I do!'

'Well, it's obviously written on that piece of paper.' He disappeared inside, leaving Syd lingering in the entrance.

'Get in here, will you?' Joseph said, head appearing round the doorframe, scaring her half to death.

'I'll keep lookout.'

'I don't need a lookout, I need you to read whatever's written in that letter, don't I?' And he dragged Syd inside before retrieving the ball of paper from the floor.

'What does it say?' he asked, thrusting it into her hand.

Syd was a good reader. One of the best at school, but for once, she wasn't fluent enough. Nowhere near.

'What are you two doing in here?' came a voice from nowhere. They spun around to see Mrs F in the doorway, her face darkening, probably due to the look of guilt on their faces.

'Looking for you,' said Joseph. Syd said nothing, just moved her hands and the letter behind her back, way too slowly.

'What's that you're hiding, Syd?'

Her mouth flapped open like a fish.

'Nothing,' Joseph said, answering for her.

'Very impressive,' said Mrs F, walking forwards. 'You said that without moving your lips, Syd. Come on, let me have it.'

Syd did as she was told. Joseph groaned. She could've tried to hide it somewhere or slip it to him. He definitely wouldn't have given it up so easily.

Mrs F smoothed out the letter's creases.

'Right,' she said, lips tight. 'Been snooping, have we?'

'Not snooping,' Joseph replied. 'Syd was worried about you, that's all.'

'And you thought the answer was written in here, did you?' She waved the letter in front of them both.

'It certainly looked like it.'

She rammed the letter into her pocket. 'Well, you're wrong. It's nothing. Mindless bureaucracy, is all. You'd think people would have better things to do than waste time writing pointless letters.' She moved away from them, picking up a broom, pushing it one-handed, but fooling no one.

'Mrs F,' said Syd, suddenly piping up. 'It's true what Joseph said. We've noti—*I've* noticed, that you've been different the last few days. Sad.'

'Sad? I don't think so.'

'Well, you've not been yourself.'

'What absolute non—'

But Joseph now believed what Syd had been getting at. He'd become so adept over time at telling lies himself that he could see Mrs F's radiating off her.

'What was it you said to me?' he reminded her. 'About letting the truth out. About things festering if they don't see the light of day?'

'I don't see what that has to do with me.'

'Yes, you do. You know exactly what I mean because you're doing the same thing yourself. Which makes you as bad as me. In fact, it makes you worse. Makes you a hypocrite.'

Mrs F was not a woman who was easily shamed, nor did she often deviate from a path once she'd embarked on it. But there was something in what Joseph said that made her stop, take a deep breath and retrieve the piece of paper from her pocket.

With a shaking hand, she held it out to the two of them, paper still quivering as Syd took it from her and read silently. 'It's from the local authority,' she said.

'But what does it say?' asked Joseph impatiently.

'It's about Adonis,' she said, breathless despite standing stock-still. 'There's been a complaint.'

'From Bert's dad?'

'Doesn't say, but it must be. It says that Adonis is dangerous. That he endangered someone's life.'

'Wasn't his fault though, was it?' Joseph said. 'Bert shouldn't have been here!'

'Powers that be don't know that,' replied Syd sadly. 'All they know is that there was an incident.' She underlined a sentence with her finger. 'That a boy could've died.'

'So, what are they going to do?'

'*They're* not going to do anything. Not yet. Says here it's up to Mrs F to find an alternative home for him. Another zoo.'

Joseph looked to Mrs F. No wonder she was looking distressed.

'How long have they given you? To find somewhere?' he asked her.

'Two weeks,' she replied, sadly.

'Or what?'

No answer.

'Or what happens?' he asked, louder.

'They'll shoot him,' Mrs F said.

Syd was the first to cry. 'They can't do that, can they?'

'Seems they can do whatever they want,' Mrs F said, her voice tense. 'I tried to speak to them, but they weren't interested in a conversation about a gorilla when there's all this other madness going on.'

'All the more reason to leave him alone!' Syd cried.

'All the more reason for them to do something about it,' Mrs F replied. 'This is probably one of the only things they *can* do something about. So, they will.'

Joseph couldn't quite believe this was happening. It all felt so final. And more importantly, unjust.

'What are you going to do about it?'

'Everything I can, though I doubt for a second any zoo will take him on. I'll be lucky to even get any responses before the authorities come knocking.'

'Well you have to go see them, then,' Joseph said. 'The other zoo people. Twist their arms. Tell them they have to.' Why was he having to gee her up? Where had her fight gone? It was almost as unbelievable as the fact that he was now protecting the ape.

'Joseph, the other zoos are hundreds of miles away and there's barely any ruddy trains running. So how am I meant to get there? Walk? Stroll up to the gate with Adonis on a lead and a suitcase tucked under his arm? Life doesn't work like that.'

'But you can't give up. If they take him, then what have you got left? Couple of wretched wolves aren't going to entertain anyone when the war ends, are they?'

If Joseph's intention was to rouse Mrs F into action, then it seemed to work.

'Do you think I don't know that? Of course I do. And so I'll tell you something, if they do come rattling the gates, then they'll have to deal with me first. Because I'll be ready for them. They can bring every gun they want; they can bring a *tank*, if they have to. But if they want to put a bullet in this one here? Well, it'll have to pass through me first.'

For once Joseph was in agreement with her. He felt his fingers tighten into a fist and his lips curl into a small smile. If it was a fight they were after, then he was more than happy to stand beside her and trade blows.

31

'How many times do I have to tell you?' the old woman yelled at Joseph. 'The answer is no. Do you honestly think I can spare you any veg?'

But Joseph would not stand down. 'Please, Missus. It's not even for me, or my family. It's for my gorilla.'

That was enough to turn the woman's brush into a deadly weapon, and she shooed both Joseph and Syd away from the front door of her shop.

'How many is that now, who've said no?' Syd asked as they slumped away.

'Too many.'

'I think you'll find the answer is everybody. Every shop in walking distance, anyway. Can we please go home now?'

'No!' he replied.

'Well if you're going to insist on keeping me out here against my will, then the least you can do is practise your reading as you walk.' She pulled Joseph's book from her coat, though he had no idea how it got there. 'Come on,' she said. 'From the beginning, go!'

He did as he was told, though it was unusual for Syd to threaten to quit anything, and besides, Joseph had one more idea. He knew Syd wouldn't like or approve of it, though, so he told her very little until they arrived at the allotments. Until recently these had been a football pitch. The goals still stood, rusting, between rows of furrowed mud.

'Why are we here?' Syd asked.

'Isn't it obvious?'

'Well, yes, but you're not going to get anything out of the owners today, are you? You've nothing to barter with.'

But Joseph wasn't interested in such a technicality. He was already swinging his leg over the wall.

'What are you doing?' she asked, pulling at his coat.

'It's all right, there's no one here, is there? It's bloomin' freezing. No one's gardening today.'

'That's not the point, Joseph. You can't go over there, stealing people's food.'

'But this is public land, isn't it? The footie pitch there, anyone could play on it, right?'

Syd nodded hesitantly.

'So, whatever grows on it belongs to all of us, really. All I'm going to do is take my share. For Adonis.'

Syd didn't know what to do with her face. But she did know there was no way she was going to change Joseph's mind.

'Do it quickly, then,' she whispered theatrically, keeping watch for any hardy gardeners who weren't already in front of their fires. At least the light was fading, she thought to herself. It would offer Joseph a bit of cover, as long as he was quick.

But he wasn't. In fact, he seemed to be in there for ages, only returning after a good five minutes, the front of his jumper so swollen it looked like he was going to give birth to a marrow.

'What on earth have you got in there?' she gasped.

'Anything I could find,' he replied. 'Hardly growing season, is it? Couldn't find any carrots at all that were worth him eating.'

'Do you not think people will miss all that?'

'Nah, I trod all the mud back down, didn't I? And don't worry, I didn't leave any footprints, Detective.'

'You don't have to be a detective to know you've been stealing. Look at you.'

'Best help me, then,' he replied, emptying half of his jumper into every pocket she owned. There were cauliflowers and broccoli heads, leeks and swede, some in better states than others.

'Do you think he'll eat any of this?' she sighed, feeling more guilty than she ever had in her life.

'God knows. Got to be better than grass, hasn't it?'

There was no answer to that, so they scampered away furtively from the allotments, to the relative warmth of their homes.

Mrs F looked at the veg with a quizzical expression.

'Are you really telling me a grocer gave you all of this for free?' she asked.

Joseph nodded, wanting to keep his lies to a minimum.

'Then they could do with you in government,' she said. 'Mr Churchill needs negotiators from what I hear.'

Whether Mrs F actually believed him was a matter for debate, but she didn't quiz him any further. 'The lad in that cage will think it's Christmas,' she said, before leaving Joseph to it.

He no longer needed prompting to feed Adonis. He made it his priority, though he never took it for granted or got lax in his approach. The sight of Bert pinned against the bars was seared into his brain.

He walked slowly to the bars, but now he didn't feel nervous. All he could hear was his own, slow breathing, mirrored by Adonis's, as the ape waited for his arrival at the bars.

They grunted and scratched, impersonating each other, all the rituals repeated almost identically. Joseph's favourite moment was always the same one: when the food passed from him to Adonis. There had never been physical contact between them, though, as usually the ape would impatiently rip the vegetables from Joseph's hand.

Today was different, for as Joseph crouched on his haunches facing Adonis, he felt the ape's fingers brush his. Joseph swallowed a gasp as a jolt of electricity ripped through him. It was thrilling. He couldn't believe it had happened, that the gap between them had disappeared entirely, even if only for a second.

Immediately Joseph wanted to feel it again, that trust, and he reached into the bucket for something fresh, choosing a head of broccoli. Would it work? He hoped desperately that it would.

Nervous again, heart pounding, Joseph dropped his head as he offered his arm slowly to the bars. There was a beat, a moment when he thought Adonis might not be interested, but it was merely that, a second, as the ape's hand moved as slowly as the boy's. Joseph held his breath in his lungs, not daring to let it out, but as Adonis's fingers met his a second time, he thought he might explode with joy. For, this time, it was more than a brush of the fingertips.

Joseph watched with eyes widening, not daring to blink as Adonis's open hand enveloped not only the broccoli, but Joseph's entire fist, squeezing gently. Adonis's palm was warm, the pads of his fingers both soft and calloused in places. The force slowly increased. Forgetting the script, Joseph lifted his head and looked Adonis squarely in the eye, the ape meeting him with the same intensity. And there they sat for seconds that lasted on into minutes, until the ape pulled away, sliding the broccoli from Joseph's grasp, leaving his fingers cold once more.

Joseph remained on his haunches, head raised high, and watched as Adonis feasted on his prize.

Rain started to fall, a storm from nowhere, plastering the hair to their skins, but still, neither of them moved, until both the bucket, and the clouds, were empty.

32

Insomnia, it seemed, was contagious.

Mrs F wasn't sleeping, that was clear. Maybe she felt she was constantly on duty, waiting for the bombs. They came often enough, after all. But Joseph reckoned it was more than that. Even when the siren didn't sound, he still heard her slippers night after night, padding softly down the stairs in the darkest hours, the sound of the poker, teasing the sleepy embers awake, and the less subtle sounds of Tweedy, excited to see his mistress unexpectedly.

But he was always awake long before she was.

His head was constantly full, too.

There was Gryce's monthly exam looming desperately close now, and the fear of his plan being exposed.

There was his anger that Mr Conaghan had followed through on his threat, and that his son had come to the zoo that day; but also that Joseph's own actions, his own *stupidity*, had led to the fight in the first place.

He was angry about the noose tightening slowly around Adonis's neck. True, he had spent the first weeks not just fearing but hating the beast. But then if it wasn't for the ape's intervention, Bert and Jimmy would have beaten him to a pulp. And after feeding the ape at such close quarters, Joseph was now more convinced than ever that Adonis had meant to help him. That the ape was sticking up for him. And that meant something to Joseph.

If this wasn't enough, there was Mrs F to think about. She hadn't wanted him here, in her home or her life, she'd said as much, and there had been her hot temper and cold words. But on the other hand, she'd stuck up for him over Bert, and she hadn't laughed or pointed or called him thick like others had when he'd told her about his reading. He'd felt himself relax around her as a result, ever so slightly. For years now, as long as he could remember, he'd been a knot that other people had tied, a knot so complicated and off-putting that no one stuck around long enough to unpick it.

But *she* hadn't given up, not yet. She'd picked at the edges, loosening them ever so slightly, but in an unexpected way. Her manner was rough and crude, but no matter how loudly Joseph shouted and pushed her away, there she was, still in his eyeline. Giving back as good as she got. Unlike the others, she hadn't walked out, or away.

And now? Now, she needed help: that much was clear.

He stood at the top of the landing; hand on the banister, left foot making nervous circles, wearing out the carpet. She wouldn't want him to appear before her, but his legs took him down the stairs and through the door before the rest of him had time to stop them. The words fell from his mouth before his feet stood still.

'I want you to read me the letter again,' he said, steel in his voice.

'What are you doing up?' she said, startled. 'You've your test thing tomorrow, for goodness' sake.'

'Yeah I know, but . . .'

'But nothing. You should be asleep.'

'So should you, then,' he said. 'Or are you not coming now?' He wasn't exactly sure if he wanted her there or not.

'Yes, I'll be there. Now, get yourself back to bed.'

'Not until you read the letter again to me. From the council. We must be missing something. Or understanding it wrong. You can't let them do this.'

But Mrs F said nothing. She was sitting at the table, alongside the tin from the shelf, with the same faded documents and creased photographs scattered in front of her.

Like the last time he'd disturbed her, she gathered the papers up, only this time with less urgency and more sadness. She pushed them into a neat pile and slid them back inside the tin, before passing a letter towards him, bearing the same official insignia that he'd seen at the zoo.

He creased his eyes, forcing them onto the words, willing them for once in his life, just to sit still, but they didn't. Of course they didn't. It didn't work like that, and they danced and swirled around the page, threatening to slither onto the hearth rug.

Joseph fought the urge to scrunch the sheet into a ball and

propel it into the fire. Mrs F put the tin back on the shelf but she turned and saw the anger written large on his face. She walked to his side, her tone kind and patient.

'It's another one,' she said. 'Arrived today. Final warning. Want a line drawn under it, apparently, before it happens again.'

'Again?' Joseph spat. 'Wouldn't have happened in the first place if Bert had stayed out.'

She said nothing, sadness weighing her down so entirely that it seemed difficult to even raise her head.

'Besides,' he went on, 'Bert's hardly likely to come back again, is he?'

'Well we've a week now,' she said. 'And if I've not arranged a new home by then, they'll be back, to put him down.'

It wasn't an image Joseph wanted to linger on.

'So what are you going to do? It's all so unfair!' he said, the power in his voice shocking him. 'I mean, Bert shouldn't have been in the zoo, should he? Or so close to the cage? Did you tell *them* that? That he'd broken in?'

'Of course, I told them. In person and in a letter.'

'Then why won't they listen?'

'Because they've already heard what they want to hear. They're not interested in an old monkey—'

'He's an ape!'

She smiled, sadly. 'I know that, as do you. But to them, in the grand scheme of things, he's just another thing to cross off their list, and they'd sooner put a bullet in him than listen to the truth. That's what this war does to people. The bombs are so loud that it makes them deaf as well as stupid.'

'Then we find him a new home. Write more letters. Telegrams. Zoos must have telephones, too. Or we start a petition. People won't let him die.'

She was looking at him funny. It wasn't normal. Her eyes weren't creased or scowling. It felt like she was looking at someone else. Like he was Syd. Or Adonis, and he didn't know how to feel about it. It made him uneasy.

'Do you not think I've thought about all this?' she said.

'Then we have to do it!'

'I've tried. I have. But the other zoos already can't cope. They've barely enough to feed the animals they have, and as for people round here? Everyone's clinging on to what they have, and even that's slipping away, every time the siren goes.'

'So that's it? You just give up? I thought the place was important. I thought Adonis was everything to you. That's what Syd said. But I guess I was *wrong*.'

He spat the last word. He hadn't meant to, but then again, he hadn't meant to say any of it, or come in the room in the first place. But he had made a lifetime habit of saying and doing the wrong thing.

'You have no idea what he or that place means to me,' she said, angrily. 'You've not been here two minutes, so don't think you know what I'm feeling, or what I've lost. I'd appreciate it if you kept your ideas to yourself in future.'

'Maybe I will,' he said. 'And don't bother coming to school tomorrow, if that's the way you feel.'

'Joseph Palmer, take yourself up to bed right now. I don't want to hear from you or see you until tomorrow. And if I want to come to school tomorrow, I ruddy well will. It will be *my* choice.'

That is where the conversation ended. She swept the tin up from the shelf and left the room without even slamming the door behind her.

Joseph didn't follow her. Instead he poked the fire back into life, watched the flames, and thought long and hard.

33

They could smell the burning from miles away. On every step of their walk to school.

'Do you think there's anything left standing over there?' Joseph asked, peering at the smoke that clung to the horizon.

'Hard to tell,' said Syd. 'Doesn't look like it.'

'I can smell it,' Joseph grimaced. 'Even from here. What bit of the city is that?'

'The docks. Auntie says they've bombed it to stop supplies getting in and out. Says Hitler won't stop till we're on our hands and knees, begging him to.'

Joseph felt himself bristle. No way he'd be doing that.

'What's she like, your auntie?'

Syd took an unusual amount of time to answer. 'She's all right,' she said, pausing again. 'She's just not my mum.'

Her response made Joseph pause too. He understood what she meant but had no idea how to say anything that would help.

'You should see her run to the underground station, though, when the siren goes. I told her she could win a gold medal.'

'You not got a shelter in her yard?'

'There's no room. Plus, the tube station is only at the bottom of the road.'

'Must be weird down there at night.'

'No weirder than being underground at the bottom of the garden. Plus, there's other people there to keep us company. People bring playing cards, or sing. If you were down there, we could practise your reading, make sure you passed Gryce's test every month!'

It didn't raise a smile, so she went on. 'It's different to being in a small shelter, that's all.'

'Enough space to hide a gorilla down there?'

Syd laughed. 'Don't think so. Unless we put him in a frock, give him a shave and teach him some manners first. It's packed down there. Not just people sleeping on the platforms and in corridors. They sleep head to foot on the tracks as well.'

'So how *do* you hide a gorilla?' he asked. He would have smiled at the absurdity had it not been such a pressing, troubling question.

It stumped Syd.

'That's just it,' he said, when she said nothing. 'You can't hide him. And I've thought about it. Whether Mrs F could move him to a different cage, build a smaller one somewhere secret, like in the cellar under the aquarium, but even if she could – and she can't – how would we even get him down there? He's hardly likely to hold my hand and follow us, is he?'

'If you could get hold of bananas any more, I reckon he'd follow you anywhere.'

'Well, we've got to come up with a plan soon. Clock's ticking, isn't it?'

'I'm just pleased you've changed your mind about him,' she said. 'I mean, I don't want to sound cruel or harsh, but you hated Adonis at the beginning. First time I met you, you were chucking stones at him.'

'Yeah, I know.'

'But you don't hate him now?'

'No.'

'Why?'

'Why, what?'

'Oh for Pete's sake, Joseph, stop being so flipping difficult. If you don't hate Adonis now, then tell me why?'

'Because . . . because . . .'

'Go on . . .'

But he didn't know how to explain it to Syd without sounding soft. How it felt when he touched his hand, how good it was to know Adonis had tried to save him from Bert and Jimmy.

'Come on, Joseph. Tell me . . .'

'Just feels like . . . I dunno, like there's enough death going on without adding another one.'

It wasn't a lie, he felt it, believed it, and it was easier to think that than trying to order all the other thoughts zooming round his head.

'There HAS to be something we're not thinking about,' she said. 'A letter, maybe, to the newspaper. Yes, that's it. Because adults like that, don't they? Stories about children and animals. We can tell them all about you, about how Adonis has been your only friend since you got here – well, apart from me, but we don't have to tell them that bit. Artistic licence, they call it. It pulls at the heartstrings. Gets everyone writing letters to the editor at the paper, dozens of them, hundreds, even, and before we know it, the government will have to listen. There's no way they'll touch Adonis, not then, when everyone's happy for once. What do you think?'

Joseph had thoughts, and plenty of them. But the speed at which she spoke meant that he needed a little bit of time to catch up. And besides, they'd reached school, just as a shrill ringing started.

'There goes the bell,' he said, realising that his big moment with Gryce was just hours away. He traipsed into class, his mind no longer on Adonis, but on Clarence instead.

An apprehensive mood hung over the classroom all morning. Joseph was aware not just of his own tension, but everyone else's too. Even Miss Doherty's. As the morning progressed, she made her way around every child, including Jimmy and Bert. Joseph watched as she bent over them, drilling them on their sums, which made him feel momentarily better. She stayed with them for some time, too: it was clear that whatever she was teaching, they still weren't grasping it.

Finally, she arrived at Joseph's shoulder, tentatively, as always. 'Now, Joseph,' she said, gently, 'I know this is the first time you've sat one of Mr Gryce's tests, and you may be, well, *nervous*. But I wanted to tell you how proud I am of the work you've done. Your maths is . . . well, phenomenal. And I've told Mr Gryce that he should look at that carefully, especially in light of . . . well . . .'

'My reading?' Joseph offered.

'I realise you don't find it easy . . .'

'I've been practising.'

'You have?' She seemed surprised and relieved, touching him lightly on the shoulder before realising what she'd done. 'That's wonderful. Would you like to practise some more with me now?'

He shook his head. He didn't want to get it wrong and expose his plan before the headmaster arrived.

'S'all right, Miss. I'll do it on my own,' he said coolly, relieved when she moved onto preparing Syd (not that she needed it).

He concentrated hard, rehearsing the lines in his head. He could hear Syd in his mind, the endless advice she'd offered him.

'You don't just have to *read* the words, remember,' she'd said, on more than one occasion, 'you have to *act* them. Make Gryce *believe* that you're reading them fresh off the page.'

'Do I look like an actor?' he'd asked her.

'I don't mean you have to be over the top, or polished. It might actually be more believable if you stumble over a few sentences. Read too well, and he might well smell a rat.'

The thought of it made him anxious. It was one thing to do this as he sat by Adonis's cage, and quite another to do it under pressure. What if Gryce wanted to grill him on more than he'd learned? He really would be in trouble then.

By lunchtime, he was beyond nervous.

'Try thinking about something else for a bit,' said Syd, but that just led him back to Adonis and an anxiety of a different kind.

She tried again. 'Try eating, then.' But every mouthful tasted like he was chewing sand.

Syd saw he was in a dark place, and wisely chose to stay out of striking distance until the bell called them back into lessons to face Gryce's judgement.

The first thing that threw Joseph when he walked back into class was the parents. They'd arrived and were milling around at the back of the classroom as Miss Doherty clucked and fussed and told them how well their children were doing. She looked flushed, apologetic even, presumably as she knew Gryce's methods caused unnecessary stress for everyone. Joseph scanned the faces present, relieved that there was no sign of Bert's father anywhere.

The second thing to affect Joseph was Mrs F's absence from the group. It was clear very quickly that she hadn't come. It wasn't unusual for an adult to let Joseph down, yet she'd been adamant that she'd be there. He felt a ridiculous mixture of disappointment and mild relief because she knew him better than Gryce, and as a result was more likely to see through his plan.

'No Mrs F?' whispered Syd, as she waved at her aunt, a

mousy-looking woman, as seemingly meek as her niece was bold.

'I knew she wouldn't come,' Joseph said.

'She'll be here. I prom—'

But there wasn't time to reassure him any further, as through the door swooshed Gryce, with Clarence twitching and flexing in his hand.

'Good afternoon, everyone!' said Gryce. There was a different tone to his voice, a theatricality, presumably for the parents' benefit. 'I'm delighted to see so many of you here again. As you know, it's important that in these difficult and uncertain times your children have the normality of school to fall back on. But more than that, that they continue to flourish. After all, the only way we will beat Hitler is through application, dedication and knowledge.'

He stopped momentarily and looked to the parents. Joseph wondered if he was expecting applause for his stirring words, but when none came, he moved swiftly on, telling both the children and adults to sit, which they all promptly did.

'We will start with mathematics. Twenty questions, each targeted at your child's individual age, and twenty minutes in which to finish them. Parents, Miss Doherty has copies of the sums for you to peruse.' Miss Doherty scuttled between them, distributing textbooks, until she had only one left in her hand. Presumably, from the embarrassed look she gave Joseph, this was meant for Mrs F.

'Twenty minutes, then, class,' Gryce barked. 'You may begin.'

Joseph did just that, relieved in some ways that they were starting with maths. He was even more relieved, when he scanned the questions in front of him. They were no different to the sorts of algebra and geometry puzzles he'd solved many times for Miss Doherty before. He was careful though, not to whizz through them too quickly and draw Gryce's attention to him. Gryce was prowling around peering over shoulders, tutting, and no doubt making every child and their parents incredibly nervous. Eventually he told everyone to stop and put their pens down.

'While Miss Doherty marks the mathematics, we will move onto reading. Oration builds confidence and character, and that is what we need these days more than ever, is it not?' he said, clicking his fingers at Tim, one of the younger children, to summon him to the front of the class.

Tim, head down, approached the front tentatively, as Gryce sat on a chair, making his gown billow with a whip of his wrists.

Joseph watched, keen to see how long each student would be tested for, but it seemed to vary. What he did notice was that Gryce grew bored if someone read well, waving them away quickly, which heaped further pressure on Joseph. Start badly, or nervously, and he ran the risk of making Gryce stretch it out. Do that, and he knew he would eventually be exposed.

He decided not to watch, hoping it would ease his nerves, and his gaze fell to Miss Doherty, who upon seeing him, lifted his maths book up discreetly and mouthed 'Brilliant,' at him.

The word soaked through his skin and warmed him, if only momentarily.

But eventually, his time in the spotlight came. Bert and Jimmy had blundered and stalled, but passed with a stern look and promises of 'greater application', while Syd was second-to-last, commanding the space with her normal poise, which seemed to bore Gryce, making her read for what seemed to be little more than thirty seconds. He tapped Clarence weakly on the desk, as close to an ovation as he could muster, before sending her away.

'Palmer!' Gryce boomed, 'I believe this leaves us with you. If you would be so kind?' He beckoned Joseph forward with Clarence, which did little for his nerves.

'Aren't you forgetting something?' Gryce asked as he arrived.

Joseph hadn't a clue and panicked. Was he supposed to thank him, or bow? What had he missed?

'Your book, boy! How on earth are you expecting to read without your book?'

The short walk back to his desk was a shameful one, but he took a small amount of solace from Syd's supportive smile as he passed.

'I'm ready, sir,' he said, when he finally stood beside Gryce.

'Well, start at the beginning then,' the headmaster replied, and stood for the first time, moving in front of Joseph, like he had bought the most expensive seat in the theatre, at the expense of the view held by anyone else.

Joseph peeled the dog-eared book open, moistening his lips with his tongue. *You can do this,* he told himself. *You know the words, you do.*

'*The night was dark,*' he began, quiet at first, but getting louder for fear of being told to start again. '*And the clouds hung low and heavy.*'

He took it slow, allowing the words to come back to him, but at the same time working hard to not be too fluent, just like Syd had said. He used his finger as a prop without actually looking at the words, pretending to trace the phrases as he read.

Five lines in, though, and he made the mistake of actually focusing on the words instead of his finger, and felt the nausea rise as they spun and rolled, forcing his tongue into what felt like a knot that he could never untie.

He felt eyes on him, saw Gryce stop prowling and tap Clarence's tip on his calf, just once. Joseph wiped at a stray bead of sweat on his nose, nodding slightly as he saw Syd do the same, encouragingly.

He started the line again.

He was doing a good job, good enough surely, and he allowed himself to look up briefly, seeing Miss Doherty willing him on like a proud parent.

Two lines later, though, and Joseph felt the tension rise again. How long until Gryce called him off? He must have read for longer than anyone else.

But finally, eventually, as Joseph neared the end of what

he had rehearsed and considered how quickly he'd have to move to outrun both Gryce and his cane, the headmaster finally said something. It wasn't aimed at Joseph, though his stare most definitely was.

'Miss Doherty.' Gryce smiled thinly. 'You are to be congratulated. Such fluency and understanding in our newest student.'

Joseph felt his blood swirl. He hadn't expected praise from Gryce, so he didn't trust it either.

'I enjoyed your performance so much, Master Palmer, that I wonder if –' he moved behind Joseph, his bony finger coming into view – 'that I wonder if you could possibly read this line again for us.'

His finger landed midway through the page, around six lines from the top.

'Why, sir?' Joseph dared ask, though he knew he shouldn't have. Challenging the man was never going to make him change his mind.

'Because you read it so beautifully. With such colour and eloquence, I think we would all benefit from hearing it again.'

Joseph's stomach capsized. He hadn't a clue what the line said.

'Come on, Master Palmer,' Gryce said as he circled endlessly, finally stopping at Joseph's left shoulder.

Joseph's head was chaos, recapping the story, trying to recall what the right line might be.

'Quickly now, boy. Come on!'

He felt sweat force itself free across his forehead before he could wipe it away.

'READ!'

So he did. He made a guess, a wild stab in the dark, knowing full well that it would take a miracle of biblical proportions to see him start in the right place.

And of course, there was no miracle. No parting of the sea or water into wine, just a boy exposing himself for what he was: a chancer and a cheat.

These were the words that Gryce bellowed at him as he ripped the book from his hands and tossed it to the floor.

'You're not reading this at all, are you? You've simply memorised it, to hide the fact that you cannot read! Did you really think you could fool me with this charade?' he roared. 'You should be ashamed. Pretending to read like that. To mock not just me, but your teacher. The teacher who expected and frankly deserved much more.'

Joseph's panicked eyes fled to Miss Doherty, her shocked expression, hands at her face. It wasn't clear if she were appalled at Joseph or fearful of what would happen to him next. She wasn't alone. The parents looked like they would rather be anywhere else than here.

'Well, let me tell you something, boy,' Gryce went on. 'If you dare to make a fool of me, I can promise you that you will never, EVER, dare do it again.'

He felt the headmaster grab at his wrist, turning his palm skywards, and then saw Clarence arc its way up.

Joseph braced. Not just his hand, but his entire body. He knew what was coming and how it would feel, but feared it anyway, and did not try to hide the pain when the cane tore at his palm, shockwaves shooting to every part of his body.

He lifted his head to the ceiling, managing to see the others through his tears, their faces uncomfortable, wincing.

But Joseph knew that wasn't it. Gryce was merely warming up, and it took every inch of courage he owned to raise his palm back up, and swallow hard, ready.

But the next blow didn't come. Clarence didn't sing as he tore through the air. Instead Gryce's arm remained at the top of its arc, held not by the strongest of arms, but by the most powerful of voices, that demanded from nowhere: 'What on *earth* is going on?'

34

As timing went, this was close to miraculous. What was also wonderful, to Joseph's eye, was how powerful Mrs F seemed, from the second she came into view.

Somehow, she seemed to tower over Gryce, stopping him and Clarence dead in their tracks. Whatever her reasons for being late, at that moment, Joseph forgave her.

'I think that will do, don't you?' she said to the headmaster. It was a demand, not a question.

Gryce didn't know how to react.

'Mrs Farrelly,' he said, with an expression he normally saved for Joseph. 'If your timekeeping wasn't so tardy, you would know exactly what I was doing. Rightfully punishing this boy for an act of deceit.'

'I don't care if he's decapitated the king, I can see that you've already struck him once, and once is clearly enough.' She turned to Joseph. 'Are you all right?'

'There's nothing wrong with the boy,' Gryce said. 'He's proved today he is more than resourceful. He is, in fact, a devious schemer.'

'Well, thank you for pulling him apart so publicly.' She looked at the other parents, who seemed to stare quickly at their shoes. 'Perhaps I should ask *them* what happened?'

'I don't think that's necessary, do you? If you'll follow me to my office, I'll be delighted to recount the whole despicable event.' And Gryce made to leave, gown swishing to maximum effect.

'Or, you can tell me right now. Just in case I need to check with Joseph's teacher here.'

Miss Doherty had been fidgeting at the back of the class, such was her level of discomfort, but this new woman appeared so strong that it galvanised her too, lifting her shoulders and chin higher than usual.

'If your wish, my dear, is to humiliate your boy still further in front of his peers and their parents, then yes, of course, I'll tell you here and now. Joseph is a cheat and a liar. He has made it his priority to ridicule both myself and his teacher, simply for his own amusement.'

On he went, talking at great length, about how Joseph had weaved a 'web of lies.'

Mrs F listened and looked uneasy, though she waited patiently until Gryce finished his rant.

'Well, if there's anyone to blame for Joseph's lying, then it's me.'

It was an admission that brought puzzlement to Gryce's face.

'Oh really?'

'That's right. Joseph came to me, weeks ago now, and explained what was going on with his reading. That when he tries to read, the words don't stay still on the page.'

Gryce scoffed loudly. 'Ridiculous.'

'So it's my fault it's come to this, not his. I should've come to you about it.' She took a deep breath and switched her attention to the boy. 'I'm sorry, Joseph. I really am. And as for you,' she said, swinging her attention back to Gryce, 'what you need to hear is that Joseph isn't lazy, or evil, or stupid, or any of the things that you've branded him. It's clear to me, to anyone who *really* knows him, that he's none of those things.'

Joseph stood, stunned. Her words, her belief in him, dulled the pain that he felt in his palm.

'What he is,' Mrs F went on, 'is different. He speaks his mind, granted; sometimes more than he should, but at least I know where I stand with him. What he isn't, is thick.'

'That's right. He isn't,' came a voice from the back of the classroom. Miss Doherty stepped forward, voice louder than ever before and clutching Joseph's maths book. 'He is exceptionally bright. His mathematical abilities are of someone two years older at least.'

'That is enough, Miss Doherty,' Gryce snapped.

'No. No, it isn't,' she replied. 'Not until you actually look at his work.' And she thrust the open book into the headmaster's hand.

Gryce looked, and looked again, but said nothing, which allowed Mrs F another window of opportunity.

'This boy would be more than happy to read, delighted to, because, first and foremost, it would keep you off his back. Problem is, he can't. Doesn't matter how hard he tries, or how many times you or I spell things out for him, the words on that page will *not – stay – still*. Now, I have no idea what that means, or what the hell to do about it, but I will work it out. Just like I should've done weeks ago when he told me. I'm sorry, Joseph. I am.'

It was impossible for Joseph to meet her gaze. Impossible because it was alien to him, the idea that anyone would ever apologise to him.

'Well,' said Gryce. 'This is all incredibly touching, and I thank you for your input. But the facts remain the same, the boy lied, and the boy cheated. And in my school, these are virtues that must be punished.'

This brought Mrs F further onto the offensive. 'So if Joseph had come forward, and told you, right from the start, that words dance on the page and stop him reading, then you would've believed him?'

'Well, I . . .'

'I'm sorry?'

'The boy has proved himself to be trouble from his very first day. And boys that cannot behave, then they need to be—'

'What? They need to be *what*?'

Gryce stood, ramrod straight, and as if by force of habit, snapped Clarence upon his own leg. 'To be shown the right path. And if that is by punishment, then so be it.'

Mrs F had seen enough, and without hesitation, she strode forward, and whipped Clarence clean out of Mr Gryce's grip.

'There's enough punishment going on already these days,' she said. 'Inside these walls and out.'

Gripping the cane at each end, she brought it whipping down, one final time, across her knee, snapping it into two glorious jagged pieces.

There was a cry. Joseph was unsure if it came from Gryce or Clarence himself, then a further noise, as the useless shards of birch clattered to the floor.

'Joseph,' Mrs F said, still looking the headmaster straight in the eye. 'Fetch your things. You'll not be coming back.'

Joseph did as he was told, feeling ten foot tall as he followed her out of the door.

'Where are we going now?' he asked.

'To the zoo,' she replied, face grave. 'There's things we need to talk about.'

35

Mrs F was quiet as they walked. There was no celebration or elation. The pace was brisk enough to make breathing the priority through the busy streets.

People queued patiently by shops, clutching their ration books; small children picked through debris and sat on doorsteps that were no longer attached to a home.

Joseph watched as a milkman approached a destroyed house with a full, creamy bottle, scratching his head, trying to work out whether to leave the milk or not. He put it on the step and stared at it, before realising it was ridiculous. If anyone had been in there when the bomb dropped, they'd have no need for milk any longer.

Joseph's mind was racing. Gryce's face as Clarence splintered before him playing again and again. Oh, the joy! His only regret was that he hadn't had the guts to do it himself.

'For a while there, I thought you weren't coming!' he said to Mrs F. 'Thought you'd forgot. I'm glad you did though. Did you see his face? And did you hear how Miss Doherty stood up to him? She's never done *that* before. Not once!'

He looked at her, wondering why she wasn't feeling the same adrenaline rush he was. Did it not feel good to her too? He hoped she wasn't regretting her actions already.

Negativity and doubt raced quickly through him. What had he been thinking? He knew better than that, to be seduced by someone's words. Perhaps she'd said them just to make herself look good.

Round the thoughts sped, quicker with every rotation, larger and more distorted, so fast that once Mrs F pushed the zoo gates open, he could barely keep them inside him. He needed to have this out with her, right now.

'What's going on?' he demanded. 'Because I don't understand. All that stuff you said back there. So, come on. Tell me.'

She said nothing, just paced on, Joseph in her wake, snapping at her heels like Tweedy. It wasn't until she arrived at Adonis's cage that she finally stopped moving, though she didn't turn round, looking through the bars with a fixed stare.

Something was wrong. There was no sign of Adonis: he was not in his normal, mournful spot. This wasn't right – where was he? Joseph walked the length of the cage, up close to the bars, pace increasing.

'Where is he?' he barked without looking at Mrs F, his eyes still roaming. 'They haven't been, they can't have. It isn't time. Mrs F?' He turned. 'Please, where is he?'

Finally, the woman broke her gaze with a single nod of her head, offered at a slight angle, to the far-left corner of the cage.

And there, from behind his hut, Adonis stalked imperiously, wearing every battle scar he had bravely collected, but thankfully no new ones.

He was alive. Relief coursed through Joseph.

'I thought they'd come for him!' He beamed, grabbing Mrs F by the arm and pulling on it playfully. 'I thought it was all over.'

But Mrs F wasn't in the same mood. Tears weren't far from her eyes.

'There's something we need to talk about, Joseph.'

'Come on.' He smiled. 'Whatever it is can wait, can't it? I mean, you broke Clarence in half! And you ripped a strip off old man Gryce. Plus, now I've got no school, we can come up with a proper plan for Adonis. With both of us on it, there's no way anyone's putting a bullet in him!'

'Joseph, I've had a letter.'

But the boy didn't care. A letter? A letter? How could a letter possibly hurt them after what she'd done today?

'Tell me later. We need to be writing our own. In fact, Syd and me have a plan, we're going to write to the paper, start a campaign.'

'Joseph . . .' but the boy went on.

'Joseph . . .'

He would not listen. Couldn't.

'JOSEPH!'

Finally, he stopped as a letter was pulled hesitantly from her pocket.

'It's from your grandmother, son.'

Joseph didn't like this. Not one bit. He felt his hands go instinctively to his ears.

'She's had news.'

His head shook but he couldn't bring himself to tell her to shut up.

'About your dad.'

He wanted an interruption. A Nazi invasion from above. But there were no bombers. There was no siren.

Yet still the sky fell.

36

Joseph didn't want to hear what she had to say.

He had feared it was coming long before his father marched off to war, leaving early one morning, planting a kiss on his forehead as he lay in bed.

Joseph had not been asleep. He'd heard his father enter his room, the floorboards betraying his approach: felt his lips gentle on his skin. Joseph had kept his eyes shut, his breathing even.

He refused to open his eyes. That would show acceptance, that he was content to see him leave, and a knowingness that he would never return. For that was what people did. He drove them to it.

'Joseph . . . ? Joseph. Come on now, son. Come away from there.'

He had almost forgotten where he was until Mrs F's hands prised his own from Adonis's bars.

The ape looked on, still some yards away, chewing slowly, intent on the two of them.

She tried to turn Joseph, but he resisted, staring on at Adonis, wishing he was on the other side of the bars too, that his life was as simple.

'This isn't easy for me, Jo—'

'Then don't say it.'

'I have to. I have to tell you what the letter says.'

'I already . . . *KNOW.*' He pulled his arms from her grip on the last word. He had to move. The charge inside him was growing, and it hurt.

His movements were random, steps in many different directions, looking for escape.

Mrs F had no idea how to tell him, what words to use, or how to even think about calming him afterwards. How did you hold a boy together, when he was already broken? There were *already* too many pieces to manage, without dropping and damaging even more.

'There's been a telegram. Delivered to your grandmother. Your father has been killed, Joseph. In France.'

Joseph continued to pace. Shorter steps, and more of them. His face was blank, unreadable, eyes fixed on anything but her.

'His regiment was marching on a town when they were attacked. He battled bravely but they were outnumbered, outgunned. There were many fatalities, and your father's injuries were too great. I'm sorry, Joseph, but your dad won't be coming home.'

At that moment, as the last of her words died away, his movements changed. Gone were the random directions. Instead he ploughed a straight line alongside the cage, in the direction of the gates, so quick and decisive that Mrs F had to trot to catch up with him.

'Joseph? Joseph!'

She made a grab for his arm to stop him, to make sure he had heard what she said. But the contact was too much for him to bear.

'Don't do that,' he said, flatly.

'Do what?'

'Touch me. It's not safe. Can't you see that?'

'What do you mean, Joseph? I don't know what you mean?'

But Joseph didn't answer. He was still on the move, the gates edging closer.

'Joseph, please,' she cried. 'I don't understand. Where are you going?'

'To pack.'

'Pack? What do you mean?'

'I was only here until he came home, wasn't I? And now he's not coming. So I can't stay here. I'll go home.'

'Joseph, it's much too soon to be thinking of that. And there's no need. You need time. Your gran just wants you—'

'Wants me? *WANTS ME?* Are you joking? She doesn't *want* me. She just wanted to be away from me. Just like everyone else.' The anger was back, a switch flicked, every word, every syllable spat with poison. 'So, I'll go somewhere else. I'll get on a train. No one will notice. I'll hide, and when I get off the train, wherever it's going, I'll look after myself. Cos nobody else wants to do it.'

'That's not true, Joseph. There's a home here for you. Here, with me.'

237

But he couldn't hear it. 'You've changed your tune, haven't you? Anyway, it won't last. You don't want me, or need me, and I certainly don't want *you*!'

He made to walk on, but as with their first meeting, Mrs F was having none of it, hanging on as he railed and thrashed.

'Joseph, listen to yourself. To what you're saying. You *do* need someone, you're only eleven, for Chr—'

'I'm *TWELVE!*' he barked, which drew a growl from Mrs F in return.

'Yes, you are. And no twelve-year-old should lose his father. Not like this, not at all. But it's happening, son, it's happening everywhere. To lots of people.'

'Yeah, well, they're not me, are they?'

This stopped her dead, her feet planted. With a single pull, she held his anger and strength, every shred of it. He couldn't move. He *had* to listen.

'No, they're not. But pain is pain. It's not limited to you, you know. Other people feel it too. Like Syd.'

Joseph thought of Syd. Her incessant talking and know-it-all attitude – but this was quickly drowned by an image that Syd had given him earlier in their friendship. The thought of her parents, thrown on top of her, their instinct to protect her so she might live.

While the image had troubled him when she first painted it, it was only now, with the news of his father, that it truly hit him.

It pulled the plug from his veins and saw him slump to the

ground. That sacrifice: the act of protection, of literally throwing yourself on top of your child, no matter what the consequences were. He saw it, clearly: the pain of it filled every cell to the point of bursting, until he had no option but to ask the question that had been racing round him for as long as he could remember. A question he'd never dared to ask.

'What did I do wrong?' he wept, defeated. 'Please, Mrs F, tell me. What did I *do*?'

37

It would be wrong, a lie, to say that Joseph had never felt pain like it.

He'd felt it years ago, as sharp and debilitating as it was now. But for a long time since he'd denied its existence, buried and smothered it with the only thing he could find that would hold it in place and out of sight: anger.

But the news of his dad had wrecked everything, creating a tremor that cracked the fortress he had built, leaving him only with the pain again.

Mrs F cupped his chin in her hand, asking, pleading with him to look her in the eyes.

'What did you do wrong? What do you mean, son? To who? I don't understand.'

'My ma.'

'Your mother?' It was the first real mention of her to leave the boy's lips in the time she'd known him.

'I must've given her a reason. To hate me like she did.' His eyes swam with tears, pupils drowning beneath them, pulling him under.

'Hate you? Joseph, that's silly. How could she hate you? A mother can't hate her child. It's not possible. I promise you.'

He pulled her hand from his chin, and she felt his anger, yet again.

'What would you know?' he yelled. 'You know nothing. Only thing you've loved in your life is in that cage. An ape. An animal!'

'That's not true. It may seem like it, but it's not, I promise you.'

'Then explain this: Syd's mother and father threw themselves on her. That's how much they loved her. That's what Syd was worth. They'd *die* for her.' He made a choking noise, almost expecting the world to end as the truth finally came tumbling out. 'My mother? I can hardly tell you what she looked or sounded like. Not really. Anything I remember clearly is from a photo. Because she left before I could remember, *that's* how much she loved me. That's how much *I* was worth.'

'Oh Joseph, that's not true. Of course she loved you.'

'Then why did she leave? What did I say or do that was so bad?'

'Your grandmother has only told me so much, because I don't think even she knows everything, but your mum wasn't happy. Not just unhappy. Ill. She'd been ill for a long time. She suffered with her mood. Black moods. And your parents, well, they argued. And it made her worse. For days, weeks sometimes, she wouldn't get out of bed. She couldn't, even if your grandmother dragged her out. She was ill, Joseph, and in the end it got to her. So badly that she had to leave.'

'Then why didn't she take me too? I wouldn't have made trouble for her.' He was pleading now, eyes wide and brimming with tears. 'I could've looked after her,' he sobbed, 'if she was ill. I wouldn't have minded.'

'You were five years old, Joseph.'

'Doesn't matter, does it? I could've hugged her. If she was sad, I could've made her laugh, told her a joke. Maybe I tried then, I don't know, cos I can't remember. All I know is that it must have been my fault, that I must have been bad. Otherwise she would have stayed, wouldn't she?'

'Don't say that. It's just not true. It's not your fault.'

'Then whose fault is it?' As his head shook, tears set themselves free, puddling in the gravel. 'Because it's not the only time, is it? Gran didn't want me either. Couldn't wait to send me away. Then I walk into school here, and it starts again, before I even open my mouth. And what about you? From the second I arrived, you made it clear you didn't want me here either. Did you? *DID YOU?*'

She should've answered quickly, lied, told him it wasn't so. But she didn't, despite the fact that she didn't feel that way any longer. And her delay poured petrol onto Joseph's already considerable fire.

'So tell me, will you?' he roared, tears coating his face no matter how many times he wiped them away. 'What did I do to you, eh? What's wrong with me?'

'There's *nothing* wrong with you, Joseph.'

'Then why do people keep leaving!' The pain in his voice

242

yanked at her like a loose thread on a jumper, unravelling her. 'Dad promised me. He *promised*, when he went to fight, that he would come back. He . . . PROMISED.'

He fell again, shattered, but would accept no arm or consolation from her.

'And he meant it, Joseph. Of course he did. It's probably the only thing that kept him going in all that madness. You'd be the first thing he thought of in the morning, and the last thing before he closed his eyes.'

He sniffed loudly. 'But it wasn't enough, was it? *I* wasn't enough.'

'I promise you, Joseph, that none of this is your fault. None of it. I know you don't want to hear it, especially from me, but it's true. Life can be hard sometimes. And it can be unkind, more unkind than you can ever possibly imagine. But you must believe me that it can get better too. You can work it out with me. Here. For as long as you need. In time, I promise, it will get better.'

'Will it? And you know that, do you?'

'I do,' she replied.

But Joseph did not believe her. 'How? I mean, what have *you* ever lost? This place? Is that it? Do you think losing a few animals is the same as losing your entire family?'

'It has NOTHING to do with this place!' she roared.

'Then tell me,' he spat. 'Tell me what you've lost?'

He watched her. And waited for a reply, trying to read all the thoughts and feelings that seemed to flash across her face.

She looked close to tears, her lips moist as they twitched and formed words that never came out. She took a step forward, lifted her arms to him before pulling back, like she'd changed her mind.

'I'm here for you, Joseph,' she said, her voice tired, sagging like her body. 'And you have a home here for as long as you want it.'

He didn't reply. He was done. Spent. He felt no better for saying what he had, didn't care or imagine that his words would have any effect on anything that followed. He was where he'd always been. Alone. And it was safer that way.

Silence followed. And when it was finally broken, it wasn't with words but by the crunch of gravel beneath Mrs F's feet as she walked reluctantly away.

Joseph didn't move until he guessed she was out of sight, and even then, he didn't go far, only back to Adonis's cage, until he could lean his forehead against the cold metal of the ape's bars.

He knew it went against what Mrs F had told him about Adonis and remaining safe, but in his mind, Adonis was the only friend left that he felt he could turn to.

So he didn't flinch or move when he heard the slow, heavy footsteps labouring closer. Instead he lifted his head and looked the ape in the eye. Adonis looked back, breathing slowly, the same low, slow, repetitive noise coming from his mouth that Joseph had heard before, in another moment of distress.

But today, the effect was different. It didn't soothe or take away the pain that Joseph felt. Instead it allowed it to come, and Joseph cried, loudly and angrily to the skies, not even stopping when Adonis tipped his own head back and roared his pained song too.

38

Winter bit, hard.

Colder, darker, angrier.

Spring might only be weeks away, but it felt like Hitler had cancelled it, choosing instead to release a new hell from the skies.

For three nights solid, bombs rained. A storm unlike any that had gone before, making devastating use of every second of darkness. Even when the sun dared poke its head above the parapet, its powers were useless against the dust and smoke that hugged the ground so stubbornly. Streets lay flattened, reducing families to sifting through endless rubble for the tiniest piece of their life before impact.

Somehow, amongst the carnage, Calmly View still stood, though two of its residents showed every sign of total devastation themselves.

Since the bombshell at the zoo, Joseph had reeled from minute to minute. In many ways, he'd reverted to type, pulling his defences as high as he could, building a barricade to repel anyone who dared to approach.

With no school to keep him busy, whenever the anger fizzed, he stalked the streets, cursing the bombers' accuracy and ruing the lack of windows left to break himself.

Instead, he picked through rubble in search of items left intact; a cup, a vase, anything he could line up and smash with a bomb of his own, be it his right foot or a lump of brick. It did little for his state of mind, though: with every explosion there came a growing frustration, an irritation that he felt no better. His father was still dead, he was still alone, and he'd exposed too much of himself to Mrs F that he couldn't take back.

'That's someone's bear!' said Syd from behind him, as he tried to separate a teddy's head from its body with only his boot. He didn't look round, knowing that a long and rambling lecture lay ahead that he didn't want to hear.

But he soon realised he didn't know Syd as well as he thought.

'I'm sorry about your dad,' she said.

He braced, waiting for the rest of it, but there wasn't another word.

He turned, wondering if she was still there. And she was, perched on a splintered three-legged chair, looking at him, but saying nothing.

'What?' she said, when he frowned. '*What?*'

'That was five words.'

'And?'

'You never use five words. Not when there are another five hundred you can tack on the end.'

'I could use five million if I wanted to, but what would be the point? Your dad's not coming back. Mine neither.'

He knew he *should* say something: thank you, perhaps. Or

ask when it would get easier. But *should* was a lot easier than *could*.

Instead, he let his mouth hang open, brain unable to focus on anything except ripping the next thing he found limb from limb. He could see Syd only wanted to help. And he saw her disappointment, a slight irritation when he couldn't bring himself to ask for it.

'There's a doll popping out over there,' she said finally, as she stood to leave, 'just by the chimney pot. I'm sure she'd love her arms pulling off. You could yank out her hair while you were at it.' She took a pace away from him. 'Or you could go home and speak to Mrs F. Sort things out.'

But Joseph wasn't listening. Her voice, and good sense, was lost to him beneath the sounds of jagged rock beneath his feet, as he ploughed quickly and clumsily to where the abandoned doll lay.

For every moment of wanton destruction, there were moments of fear and panic, of waiting and expecting something else to be taken from him. It felt so cruel that the only thing he felt a pull towards was the thing most in danger.

Joseph knew the clock was ticking for Adonis, and he hadn't a clue what he could do, if anything, when they came to end the ape's life. So in the moments when he couldn't find more objects to smash, he roamed the streets for something to bring joy to the animal for as long as he still had him.

His bartering at the allotments went to another league.

Three pieces of veg became six, then seven and eight. He worked out not only when all the greengrocers in their area opened and closed, but also the times of day when the shopkeepers arrived and left, dashing between them as they binned any vegetables too decayed to sell on, or doorstepping them directly.

'It's for my ape,' he'd explain, which would either earn him the threat of a thick ear, or the occasional rotting turnip, just to be rid of him.

Adonis didn't mind where it came from, though: he became so used to seeing Joseph approach, full bucket in hand, that he sauntered to the bars happily, ready to be fed, an act that filled Joseph with momentary joy. While Joseph was always cautious, he didn't fear Adonis any more. The ape fed happily from his hand, his fingers brushing his as a matter of course now, and Joseph wanted more. Adonis's touch felt like the only act of warmth he received, and as a result he craved it.

Joseph felt a bond with Adonis in these dark days of his life and this filled him with happiness, but also dread. Happiness that Adonis finally trusted him, but dread that their friendship might soon be over.

The two emotions fought a constant battle inside him. Should he allow himself to love the animal? Of course he should, but that left him wide open to yet more pain and loss as the death sentence hung over Adonis.

The dread was too great a thing to live with. It was like a parasite, worming its way through him, consuming any hope that he'd stored up in his darkest corners. It took every bit of strength Joseph had to keep it at bay, to not worry about if or when the executioner would come calling, and he did this by spending as much time with the animal as he could. It was harder to grieve for something that was standing right in front of you.

Eventually, simply feeding the ape through the bars wasn't enough for him, and it wasn't helped by what he saw as he looked through them.

Adonis's enclosure was in dire need of cleaning out again, and Mrs F was once more out of sight. Joseph wasn't angry about that: he knew exactly where the woman was: in the office, fretting, chewing on her pen as she wrote yet another letter to anyone who might listen. And if she was going to take that approach, then in Joseph's mind, he had to be the one to take control out here, and keep the place clean.

He knew full well Mrs F would be apoplectic if she got so much as a whiff of him being on the other side of Adonis's bars, though. Should he wait for Syd to turn up, he thought? Rope her in, make her stand guard? But as quickly as the thought arrived, he dismissed it, as she'd never play along. In fact, knowing her, she'd scuttle off to Mrs F and tell her what he was planning.

No, if he was going to do this, he had to do it now, while there was no one else around. Especially Adonis, who was sleeping in his hut.

Gathering his shovel and bucket, he filled his pockets with as much food as he could, remembering how Mrs F had it as her backup if she disturbed Adonis.

As his hands wrestled with the lock to the enclosure, he found himself shaking, which made him pause. Was he doing the right thing? Did he trust himself, or Adonis to share the same space like this safely?

But he knew he wanted to do this. To be closer to Adonis. It might be his last chance before Adonis's life was snuffed out.

So, with one last, deep breath, he let himself inside the cage, not forgetting to secure the door behind him, flinching when it slammed shut much more noisily than he had intended. His own breath loud in his ears, Joseph turned and walked quietly, senses adjusting, seeing Adonis's lair so differently from this new perspective.

The first thing that hit him was how small it felt inside, how the world outside the bars seemed to stretch in all directions, and how trapped he felt as a result. It took every bit of bravery he owned not to retrace his steps back to the gate and let himself out.

'Come on,' he told himself, 'you can do this.' And he reminded himself of why he was here, heading to the first piece of dung he could find, scooping it into his bucket, before heading to the next.

He built up a steady rhythm, combing the ground forensically, concentrating on one area at a time, not even hesitating when he found himself edging closer to Adonis's hut. It was so quiet in there that it would be easy to believe you were actually alone, yet Joseph knew that would be a mistake. He had to keep his wits about him. So as he tidied around the

251

hut, he never once turned his back on its door, making sure the metal of the shovel made as little noise as possible against the ground or the side of the pail.

Area complete, he moved towards the front of the cage: clear this, and his work would be done. As he registered this he felt a pang of disappointment that Adonis hadn't put in an appearance, that he hadn't even seen that Joseph was so close.

Then, as he closed in on the final shovelfuls, he heard a rustling, and saw Adonis's bulk filling the doorway to the hut.

The ape seemed groggy. He leaned against the frame to stretch his considerable bulk, eyes only widening when he finally saw the child.

'Oh, boy,' whispered Joseph. He eyed the distance he'd have to travel to make it to the gate, but knew that however quickly he covered the ground, Adonis could travel faster. All he could do was stay where he was as the ape approached, remembering quickly what Mrs F had done when she found herself in the same situation.

Putting the shovel and bucket quietly on the ground, Joseph kept his body low, one hand snaking into his pocket, filling a fist with the most appealing vegetable he could find there.

Adonis edged closer, movements slow and considered, his low rumbling tones reaching Joseph as he moved nearer still. Joseph instinctively did the same, applying the routine that had served him so well from outside the bars.

Adonis was close now, very close. Joseph could hear his

every breath, feel every pace in the ground beneath his feet. He wanted to look up to watch the ape's approach, but it would be folly to do so. He had to remain subservient, the waiter to the king. With his head kept low and his breathing echoing the ape's, Joseph lifted his arm, fist still clenched as he offered up the food.

Adonis didn't take it straightaway. Instead, he leaned forward and sniffed at it, nose so close that Joseph allowed his fist to unfurl, his hand becoming a plate. The ape sniffed a second time, then a third, and after a small appreciative grunt, he took the vegetable from Joseph's hand, not with his own fingers, but with his mouth, his tongue making contact with the boy's palm as he sucked the food up.

Joseph felt excitement kick within him. He couldn't believe Adonis had done that. He hadn't seen it happen to Mrs F, and it thrilled him. His hand returned quickly to his pocket for more food, slowing when he sensed Adonis recoil a touch.

He found a wedge of turnip there, not something he'd eat happily at any time, but to Adonis it was heavenly, and he wasted no time in taking it from Joseph in exactly the same way, tongue tickling his fingers as he did so. It took every bit of self-control Joseph had not to laugh or shout for Mrs F and Syd, or even the council. He wanted *everyone* to see what was happening, that here was a life worth saving.

Three helpings in and Adonis sat himself next to Joseph; four servings and the ape didn't even wait for the food to come out of his pockets, shoving his fingers in there himself, like it was a buffet service.

'Hey,' said Joseph, forgetting himself, 'that tickles.' But the ape didn't care, emptying the first pocket before reaching across Joseph to delve into the other. As Adonis's arm moved in front of him, Joseph brushed his palm lightly against his fur, feeling its wiriness and age, but also its warmth. What made it even better was that Adonis didn't try to stop him or react to his touch.

Instead, the pair sat together, side by side, Adonis taking food at will, while Joseph marvelled at the beast beside him, slowly, carefully allowing himself to steal glimpses as his friend ate.

Too soon, his pockets emptied, and Joseph felt a sense of fear wash over him again. How would Adonis react when the food was gone? Would he be angry? Violent, even?

Joseph's mind turned quickly to the way out. The gate remained too far away to rush to, and he knew that he was completely at Adonis's mercy. But when the ape realised there was nothing left in Joseph's pockets, he sighed long and low, once, then twice, before slowly lifting his hands and placing them gently on either side of Joseph's head.

Joseph's heart rattled like a snare drum, then threatened to explode as Adonis patted his head gently, not with one hand, but with both. He felt tears spring to his eyes at the gentleness of the act, then fall down his cheeks as Adonis lifted his chin, resting Joseph's forehead against his own.

It was an extraordinary thing to share, and although their heads were only touching for seconds, it felt like so much longer. Joseph looked at the ape, at the burning flames of his orange eyes, and felt a sense of calm that he had too seldom experienced in his life: a sense that everything was all right.

But as soon as he felt it, it was gone. With one final pat of his head, Adonis pulled away, and made for the sanctuary of his hut.

Joseph's route to the gate was unguarded: he could be there in seconds without fear of attack or disruption, but he didn't move, not yet. Not until he'd fully savoured what had just occurred between him and his friend Adonis.

39

Relations at Calmly View were not so cordial.

Joseph, rubbed raw by the news of his father's death and his confessions to Mrs F, did everything he could to keep his barriers high.

She tried to bring him round, managing somehow to hoard and barter the ingredients for a cake.

'I thought perhaps we could make it together,' she said one night after dinner.

Joseph, hands in suds as he washed the dishes, felt trapped.

'If you want to,' she added. 'I thought it would be nice. We could . . . talk, as we make it.'

But the strange thing was, her lips were saying one thing, but her body language something else altogether. She certainly wasn't demanding him to do it, nor did she push him when he kept his lips tightly closed, despite the rare prospect of cake. Instead, she retreated to the fire, which spluttered pitifully as always, and she sat poking it without conviction.

Joseph had seen more change in her that past week. It felt like she was keeping her guard high too, though Joseph hadn't a clue what she was protecting.

There were moments when he found her looking at him

intently, like words were balanced on her lips, but if they were, she soon swallowed them.

As a result, the house was often stripped to an odd and uncomfortable tension, and with the wireless reporting news of Hitler's continued pressure, they found themselves choosing silence, Joseph within the confines of his room, ruminating on when he would be sent back home. He could think of nothing else. Felt the instruction was coming any time now.

It was here, after yet another tense dinner downstairs, that Joseph heard a soft knock at his door. He wiped at his eyes, confused by the gentleness of the rap. When he opened the door, peeking around it, there stood Mrs F, dressing gown pulled tight around her.

'You're awake, then,' she said.

Joseph nodded.

'I was hoping you'd come with me. There's something I'd like to talk to you about.'

Joseph looked over his shoulder for something he could use as an excuse. But there was nothing, so he followed her down the stairs, already sure of what she was about to say.

'You don't have to explain it, you know? I can save you the bother,' he said quickly. 'I've already packed my case.'

He hadn't, but she didn't know that.

As Mrs F walked past the table and Joseph saw what was laid upon it, he realised that he wasn't being kicked out quite yet.

Practically every inch was covered in a paper patchwork: letters, photographs and telegrams from the mysterious tin.

'I've realised,' she said, her voice thick with uncertainty, 'that I've not been entirely honest with you lately. In light of what you're going through, with your father, and your mother, too, it seems only fair I tell you some truths of my own. Truths that might help you.'

'Is this about Adonis?' he asked, though he had a strong feeling it was not. A lot of the documents appeared old and faded.

'No, Joseph, this is about me. About my family.'

Family? He thought. There had been talk of a brother and a father, but as his eyes flicked across the table, they didn't seem to obviously feature. He let his hand fall on the photograph nearest to him, and picked it up, seeing Mrs F flinch as he did so.

'Is this you?' he asked, squinting at the photo, seeing a resemblance.

'No, no,' she replied, teasing the photo from his hand as if it had been a mistake to let him see. 'I've no photos of me at that age.'

'Then who is it?' he said, noticing that the same little girl appeared in the majority of the snaps laid out.

'My daughter,' she replied.

His instinct was to laugh, and he had to stifle his surprise as he spoke. 'But you don't have a daughter. Is she grown up now?' He looked for more evidence of her on the table, but not in any of the snaps did she seem to grow older. 'I mean, she can't live round here, otherwise I would've met her, wouldn't I? She a nurse or something?'

Mrs F didn't answer immediately. Instead she reached for another photograph where there was no sign of the little girl, just a man and a woman, and there was no doubting who the woman was: the explosion of untamable hair gave it away.

'I met Wilf when I was fifteen,' she said. 'At a dance.' She seemed to leave the room for a moment as she spoke. 'Not that we danced that night. We were both too shy. I could feel him looking at me, could hear his pals ribbing him, telling him to come over. But he was blushing more than *me*. In the end I said hello as we collected our coats.'

She finally looked up from the photograph, her face flushed. Joseph could see her discomfort.

'Oh, this is silly,' she said, a touch of ice back in her voice as she started to sweep the memories back into a pile. 'It doesn't matter.'

But Joseph thought otherwise. 'Bloomin' does,' he replied. 'You can't not tell me now, can you? I mean, look at the way you're staring at him in this one. You clearly loved him.'

'I didn't straightaway,' she said, struggling to meet his eye. 'Love him. And I should've done. Any time I spent *not* loving him was wasted time, given how little we ended up having. I turned him down at first, when he asked me out. So he took a different tack, left a flower on my doorstep every day for a week, same flower I had pinned to my dress at that first dance.

No note or anything attached, but I knew it was him. Said yes in the end, just so my brother would stop pulling my leg about it. Then the daft beggar turned up with a bunch of them when he picked me up.'

Joseph wasn't much of a romantic. What twelve-year-old was? But he knew what he was hearing meant a lot to her.

'I think we both knew we'd get married,' she went on, 'you do know, when it happens to you. But we wouldn't have done it so quickly had war not broken out. He proposed to me on the day he joined up. Maybe he thought it'd soften the blow, but to be honest, stupidly, I don't think either of us worried about what would happen. Lads joined up for the adventure, everyone thought it'd be over in weeks.'

She picked up another photograph.

'This was our wedding day, the twenty-sixth of October, nineteen-fourteen,' she said, her face managing somehow to look both happy and heartbroken. 'The age of us, though. Looks like that uniform belongs to his dad. Not him.'

He *did* look young, and Joseph wondered if Wilf felt like he did, the first time he held a rifle.

'Did he go off to fight straightaway?'

'Nearly. We had several weeks while he finished his training. He moved in with my family. It was strange, becoming a wife, when I still had my dolls sat at the bottom of the bed. Not as strange as it was when he suddenly wasn't there any more.'

'Did he write to you?'

She smiled again. 'He did. Often. Though after a while they became more erratic. I'd get two in a week, but find they'd been written a month apart. Then it would be weeks and weeks. It was hard. I was waiting for him to respond to a very important letter I'd written.'

'About what?'

'Expecting a baby.' She paused. 'I waited three months before telling him. In case something went wrong. Plus I hoped that the war would be over quickly so I could tell him in person. I wanted to see his face. Wanted him to see mine.'

'He must have been pleased then, when he got the letter?'

The question seemed to knock the air out of Mrs F. 'I don't know if he ever received it. No letter came back. Not for months. Then, when I was five weeks from giving birth, I got a telegram telling me his regiment had fallen under fire. That he'd been killed.'

Now it wasn't just Mrs F who was winded. He was too. The closeness of it, the pain he'd felt at the same message.

'Why didn't you tell me?' he asked her. 'When you told me about my dad?'

'I couldn't,' she replied sadly, shame keeping her head held low. 'I know I should've, when I've told you distinctly to talk about things. But the truth is, Joseph, I've buried this for so long that I didn't think I could reach the words any more, not without it being too difficult and painful.'

'I would've understood,' he said. 'I would.'

'I know that.' She sighed. 'But it's not just Wilf that I

261

lost. You saw the photo, of our daughter . . . Violet. She was wonderful. I wanted her more than anything to be the mirror of her father, and though she didn't have his eyes, every time I looked at her, all I saw was him. And although it hurt, it kept me alive, meant I had something to fight on for.'

'So where is she?'

'She was taken, too.' Joseph felt the pain in each of those four words, saw it in every crease and line on Mrs F's face. 'Not immediately. I saw her walk. And talk. Saw her play with my dolls, but when she was four, she got influenza. Thousands did. It took a liking to Violet, and it didn't matter what I did, it wouldn't let her go. We fought it, but it won in the end. She died too.'

Joseph heard what she was saying, and knew what it meant, but had no idea what to say.

'I'm sorry,' was all he could find.

'No, my lad, I'm the one who should be sorry. Because it's affected me every second since you've been here. But that's not your fault,' she added quickly. 'For years now, I've buried all trace of them. At first, I kept photographs out on the walls, but it was too much. I couldn't stop being sad at the fact they weren't here any more, so I put them in the tin, out of sight.'

'Did it help?'

'Well I didn't feel as *sad*. Just angry instead. Raging, most of the time. But at least using the tin meant I was in control of when I saw them. They weren't following me as I walked round the house every day. But then . . . well, then you turned up.'

'I'm sorry about that too.'

'Well, you mustn't be. It's hardly your fault. I know you don't want to hear that, but it's true. I owed your grandmother so much. When Violet passed, I lost my mind. Saw things, said things that scared my family so much they put me in hospital. Which is where I met your grandmother. She was a nurse, *my* nurse. With all the soldiers coming home not just injured, but ill, screaming and crying and living with nightmares from the war, they drafted in nurses from all over the country to help cope. I don't remember a lot of what I said to her, but she never abandoned me. She listened and talked, and though she never had any answers, she never walked away. She got me well again, more than any doctor did, and I made her a promise that I'd always help her back if she needed it. And that promise, well, it turned out to be you.'

'You really *were* lucky, weren't you?' Joseph said sarcastically.

'Well, you've hardly been easy,' she said. 'But that isn't all your doing. It's mine, too. When you first arrived, I wasn't ready to be a parent again, to care about another child. It had been a long time since I'd opened the tin and allowed myself to think about the family I've lost.'

'Didn't help me being here, then?'

'No.' She smiled sadly. 'Not at first. It hurt like hell, but it also made me realise how tired I was. How tiring it is to carry all that anger around every day. You know that feeling, don't you?'

Joseph said nothing, though he felt it all.

'So I've decided I'm not going to hide them away from now on. That's why I'm telling you. Because I don't want to be tired or angry any longer, and I don't want you to be either. Do you hear me?'

Joseph nodded and sighed. 'I don't feel angry. Not right now. Just sad.'

'Me too,' she replied. 'And maybe that's all right. Maybe it'll pass, if we both allow ourselves to feel it.'

Nothing was said for a minute. And Joseph was fine with that. It let him feel things, things other than just sadness and loss.

He felt hungry.

'How long does it take to actually bake a cake?' he asked.

'Depends how good you are at taking orders,' she replied. 'You'll find the eggs in the larder. And don't be dropping them, do you hear? Cost me a king's ransom, they did.'

He walked to the larder without saying a word. He had no need for an argument. And besides, he knew he wouldn't win it anyway.

40

When the executioner came, Joseph noticed two things.

He was a weasel of a man wearing a grey suit. In fact, the suit was so ill-fitting that it would be fairer to say that the suit was wearing *him*. He had the look of a boy left alone to play in his father's wardrobe.

The other thing Joseph noted, within minutes of the executioner and his associate arriving at the zoo gates, was that the suited man had clearly never met anyone like Mrs F before.

And this, more than anything, was to be his downfall.

When they arrived, Joseph had been feeding Adonis his evening meal through the bars while Mrs F watched from the bench. The ape was delighting in hurling carrot tops back through the bars, which brought a smile to her face. But her mood changed with the sound of rattling gates.

'Yes?' she said, in her regulation bark as she approached. But she knew what they were doing there.

The party, if you could call it that, was only two strong, the man-child in the giant's suit, and another man in army attire, a rifle swung across his shoulder.

'Mrs Farrelly?' the weasel man enquired, making a meal of reading the name from a letter in his hand.

'If you say so. Question is, who might you be? Because I'm

265

guessing you're not here to read the meters,' she said with a nod to the soldier's rifle.

The weasel laughed, revealing a set of teeth well on their way to an early death. If the rest of him was as unhealthy, then it was no surprise he was here doing this, rather than bearing arms abroad.

'Well, quite. I wish it were only meters I was here for, Madam, but sadly that's not the case.'

'So, what is it, then? I've things to be doing.'

If the man *was* coming to do the unspeakable, then she wanted to hear it from his lips.

'My name is Ingleford. From the council. I'm afraid it's about the ongoing issue of the danger to the public residing at this address.'

'Well, that's a first,' she said, turning to smile at Joseph. 'I've never been called that before.' She turned back to the man. 'And besides, my house is twenty minutes that way.'

Another laugh, yet this one was fattened by nerves.

'Yes, very good. But back to the matter in hand. You have, I'm sure, received various correspondences relating to the dangerous ape which attacked a boy some weeks hence.'

Joseph scrunched his eyes up. *Hence?* Had the man been reading the Old Testament before he came?

'I've received them, yes.'

'And digested them, also?'

'On many occasions. Though I must say, they left me with a rather bitter aftertaste.'

266

This time, the man did not smile.

'Well, I'm afraid that the deadline for finding alternative residence for the animal has passed. So we have no option but to make the area safe ourselves.'

And that, was that. The last word was everything Mrs F needed to respond.

'*SAFE?* Are you really telling me that ending the life of an ape in a cage is going to make this city *safe*?'

'Well, that is of cours—'

'Because for a second there, it occurred to me that you might not have been awake for the past year. Or perhaps you've been so busy down your little hole, hunched over your typewriter, punching out ridiculous, petty letters, to notice that the REAL danger we face in this city is absolutely nothing to do with Adonis.'

'Madam, the monkey attac—'

'He's an ape. A silverback,' interrupted Joseph, which drew a proud nod of approval from Mrs F.

The man corrected himself, both his stance and his words.

'The *ape* attacked a boy. And but for God's will, could easily have ended his life.'

'A boy who was trespassing in a dangerous place, a place that was also closed to the public at the time it happened. Now, Sir, if you look above the gates, you'll see quite clearly the letters that spell out what place this is.'

Joseph hoped the man *didn't* look at the sign. He looked officious enough to point out that the *Z* was still missing.

Regardless, Mrs F went on. 'The boy chose, very unwisely, to ignore this and having climbed over the wall, went on to attack Joseph here, before simply walking too close to the ape's enclosure.'

'There should be signs to warn people. There should be railings to keep people at a safe distance.'

'And there were. Both of those things. The signs are there still, you can see them from here. And as for railings, they were taken and melted for the war effort. Far as I know they were last spotted in France being fired at Nazis. That's why the zoo's not open. That's why the gates are locked.'

'Mrs Farrelly, please.' The man sighed. 'Might we come in? There's little dignity in us conversing with a gate between us.'

To some individuals, this would've worked. But to Mrs F these things didn't matter a jot.

'Anything you have to say to me can be said from there. I'll not be letting you in. Not by choice, not today nor any other day, for that matter.'

'Madam, please, this isn't something that is going to just go away. It is, in fact, a matter that could be resolved very . . . very quickly.' He gestured behind him, not so much to the soldier, but to the rifle on his shoulder.

'I doubt he'll have much success shooting from there.'

'Such range wouldn't be a problem, I can assure you.'

'Maybe not. But you can't shoot what you can't see.'

'I'm sorry, I don't understand.'

'Then understand this. Pull that rifle on my animal, and any bullet will have to pass through me first.'

'And me,' chimed in Joseph, pushing his chest out.

'Mrs Farrelly, please! There's been too many deaths around here already.'

'You're absolutely right. And you'll not be adding to them today.'

The man sighed theatrically. 'Then I am afraid we will be back tomorrow. And if you refuse, again, to let us in, then we will have no option but to gain entry by force.'

'I'm looking forward to it already,' she answered, though she didn't move. In fact, she made a point of blocking any semblance of a view to the cage that either man may have had: she and Joseph both. This left Ingleford to sigh in the boy's direction, as if offering his condolences, before striding officiously away, his suit somehow looking even bigger in his defeat.

No one said a word until they disappeared from view.

'I hope you know what you're doing,' Joseph said.

'Not a clue,' she replied.

And he watched her walk away, legs moving so slowly, and shoulders so rounded, that it appeared she carried not just him or Adonis, but the weight of the entire city on her back.

41

When they came, they came from nowhere, and they came with fury.

They hunted in packs, terrorising single houses first, then whole streets at a time, not moving on until every semblance of life had been snuffed out.

The first explosion blew Joseph from his bed, the second hitting by the time he rose from the floor: plaster fell from the ceiling, the walls groaned in terror.

The siren played as it always did, but it was an apology of a warning, a whisper eaten by a Nazi roar.

Joseph was afraid. Perhaps he'd become blasé with the bombs only ever landing in the distance, putting on a firework display without him ever feeling under any real threat. But this was different. It was loud, deafening. He could hear walls tumbling, people screaming, the incessant, looping howl of Tweedy from downstairs.

Pulling on his shorts and socks, he tore on to the landing, but there was no sign of Mrs F. Normally, they met at the top of the stairs as she forced shocks of hair inside her coarse woollen hat. But tonight, nothing: though her bedroom door was open, bed covers neat, unbothered.

He thundered down the stairs, two at a time, vaulting the

final three. He did not need to open the kitchen door as another blast saw the walls shake and the door open onto a scene he had not expected.

The top of the kitchen table was covered in the contents of Mrs F's tin. There was also a glass tumbler knocked onto its side, spilling red liquid across the documents. And there amongst the mess, was a sleeping Mrs F, head on the table, arms splayed either side of her, left hand gripping a scrunched-up document.

The only life in the room came from Tweedy, howling as he made his way through an obstacle course of chair legs, weaving and diving between them, stopping occasionally to nudge at his lifeless mistress.

For one awful instant, Joseph thought her dead, mistaking the spilled liquid for blood. But his fears were soon allayed. He dipped his head to hers, scraping the stained, sticky hair from her cheek, which woke something in her: a thick, sloppy cough that reeked of booze.

She wasn't dead, just dead drunk.

Another bomb landed, closer, causing the lights to flicker and the walls to quiver. It didn't put a dent in Mrs F's slumber, but Joseph needed to, and quickly. Who knew how long it would be until the walls tumbled?

'Mrs F?' he said, in hushed tones, before wondering why. Did he think the Nazis were listening in? He shouted, louder, but to no avail. Her eyes remained shut. So he shook her, her shoulders heavy and lifeless.

'Mrs F, wake up, come on. They're coming. They're COMING!' What was she doing? Why get herself into such a state when the threat of a raid was always hanging over them? It wasn't like her, that was for sure.

He tried to lift her head and prise her eyelids open, but if she could see him, then she was doing a damned good job of pretending otherwise.

Another bomb, closer again, edging Joseph towards blind panic.

In all the nights past, he'd never truly believed that a bomb would land on them, he was too cocky for that, and Mrs F had played her part in his naivety too. He thought Adolf wouldn't dare flatten her house.

But finding her like this changed everything. No one was keeping guard, of the house, of him, of . . . the zoo.

The zoo!

The thought of the place jolted him upright. If she was drunk and unmovable, then who the hell was going to stand guard there? What if that bomb *did* finally fall on Adonis's cage and set him free? There'd be a whole lot more than just Bert's coat being ripped to shreds.

He had to wake her, sober her up and get her through the streets until she stood sentry, rifle in hand. He'd push her in a wheelbarrow if he had to, but first he must get her to her feet.

He tried to lever her up, before his mind was pulled elsewhere. The photos. He had to do something about them! So he threw them hurriedly back into the tin, safe from the bombs' clutches. Then he pulled her upright, her head lolling backwards, unintelligible slurs shooting to the ceiling.

Joseph wasn't listening. 'Come on, Mrs F!' he yelled into her ear. 'We have to move. Please!' But no matter how hard he tried, he couldn't shift the weight of her, and she flatly refused to wake up.

So he went looking for help, out into the back yard, feet thundering towards the shelter, ripping the door open so quickly it threatened to come off in his hand.

'Help me!' he cried, spotting three silhouettes already crouched and cowering in the far corner.

'What is it?' replied Mrs Twyford.

'Mrs F . . . she's passed out and I can't move her.' He made no reference to the alcohol. He didn't want the Twyfords to judge her any more than they already did.

Sylvie didn't move, but her husband did – once he'd been shoved by his wife. Within seconds he and Joseph were back in the kitchen.

'What the hell's wrong with her?' Mr Twyford asked.

'Dunno. Found her like this, and I can't move her.'

Fortunately, the man could, out the back door and through the yard, though he made quite a meal of it, the darkness of the shelter hiding his beetroot complexion, Joseph clutching Mrs F's tin like it contained the Crown Jewels.

'She's not ill, Thomas,' Mrs Twyford spat, leaning over to inspect her, while Tweedy tried to revive her with endless licks to the face, 'she's drunk!'

'Could do with a tipple myself after that,' said her husband, though he was so out of breath only Joseph heard him.

There was more tutting, and questions and judgements, but Joseph heard none of them. The bombs still rang in his ears, focusing his mind on getting Mrs F comfortable and safe. Falling plaster inside the house was replaced by falling mud here, snuffing out the candles as quickly as they could light them.

Joseph reached for a blanket to keep her warm, but as he tucked her hand beneath it, he realised he had missed one final piece of paper, still scrunched inside her fist.

Whatever it was, she didn't want to let go of it, her fingers locked, corpse-like. But if it was important, then Joseph needed to keep it safe with the rest of her memories. When her fingers finally opened under more pressure, the crumpled sheet slid into Joseph's hand. It was old, but well-preserved, another official-looking item, so austere that it filled him with fear as soon as he saw it.

Printed in bold at the top were three words. Words he couldn't read.

'What does this say?' he said, pointing at them as he thrust the paper under Mrs Twyford's nose.

'What?' she replied, confused.

'These words at the top here. What do they say? Quickly!'

'Certificate of Death.'

Joseph felt sick. But who did it belong to?

'Can you see a name on there? Can you read it to me?' He

didn't want this woman's help, far from it, but there was no time for his pride to get in the way.

Mrs Twyford read, eyes squinting in the poor light. 'It says *Violet*. Violet Evelyn Farrelly. Died . . . fourteenth of March, nineteen-nineteen.'

Violet. Mrs F's daughter. But why today? Why did Mrs F drink herself silly today?

'What's the date?' Joseph asked suddenly.

'I beg your pardon?' came Mrs Twyford's reply.

'The date. Today's date.'

'The fourteenth of March.'

He felt his body sag. Today was the anniversary of Violet's death. No wonder Mrs F had got herself into such a state, he thought. Especially as she'd dragged the whole thing up again so recently. He wanted to be angry with her for resorting to such extremes, but he couldn't. After all, *she* hadn't got angry. Just drunk. Joseph couldn't help but feel responsible, because she'd opened up all those old wounds to help him. To make him see that he wasn't alone in what he was going through.

And if that were the case, then it was up to him to help her. He had to do what she couldn't do tonight. He had to get to the zoo.

Kneeling beside her, he made sure the tin was discreetly within her grasp and put his mouth by her ear, ignoring the stale stink of wine as he whispered, 'I've got to go now. But I'll be back, I promise. Just as soon as I've taken care of Adonis.'

What that statement actually meant, he couldn't be sure.

Different outcomes lay ahead of him, depending on just how angry and accurate the bombers were.

He breathed deeply as reality hit him in the face. What on earth was he going to do if a bomb dropped on the zoo?

'Look after Mrs F for me,' he announced to the Twyfords. 'And keep Tweedy here, will you? If you can.'

And before Sylvie's protests could reach his ears, Joseph Palmer ploughed through the doors of the shelter, straight into the jaws of hell.

42

The devil ran alongside him, every step of the way, tossing firecrackers under his feet, singeing his face with flames.

Joseph had never seen devastation like it, regardless of how much he had felt.

Everywhere he looked he saw the same thing: explosions, rubble, clouds, the sky so red, so orange, so white, that the time of night ceased to matter.

It felt like the end of the world, but still, he ran, and after only a few minutes, he realised he wasn't alone. The devil was there, yes, but so was something else, a beast on four legs, gaining ground with every corner he turned, until, still a mile from the zoo, Tweedy burst past him, affording him not a glance or a pause, just four legs determined to get there before him.

It spurred Joseph on, though he really had little time to feel anything other than exhaustion. He should've been terrified, of course he should, the world was tumbling mere feet from where he ran, but he knew that if he gave it any kind of thought, then he risked being swallowed by it before he arrived. And he wouldn't have that. Mrs F wouldn't forgive him for it. And neither would he.

So on he went, ignoring the flames licking his heels. He

saw houses tumble all around. He had to change course in a split second to avoid debris as it fell: he felt the wind whip him, not knowing if it came from the destruction or direct from the bombers' propellers as they surged by. It didn't matter, none of it did. As long as his lungs kept pumping and his feet kept pounding the road, there was nothing that Hitler or his minions could do to stop him.

Finally he arrived, the locked gates greeting him with bad news: Joseph realised, to his fury, that he had failed to bring Mrs F's keys.

It hadn't stopped Tweedy though, who was somehow already inside, barking at him, chivvying him along.

Joseph remembered that Bert Conaghan had made it over the wall on that awful night. Anything Bert could do, then he could do better. And faster.

Two minutes later, Joseph ran alongside Tweedy. It had cost him the skin on his left knee but given the injuries that were occurring all over the city, he considered it a badge of honour instead of a hindrance.

All he could think about was reaching the office, grabbing the rifle and getting to where he needed to be.

When at last the rifle lay heavily in his arms the gravity of the situation hit him. Then, and only then, did he stop and think, *Can I do it? If that bomb finally falls, and takes out Adonis's cage, would I, could I, really, pull the trigger?*

He didn't know, he hadn't a clue, but he knew he couldn't

make a decision unless he was there, staring his friend in the eye. And so, for one final time, he ran.

He found Adonis where he'd left him earlier, and where Aphrodite left him too, stock-still, eyes not on the skies but on the exit they'd taken her through.

He showed no clear sign of agitation or distress, didn't acknowledge Joseph or even Tweedy when the mad dog yelped through his bars. Joseph fussed the dog with his free hand, telling him it would be all right, which only served to make him more frantic.

'You'll be all right, too,' the boy shouted to the ape. 'I'll make sure of that.' He was edging closer to the bars, passing Adonis the biggest vegetable left in the bucket. As always, he felt the same shiver of excitement when the ape's fingers brushed his.

Joseph considered feeding him more, only to be interrupted by a cluster of explosions back in the direction of the office that tested the ground on which he stood, prompting Adonis to retreat and howl in fear.

'It's all right! Stay there, don't move!' he yelled uselessly at Adonis, before dashing back from where he came and seeing almost immediately that not just the office, but the aquarium too, had taken direct hits. He felt the heat of the flames on his face.

What should he do?

There was a hose, coiled thirty yards away, and instinctively he raced towards it, only realising as he reached it that it was pointless, like stirring a teaspoon in the ocean to try and make a wave. It would take a couple of fire engines to douse the flames that raged. Besides, he was there for one reason only, and it wasn't that.

So, arms pumping and rifle clutched in his sweaty palms, he sprinted back to Adonis, chewing over the challenges that faced him.

Where should he stand? He'd never fired a rifle in his life, so how accurate should he expect himself to be? Should he stand close to the bars, and poke the barrel through them to improve his chances of success? No, that was ridiculous. What was he thinking? He only had to pull the trigger if the bars were blown out, and if that happened while he was stood right by them, then he'd be flat on his back. How could he possibly be useful then?

He took a dozen paces back, rifle slippery in his grip, tucking it between his chin and shoulder. It felt rigid, lifeless, like a scaffolding pole rather than a weapon. He closed one eye as he looked down the barrel, training it on Adonis, an act that made his stomach lurch. He dropped his chin further until it lined up the sights, realising the wrong eye was closed, so he tried the other: better, but still blurred, not helped by the sweat running off his brow.

He let the gun fall against his side and pulled his coat up to mop his face, only to hear the roar of a plane overhead, and find himself thrown to the floor by yet another explosion, the closest yet. It smothered him in dust, the heat so intense that he beat at his clothes with his hands, convinced that he was on fire.

It was hard to breathe, the fog thick and cloying, coating his tongue as he gulped in air. He had to get to his feet, work out which way the cage was and somehow pick out Adonis in all the chaos. Who knew when the next bomb would fall, whether it could possibly be *the* bomb, the one that truly tested his resolve?

He pulled himself upright, ground still tilting, ears screaming with a high-pitched wail that must've been piercing Tweedy's brain, wherever the dog was now.

But just as he righted himself, he was thrown again, as the bombers doubled back, throwing their fiery blanket in every direction.

A scream left his lungs, but it was useless. He lay, crumpled, unsure of which way the sky was, worrying that there was little point in trying to stand if this was simply going to happen again and again. Perhaps he was safer down here: maybe he should burrow beneath the rubble instead, but then he thought of Mrs F, and the promise he'd made to her.

Would she lie down and hide? No, she would not, and so it wasn't an option for him either.

Sweeping debris from his clothes, he pulled himself to his feet, picking his way out to the right, to Adonis's cage. But as he clambered forwards, he realised he didn't have the rifle.

The rifle! How could he be so stupid? How could he aim the damn thing, if he couldn't even be trusted to keep it in his grasp?

He fell to his knees, crawling like a baby, raking at the ground and ignoring the jagged edges of stones as they snapped at his fingertips. He *had* to find it.

'Come on!' he wailed. 'Where are you?' He bit back tears, feeling like a failure again.

But just as he was ready to quit, his right leg became entwined in something. He cursed, trying to free himself from its grasp when he realised he'd stumbled right into the rifle's strap! He unearthed it frantically, running his hands along the barrel, feeling for dents.

It felt all right, but what would he know? Maybe if it *were* damaged, then it offered him a way out, a way of not pulling the trigger even if the situation demanded it.

Because the truth was, he didn't think he could. As old and dangerous as he was, the ape on the other side of the bars was the only thing that both Joseph and Mrs F had left. The only thing they loved.

His mind was being torn just as the landscape was, in every direction imaginable.

And all he could do was stumble, rifle in hand, back towards the cage, hoping against hope that when the moment came he would know what to do.

43

The sky raged on.

With every breath it spat its bombs, each one falling closer, with greater venom.

Down they screamed, ripping holes in the clouds, eating into the earth, stealing something precious with every bite.

The ground shrieked back, tearing the sky in half with a blinding light, followed by a volcano of fire.

The world was ablaze, its flames licking closer: to the boy, to the cage.

His face burnt. Not just from the flames, but with panic. The rifle was not heavy, not really, but at that moment it felt like a sledgehammer, its butt tucked under his chin, barrel trained on the cage, shaking as his arms trembled with the pressure: with his desire to drop the weapon to the floor.

Another bomb fell.

Closer.

Close.

His ears screamed in pain at the moment of impact, forcing his eyes to close and release the tears that he had been holding in.

He knew what he had to do, and for a while he'd have been happy to do it, but not now.

Not ever.

But he didn't put the rifle down.

He couldn't, because in his head was the image of her, standing in the same position, the same tears on her face. Never once did *her* rifle waver, nor the love for the life she was about to snuff out.

This was simply what the war did: it took the power from the people on the ground and gave every bit of it to those in the sky. All they could do was respond to what was thrown at them, to try and keep everyone else alive, even if in this awful act, the last part of themselves died.

The boy choked down a sob, swirling with the anger that congested his chest, creating an emotion he couldn't name nor wished to experience again as long as he lived.

Another explosion. The noise different again.

This time he heard stone cracking and falling, and within seconds he could feel the dust in his eyes and on his tongue.

He might not be able to see much, but he knew how close they were now, and as he squinted into the darkness, he could see smoke billowing from the tower at the southern end of the zoo, the iron of the empty cage in front of it mangled in defeat.

They weren't finished yet, though; a deafening metallic roar fell from above, fighting against the animal noise that ripped through the bars in front of him.

It wasn't just the boy panicking; it was Adonis now, too. And while the beast had never lost a fight yet, Joseph knew that if he had to, he would be the one to end his reign. That was his job, whatever it might cost him.

The noise was dizzying, and as he squinted upwards he saw them, the bombers, wings outstretched almost in relaxation as they cut effortlessly through the clouds.

He raised his rifle, wanted more than anything to be brave enough to fire, to save the day as the heroes did every Saturday morning at the Empire, but those films weren't real and his bullets were few, and who knew how many he would need to bring Adonis down if necessary.

Instead he heaved the barrel back to the bars, sobs wracking him, face lit up by the carnage around him.

He was consumed by a sense of inevitability, that he would have to be the one to pull the trigger, though where he would find the conviction or strength for even that smallest of movements, he had no idea.

But as his finger tightened and curled, the world howled. It was a din heard by many but never spoken of, as all too often it was the last noise to fill their ears.

It filled Joseph in his entirety, knocking him off balance, priming him for the blast that threw him in the opposite direction, tearing his clothes.

But not his will.

For as much as he wanted to throw the rifle down in defeat and disgust, his right hand refused to let it go.

The world was on fire, the nightmare had landed on top of him, and the boy went to ground, still fighting . . .

44

At first, there was nothing.

Then a breath, a gasp that lifted his head and shoulders, and a blue flash of pain from temple to jaw that knocked him unconscious again.

Nothing . . . then more breathing. Not his own, but close to him: low grunting, slightly out of breath.

Is someone carrying me? he thought to himself, *I'm on a stretcher, to hospital . . .*

Where's Adonis?

The thought was too much, and he went under once more.

If he was expecting starched cotton sheets and a calm bedside manner when he next opened his eyes then he was in for a shock, as he found himself where he'd fallen, on a mattress of brick and rubble.

It was still night. The sky high above him was black and empty, only giving way to reds and oranges as he turned his head and saw where the city burned. The flames stung his eyes, forcing them shut again, hiding the grim reality if only for a short time, until he was ready, stronger.

Hesitantly, he tested himself, moving one arm then another, expecting pain, but miraculously feeling nothing but the vague sting of cuts and grazes.

He moved his attention to his legs: his right knee bending with little more than an ache, though when he tried his left, submerged by brick and stone, nothing moved. He strained. Nothing.

He tried to sit up and see what was going on, but the second he lifted his head, pain flashed the length of his face, threatening to force its way through the top of his skull. He raised his hand to his cheek, feeling it come away wet and clammy, not needing to look to know that it was covered in blood.

Fearfully, Joseph kept his head still and moved his arm down his body to where his left leg lay trapped. He tried to dislodge some stones to allow himself to slide free, but he didn't have the strength or coordination to do it, not without waking the pain in his head.

Frustrated and scared, he let his eyes close once more, and gently, gently allowed his head to fall to the left, trying to relieve the pressure that he felt building in his forehead. But when he opened his eyes, he faced a sight that he'd often thought about, but had never been able to really picture.

Adonis's lair as never before.

His hut still stood, but something was missing: a twenty-foot stretch of bars, now warped into a tangled mess and lying flat on the ground, where Bert Conaghan had once stood, fist clenched.

Joseph let out a cry. This couldn't be happening, but it was, and as much as it hurt him, he tried desperately to remember what had happened before everything cut to black. There had been a final explosion, he knew that, but whether it came from a bomb or the end of his rifle as he pulled the trigger, he had no idea. All he knew was that the wall was down, and that there was no sign of Adonis.

He panicked, the tensing of his body bringing another wave of pain and terror, though he didn't know what terrified him more, the thought that Adonis could already be dead, or the prospect of him walking free, and what he might have to do as a consequence.

His eyes scanned every inch of the enclosure but there was no sign of him. He craned his neck back still further to work out if Adonis was perched in his normal grieving spot, but there was nobody there.

He could be in his hut, Joseph thought, though he reckoned it was unlikely. If *he'd* been locked away his entire life then, given a chance at freedom, he would grab it without hesitation.

But if Adonis *was* free, then where was he? In the shadows, scared or angry? Or had he bolted, found a way over the walls and into the streets beyond? And if he'd done that, how long till he created pandemonium? How long till someone else pulled the trigger on him? Joseph was scared, but also furious with himself. He'd had one job to do but had fallen woefully short. How would he tell Mrs F?

He was finding it difficult to keep his eyes open. Any effort to focus brought yet more shooting pains, so he let his lids close and swept his arms around him in an arc to find a trace of the rifle. He'd got lucky once before, so why not again? He had to believe that, he had no other choice.

But there was nothing. His searching was fruitless. The rifle was buried, like his leg. He allowed himself a moment to take stock and work out what the hell he was going to do: what options did he have? His mind raced to Syd, hunkered down in the underground station. What would she do? Because she certainly wouldn't just lie there, that was for sure. He'd never met anyone more determined than her. He had to be more like her, let her inspire him.

It came to him quickly. It was clear what he needed to do. He had to free himself. He had to ignore any pain that he was feeling and drag his leg free.

Then he could look for the rifle properly, look for Adonis properly, find a way, somehow, to keep the promise that he'd made to Mrs F.

He pulled air deep into his chest, seeing stars as he wedged his elbows into the ground and hoisted himself to a sitting position. His head throbbed and swam, and he tasted sick in his mouth. He looked where his leg should be, replaced by an avalanche of brick, and with a clumsy arm he brushed away the smaller rocks, laying bare the size of the job in front of him: a slab of concrete that would challenge Goliath.

His spirits sank. What now? He looked around him, and could see the flames intensifying. He tried to guess how long he had before they snaked closer, putting him out of his misery.

But just as his mind turned to the most gruesome way to die, there came a lifeline. As out of the shadows lurched the most unlikely of saviours.

Out of the shadows, came Adonis.

45

Joseph cried.

Huge, racking sobs, made up of too many emotions.

Fear, of course: there was no cage door for him to exit through or lock any more, but more relief. Relief that his friend was alive!

But with that recognition came more fear. What would Adonis do now he was free? Would he run? Hurt others? Hurt him, even?

Joseph pulled again at the slab on his leg, but it wouldn't give an inch, not even when he ignored every jolt of pain in his head and heaved with everything he had left.

'MOVE!' he begged the stone. 'Please!'

It was no good, though he battled futilely on, while Adonis moved closer, his steps still slow. Joseph watched him with concern: a deep gash by Adonis's temple was bleeding heavily. He seemed disorientated, dizzy, even.

'Adonis!' he cried. 'I'm stuck. Can't move.' He didn't expect help, but he needed his friend to know. 'Are you all right? You're bleeding!'

The ape staggered closer, only pausing to wipe blood away as it reached his eye, and despite his wounds he climbed piles of rocks that would've had Joseph stumbling. When he reached

Joseph, whose eyes were wide at the power and magnificence of his friend, he sat. By Joseph's side.

But the ape didn't look in Joseph's direction, not even for a second. Instead, he stared beyond him, head turning slowly from side to side.

Joseph tried to follow his gaze, to make out what Adonis was looking at, but there was nothing but flames, kissing and smothering every piece of wood they came into contact with.

That didn't stop Adonis looking, though, and the longer it went on, head swinging left to right like searchlights sweeping for bombers, Joseph started to realise what was happening.

Adonis was playing sentry. Keeping Joseph safe.

Tears stung his eyes. He was overwhelmed by this act of care and love. All his life, Adonis had been held captive, but when his moment for freedom had come, he hadn't bolted. He hadn't left Joseph. He'd stood guard instead.

'Thank you,' Joseph wept, 'thank you, thank you, thank you.'

Suddenly he felt a movement beside him, as Adonis shifted his weight, his eyes lingering on Joseph's face before moving down his body, stopping as he reached his leg.

'That rock —' Joseph pointed at it — 'it's trapped my leg. I can't move it.'

He had no idea what Adonis could really, truly understand, but he didn't believe it was a coincidence that with the greatest of ease, Adonis flicked the slab away, as if it were a mere pebble.

As the slab rattled to the ground, Joseph felt a shriek in his knee. He wanted to cry again, and did, though not just in pain or relief, but now in gratitude too.

Their eyes locked for a second time, and Joseph saw a softening in the ape's face that was undeniable, however unlikely it seemed. If they *did* share a moment, and there would be many in the future who would refute it, it passed in a flash, as a new shriek filled the night.

The change in Adonis was immediate, every muscle in his frame tensing as he thrust his weight forward, front arms landing on the other side of Joseph's body, building a barrier between the boy and whatever was out there.

There was a new urgency to him: on high alert, his eyes scanned the surroundings, but nothing moved, nothing stirred, only the flames.

Until, from nowhere, loped a four-legged shadow, forcing Adonis to stride over Joseph, putting himself entirely between the threat and the boy lying injured.

Joseph was scared to look but couldn't help himself, eyes straining until he could make out a skeletal wolf, tongue lolling from its mouth, realising that it was the prospect of *him* that was making it salivate.

But Joseph had nothing to worry about, as in front of him, Adonis rose majestically onto his back legs, using every inch of his bulk to dominate the landscape, letting loose a roar that rolled all the way to the heavens.

The ape was a king. There was no other word for it. Joseph

watched for the wolf's response, but there was no retreat. In fact, Adonis's call merely summoned a second wolf from the shadows; equally stupid, but equally famished.

Joseph felt any kind of stand-off could never end well for the wolves, yet all he could do was watch Adonis take another pace forward and repeat his instructions, deafening the sky as he did so.

Still the wolves didn't retreat. Instead they split up, one stalking left, one right, dividing Adonis's focus, making it impossible for him to cover every route to the boy.

Joseph felt his heart quicken, ignoring the pain in his body as he started another search for the rifle, though this time, with different targets in mind.

The wolves moved quickly, their bodies close to the ground, so close that they appeared to almost slither over the debris. Adonis moved left and then right, barking and yowling warning after warning, all of which were ignored.

Joseph was panicking now, so much so that he tried to stand. But it was a fruitless attempt, pain in too many places made it impossible, and he was forced to watch as Adonis made a decisive move to the wolf on the left who had edged the closest. His speed was mesmorising, made even more so by his size.

Joseph gasped as Adonis bounded into the shadows. The fight was brief, but he took no delight in seeing the first wolf throw itself at Adonis in the darkness, nor in seeing it fall to the ground seconds later, not just defeated, but broken, dead.

Joseph's attention turned to its mate, who, seeing an unbroken path between it and dinnertime, was now tearing towards Joseph, jaws wide, eyes ecstatic.

This was it. He was exposed. Powerless. Even Adonis couldn't save him now.

46

Joseph didn't see what happened. His eyes were closed, hidden beneath his arms. But he heard it: a single crack, like thunder.

There was a second crack, then a howl and a thump, and the wind seemed to change direction. Joseph opened his eyes in shock to see, mere yards from him, a mass of fur, bone and blood, as the second wolf lay dead.

But how? thought Joseph. Was it a rifle he'd heard? And he winced against the flames, trying to see.

A voice came first, faintly.

'Over here!' he heard, though he couldn't be sure, as the voice had to fight against the noise of everything else.

He saw a man, just inside the gates, rifle still tucked beneath his chin. Joseph gasped, his instinct to shout and wave stopped by the sound of Adonis from the shadows.

He heard the sound of debris beneath the ape's feet but doubted the man would be able to either hear or see him too. And what if he did? How could Joseph possibly calmly warn him that there was a gorilla on the loose, but that there was nothing to fear? That the ape had saved him just moments before?

Matters got worse as a second figure appeared at the gate, then a third: footsteps echoing, voices slicing through the air.

'There's a boy!' the first man yelled over his shoulder as he advanced. 'Look, over there!'

Joseph's eyes focused on the leader, a man wearing an air-raid warden's helmet. An older man, perhaps. Not that it mattered. If Adonis spotted him and saw him as a threat, the result would be the same, regardless of age.

'Can you see him? There!' The warden called over his shoulder again, and for the first time Joseph could make out the others clearly, see the rifles slung over their shoulders. He looked to his left and heard Adonis's soft, laboured grunting, though he was hard to see in the darkness. How long did Joseph have until the ape made himself visible? How long until the men saw him and panicked, reaching for their rifles?

He had to find a way to communicate to them without alerting Adonis, but how he could do that was a mystery. He waved his hands in front of him, mouthing silently at them to stop. But why would they take any notice? How on earth could they make the leap to realising that moving any closer put them in the gravest of danger?

'It's all right!' the warden shouted, stumbling. 'There's nothing to worry about. We'll get you out of here, lad. The danger has passed!'

But this of course, was simply not true, and he, and the other men recognised this only seconds later, as Adonis announced himself for the first time, bounding from the darkness.

He did not howl or yell first, though. That was Joseph, as

he bellowed out a warning for the men to put down the guns that were being swung towards the ape.

The men didn't listen. How could they, when every sense they had was fixed on the huge ape galloping forwards, barking its hellish intent?

The effect was instantaneous. The first warden fell backwards, causing the soldiers behind him to teeter too, like drunks at closing time.

'Get BACK!' Joseph yelled from his knees. His hands waved wildly. 'Go now! Get back . . . PLEASE!'

But his words did not reach them. They could hear and see only danger.

What Joseph alone knew, as he faced the men, was that Adonis wasn't running at *them*, he was running to *him*, to protect him, just as he had with the wolves.

The greatest tragedy was that the men didn't know that. How could they? Whoever would've believed such a thing?

The first bullet sounded. Louder to Joseph's ears than any bomb that had landed that night.

He couldn't follow its path, but he heard a crack as it embedded itself deep inside the wall of Adonis's enclosure behind him.

Adonis heard it too, arriving beside Joseph at exactly the same time, rearing on two legs, muzzle aimed skywards as he bellowed again. They would not take the boy; he would not let them. This was *his* kingdom.

He was a fearsome sight, and even from a distance, Joseph could see the horror written on the men's faces.

Joseph watched in slow motion as the rifles quivered in their terrified grasps, and saw single eyes close against a backdrop of flames, and no matter how loudly he yelled or how many times he yelled it, it was never going to be enough. The soldiers saw their truth, and they unloaded on it.

Joseph reared up too, echoing the stance of Adonis beside him. He made himself big, as big as he could, trying to get in front of the ape. He would take a bullet, take all of them, if it would just stop them from hitting his friend.

But he was not big enough, and Adonis made himself impossible to miss.

Joseph heard the first bullet enter the ape. A thud: a sickening, echoless thud to the left arm, followed by a second, and a third tearing at the top of his right thigh and shoulder.

Adonis howled in pain and fury. How dare they? Who were they to do this to him? Joseph felt the same, screaming in the soldiers' direction, imploring them to stop. And for a brief while, they did, rifles dropping as they reloaded.

Joseph screamed. He needed a miracle, an intervention from God, and as the first marksman lifted his rifle once more, it seemed like someone was listening.

A final figure had arrived, stage left: running down the gunman and swiping his barrel skywards, just as he fired. The bullet arced blindly into the night.

The soldier reacted angrily, spinning to confront the

newcomer, rifle now raised as a club, but when he was faced by a bedraggled middle-aged woman, anger was replaced by confusion.

'Don't shoot!' Mrs F yelled at the two soldiers out of her reach. 'You'll hit the boy!'

Whether that was her one true worry didn't matter, as it was already too late.

The bullets were away, racing each other, competing for maximum damage.

Both hit Adonis in the chest with such ferocity that they burrowed deep within him, tearing at his flesh, ripping his right lung apart.

He staggered backwards, wracked with pain, but still raging at their audacity. He fell to his knees, then saw the boy terrified in front of him, which drove him skywards one last time.

And there he stood, against a hellish backdrop, the most powerful beast in his kingdom. He would not go down until he had to, until his body told him no more, until that one last bullet struck him.

Mrs F was powerless to stop it. She had done everything she could to keep Adonis safe, everything, but she couldn't stop the final shot from firing.

She ran fast, faster than any woman her age should, regardless of what she had drunk earlier in the evening, but it could never be fast enough to intercept the bullet. By the time she reached them, Adonis was already on his back, blood matting his fur and filling his lungs.

Joseph was draped over him, cheek pressed hard against his belly, tears mixing with the ape's blood.

'Give me your hands!' she yelled at him, but he didn't move. 'Joseph. Please, your hands.' She pulled him into a crouch, thrusting his palms down upon the jagged hole in Adonis's chest. 'Now, press, do you hear me? Press hard and don't stop until I tell you otherwise.'

Joseph did as he was told, not believing that this was happening. Any of it. He pressed with every bit of strength he had left, but no matter how much pressure he applied, the blood still came, seeping through the cracks between his fingers, pooling until he could barely see them.

'It's not working, Mrs F, do something. Please!'

Mrs F had been trying to stem the other wounds, and she shouted over her shoulder to the men, imploring them for help, for dressings, whatever they could find.

But the soldiers didn't want to get too close, not out of fear at what they'd see, but at the possibility that Adonis would rise and seek his revenge.

'Find me a vet, then. NOW!'

'You'll be lucky. Anyone who knows their way round a body is already down the hospital,' one of them replied. 'The city's burning, in case you hadn't noticed. They don't have time for an animal.'

'Then get out of my zoo!' Mrs F thundered. 'NOW.'

This saw the men stumble backwards and away. They'd seen enough crazy animals without getting close to another.

'Mrs F, it's not working,' Joseph cried again, feeling utterly powerless and afraid. 'You've got to do something. Help me. Help him.'

She lifted her hands from Adonis. She didn't want to, but she had no choice. She needed to remove her cardigan and rip it into strips.

'Here,' she thrust some material into his hands. 'Ball it up and press down hard. Stem the bleeding. DO NOT STOP PRESSING.'

He didn't. He daren't. He pressed, and pushed, and he listened. Adonis's eyes were open but lolling backwards, pupils disappearing to the top of his head. He was breathing, chest rising and falling, but without any great rhythm, and with less and less conviction.

And then, it happened.

Joseph saw it.

The strip of cream wool in his hand, which had fought as hard as him, gave up: a crimson bloom flowering from the middle outwards, until every last fibre had blossomed, and it glowed, like it was the height of summer. Adonis's chest rose once more, and fell just as gently, but there it stayed. Still. Defeated.

'Don't die on me, Adonis,' Joseph sobbed angrily, incredulous at what he was seeing. 'Don't you dare. Don't you dare leave me. Not you, too.'

He couldn't believe it. Whatever he had once felt about the animal, he had thought him indestructible, carved from stone.

To see him like this, reduced to such an undignified death, it turned him inside out.

'You've got to get someone, Mrs F. Fetch someone, *anyone*. Please.'

Mrs F was standing now, on the other side of her beloved ape. But she didn't move, not a single step. Nor did she shout.

'He's dead, Joseph,' she said. 'There's nothing more you can do, nothing I can do either. He's gone.'

He didn't want to hear it. Didn't want a single word of it to be true. But if he knew one thing about the woman beside him, it was that she would only tell him the truth. There would be no more lies between them. Not any more.

For as long as he could remember, Joseph had felt abandoned. And for too long, it had caused him such pain that he'd turned it into anger, which he carried secretly on his own.

But tonight, with the body of Adonis lying lifeless between them, he chose to do things differently, and threw himself into the arms of Mrs F with such force that he nearly took her off her feet.

And from the moment he felt her arms envelop him, he knew that he was safe. Finally, *finally*, Joseph allowed himself to let go.

He cried. Without hesitation or fear of being pushed away. And as the woman hugged him, he realised he was crying for everything. For Adonis, and the shell of the zoo he left behind, but also for his mother and his father.

'It's all right,' Mrs F said gently in his ear. 'You cry. Cry as much as you want. I promise, I won't try and stop you.'

So Joseph did exactly that. He pushed himself further against her, head burrowed into her shoulder, tears mixing with hers as she pulled him closer still.

'That's it,' she whispered. 'That's it, son.'

They didn't move for what felt like an age, and together, amongst the dancing flames, they both cried: for what they had lost, for who they had lost, but most importantly, for what they had finally found.

The End

AFTERWORD

The moment when a story presents itself is always special, so it's no surprise to say that I remember exactly where I was when Joseph's and Adonis's tale first took hold of me. I was sitting in a campsite in France, on a hot late afternoon, with a friend who I love very much. Let's say this friend was called Pete (because that was his name).

As we sat, Pete told me a story about his dad during the Second World War. Unable to fight because of poor health, his dad was part of Manchester's home guard and had been given a very specific job. Every time the air-raid siren sounded, his dad had to pick up a rifle and run to Manchester Zoo. Once there, he had to sit outside the lion's cage, his rifle trained on the animal. Why? Because if the bombers destroyed the cage and the lion ran free, then his dad's mission was to shoot the animal before it went on the rampage.

That was it. That was the moment when the hair on my arms stood to attention and my brain started firing. Immediately I had questions: *Did he ever have to pull the trigger? Could he have done it if necessity demanded it?*

What a story! What a gift, and one that I really wanted to tackle.

I didn't tell it straightaway, though. I carried it around with me for a long time, asking myself questions like: *What would happen if the rifle ended up in the hands of angry boy instead of a responsible adult? What if it wasn't a lion any more? What if it was a gorilla instead?*

The story was never far from my mind and every time it came to the fore, I had the same reaction as the first time: goosebumps, hairs standing on end, excitement.

Then, four years ago, I stopped writing, and didn't think I would start again. It felt too difficult. There were too many other things to sort out in my head to consider telling a story, and that left me feeling very low.

One of the greatest things I've learned as a writer though, is that stories, great ones, are persuasive, they get under your skin and tend to not let go of you until you tell them properly. And if there was one story that was going to start me writing again, it was this one, especially as Pete had gifted me it. So, thank you, Pete, not just for the idea, but for the twenty years of friendship and laughs and love.

I also wanted to mention here Joseph's dyslexia, which is a strand in the book that isn't tied off neatly, as understanding of the condition in the 1940s was not what it is today. Far from it. Having worked with many dyslexic children over the years, I've always been gobsmacked by the challenges they face, and the resilience they have in facing it. If dyslexia is a challenge that you are facing, or if you would like to know more about it, you'll find information and resources here: https://www. bdadyslexia.org.uk

Thanks so much for reading *When the Sky Falls*. I really hope you enjoyed it.

ACKNOWLEDGEMENTS

I'd like to thank the following people, who have supported me in the writing of this book.

The early readers – Chaz and Dave (a chapter at a time), Shannon Cullen, Simon Mason and Dr Tony, you kept me writing. Thank you. Thanks also to David Fickling and Sarah Crossan, who encouraged me so generously.

My agent, Jodie Hodges, who has been unbelievably patient with me for the past few years, as well as kind, empathetic and steely. Thanks also to Emily, Molly and Jane who work so hard on my behalf at UA.

My publishers, Andersen Press: Klaus, Mark, Paul, Jack, Chloe, Eloise and especially Charlie Sheppard. Charlie was the first editor to ever read anything I'd written (nearly twenty years ago), and these three words she said to me, 'You can write', kept me going for a long time. Charlie embraced this story from the word go, and if it has been enjoyable to read, then much of the credit rests with her. Thank you, friend.

Levente Szabó, for creating a cover that I will never tire of looking at. Thank you so much.

Thanks and love as always to Mum, Dad, Jon and Angela. Let's raise a glass soon.

Finally, I want to thank Louise, Albie, Elsie, Stanley, Rufus and Bebe. You lot are fabulous. I don't half love you.

Hebden Bridge, July 2020

BERLIE DOHERTY
TREASON

Will Montague is a page to Prince Edward, son of King Henry VIII. As the King's favourite, Will gains many enemies in Court. His enemies convince the King that Will's father has committed treason and he is thrown into Newgate Prison. Will flees Hampton Court and goes into hiding in the back streets of London. Lost and in mortal danger, he is rescued by a poor boy, Nick Drew. Together they must brave imprisonment and death as they embark on a great adventure to set Will's father free.

'Doherty paints a very vivid picture . . . almost Shardlake for young readers.'
Independent on Sunday

'A beautifully paced and measured story. 5 stars.'
Books for Keeps

9781849391214